WRITTEN IN STONE

ALSO BY PAIGE SHELTON

WRITTEN IN STONE

A SCOTTISH BOOKSHOP MYSTERY

Paige Shelton

MINOTAUR
BOOKS
NEW YORK

First published in the United States by Minotaur Books, an imprint of St. Martin's Publishing Group

WRITTEN IN STONE. Copyright © 2025 by Paige Shelton-Ferrell. All rights reserved. Printed in the United States of America. For information, address St. Martin's Publishing Group, 120 Broadway, New York, NY 10271.

www.minotaurbooks.com

Library of Congress Cataloging-in-Publication Data

Names: Shelton, Paige, author.
Title: Written in stone / Paige Shelton.
Description: First edition. | New York : Minotaur Books, 2025. | Series: Scottish bookshop mystery series
Identifiers: LCCN 2024055114 | ISBN 9781250336613 (hardcover) | ISBN 9781250336620 (ebook)
Subjects: LCGFT: Detective and mystery fiction. | Novels.
Classification: LCC PS3619.H45345 W75 2025 | DDC 813/.6—dc23/eng/20241122
LC record available at https://lccn.loc.gov/2024055114

Our books may be purchased in bulk for promotional, educational, or business use. Please contact your local bookseller or the Macmillan Corporate and Premium Sales Department at 1-800-221-7945, extension 5442, or by email at MacmillanSpecialMarkets@macmillan.com.

First Edition: 2025

10 9 8 7 6 5 4 3 2 1

For Charlie, my ride or die, my other half,
and the guy who is always there for my questions
that begin with, "What's that word . . . ?"

WRITTEN IN STONE

CHAPTER ONE

As the sprinkle of rain threatened to rev up to a late spring downpour, Tom and I increased our pace.

"I can't believe it's been almost a whole year." I sighed.

"It seems like yesterday," he replied.

"And forever. In a good way."

"Aye."

Tom had just asked me what I'd like to do for our one-year anniversary. It was still a couple months away, but time flew so quickly and he didn't want the date to pass by without planning something special.

"I don't know," I said. "Something quiet would work just fine."

"Well, I don't disagree, but I think I'd like to mark the occasion with something less quiet."

"Like what?"

"I don't know yet. I'm thinking. Let me know if something comes to you, something you'd really like to do, a place you'd like to see."

"Surprise me," I said.

"Aye?" he said doubtfully.

"Sure. Why not?"

"I'm a wee bit clueless when it comes to such things. I would hate to disappoint you."

I laughed. "Not possible."

"I guess we'll see." He slowed his steps, so I did too. "I think we're here."

The rain wasn't going to cease anytime soon, so we hurried down the close and counted doors.

We looked up at the building, at its medieval architecture, something I'd become used to seeing all around Edinburgh. "I guess this is it?"

"I think so."

We looked back at the door we'd stopped in front of. "It's not much to go on, but it seems to fit," I said.

The majority of the Hidden Door Festival was being held in an old, much larger, long unused building on Dalkeith Road. But this event was a special, invitation-only offsite experience. The "auxiliary annex," as it was described in the festival's program, belonged to artist Ryory Bennigan, and I had been intrigued since first reading about it.

Ryory, an elusive man who was often discussed amid Edinburgh artist circles—well, lots of different Edinburgh circles— didn't like to show his work.

While that might seem counterintuitive, Ryory himself had explained—

I admit that I am compulsive and have enough money not to care what anyone thinks about my life's obsession. I shall continue to immerse myself in my art, which is, frankly, where I live, not what I do.

His mysterious ways, along with how he used his body as a canvas, had been the building blocks of his reputation as a local celebrity, more than just an elusive man rarely seen in public. No one really knew where his money came from, and his ancestry was frequently the subject of speculation. Even my boss, the well-connected Edwin MacAlister, didn't know much about Ryory's history, and he was keyed in to almost everyone in Scotland, especially in Edinburgh. He made the history of the place he loved, as well as its people, his business.

When Ryory was spotted walking the streets of the city, maybe once or twice a year, cameras couldn't be opened fast enough. Pictures tagged with #ryorybennigan quickly became viral, unbeknownst to him because he was, as he claimed, "not a user of social media." Everyone wanted to see what Ryory looked like now—how he'd changed. Could they spot the differences?

The Hidden Door Festival was a yearly pop-up artistic event, always held in a place that had been left empty for whatever reason. Much of the event was musical, giving local singers and bands opportunities to introduce their music. Some of the festival was literary, filled with essayists and poets; some were exhibits—paintings, sculptures, any sort of artistic creation, really.

I'd attended my first Hidden Door Festival a year earlier and hadn't been able to get enough. I'd downloaded music from a few bands and still listened to them, watched as their popularity continued to rise. One of the paintings I'd purchased had been put on the wall above Tom's and my sofa in our blue house by the sea. He loved it as much as I did.

Though the subject of the painting was also a blue house

by the sea, it wasn't our home being portrayed. Nevertheless, it seemed perfect and neither of us had been able to resist it.

This year, the big news of the event was that Ryory had decided to open his studio to a limited number of visitors. He'd asked those who wanted to see his place to snail mail him a request. If you were chosen, you would receive a confirmation with directions and a specific time and date of your slot. There was no option to reschedule. I'd received my confirmation two days earlier. Tom and I had moved around some less-than-crucial calendar events to make our assigned time slot work. Even if it turned out to be boring, it would be more than worth it. How could it possibly turn out to be boring, though?

It was Ryory Bennigan, after all.

His art was carved stone. He took what had become Scottish historical intrigue regarding a lost population, the Picts, and reproduced what they'd left behind, with some artistic license thrown in, of course.

The Pictish people had populated Scotland a long time ago, from about 300 to 900 CE, a short six hundred years. Their historical record is scant and artistically intriguing, though not very clear, which gives them an air of mystery. Their existence is marked only by the stones they left behind, carved with a variety of symbols—some animals, some geometric, and others that historians assume were just of everyday items they used. Though again, no one is sure about much of anything when it comes to the Picts.

However, what we do know is that tattoos were a traditional part of the Picts' lives, which, some say, is where the later carved symbols originated. The name Pict comes from picti, a Latin word meaning painted people. They were warriors, many of them covering their entire bodies in tattoos, possibly to make themselves more intimidating.

The Picts used an indigo ink to create their body art. Most likely, it was dyer's woad, a plant whose flowers are yellow but turn blue green after being dried, powdered, and fermented. Woad also has antiseptic properties that might have assisted with healing injuries or preventing infection. Ochre and soot might also have been used to add other pigments or create other designs. We can guess about some of the designs that covered their bodies based on the standing stones they left behind throughout Scotland, mostly in the northeastern part of the country.

Ryory not only carved stones like the Picts had, but he also used his own body as a canvas for the blue symbols. He was quite a sight to behold, though nothing like a warrior. In fact, his mysterious reputation included lots of positive attributes— I'd heard he was kind, helpful, a great tipper. From all accounts, he was a good, if elusive, guy.

And rumor was that he'd taught himself the art of tattooing and had done many of his own tattoos himself. It was another point of speculation, and a question I hoped to ask him. If he was up to answering questions, that was.

He was almost as much of an enigma as the Picts were. No one really knows with certainty what the symbols mean, where the tattoo ink came from, what the Picts were really like. And no one knows what happened to them. They just disappeared from all historical records and never came back.

The Picts fought many battles during their time on the planet. There is no real record of them dying out or migrating. It's likely that they just melded into the other Scottish communities, though we don't know how any of that happened.

Though I found their sparse history fascinating, my favorite part of the Picts' story was their hair. Apparently, many of those in the original tribes were notably topped off by the reddest of red hair, a trait that I also carried, most of the time proudly, and much of the time with a frizz that couldn't be tamed, more pronounced than ever since I'd moved to rainy Scotland.

My hair had been one of the things that originally prompted me to take a deep dive into the Picts, led by a discussion that I'd had months ago with my boss, Edwin, the man who owned The Cracked Spine, the bookshop where I worked. He'd also told me about Ryory Bennigan at the same time.

Edwin had, in his words, "been so bold" as to invite the artist out for dinner or perhaps a get-together at the bookshop. Apparently, Ryory had shopped at The Cracked Spine, but the only person who'd ever been in when he was there was my grandmotherly coworker, Rosie. She'd try to contact Edwin as Ryory shopped, but the artist wasn't a lingering browser. He was in and out quickly, finding a book, paying for it as he and Rosie exchanged pleasantries, and then leaving, sometimes before Rosie could even manage a quick text to Edwin.

Rosie had said, "I've done my best trying to chat that man up, but as friendly as he is, he clearly doesnae like small talk. We'll just have to hope he stops by one day when Edwin is in."

He still hadn't.

When I got the invitation, Tom, knowing Edwin's intrigue, had insisted that I first invite my boss on this sojourn. But Edwin had declined, telling me he had other plans, even though I was sure he didn't. He was just stepping aside so Tom and I might enjoy the event together. I appreciated it, and Tom was having fun too, though he wasn't as intrigued by Ryory Bennigan as either I or Edwin.

The directions to the studio had been mostly clear. "Third building down the Friar's Close. The one with the interesting door."

Looking up the location of the close was easy enough. Tom and I had taken a bus from Grassmarket and then walked a short block to reach it. We found three doors on each side of an unadorned alleyway flanked by a four-story, stone medieval building on each side.

We glanced at the third door of each building. At first, neither door had seemed more interesting than the other one until we looked very closely. The only real difference was a small carved symbol in the darkly stained wood above an old brass knob on the southerly building. The symbol, a bird, was a crude representation of a Pict symbol: a disc shape atop a rectangle. Many speculated that this symbol represented the sun. Though he didn't show his work publicly, pictures of it somehow surfaced, and then he dodged the social media that shared it with great skill. I had looked at the pictures on the internet; Ryory had carved lots of symbols over the years, but this one didn't represent his skill. He was very good at his art.

The symbol on the door might have been scratched with a dull knife, but, still, it was a symbol, and the other door was plain. It seemed like an obvious clue.

"Should we knock or just go in?" I said.

"I would probably knock first if the invitation doesn't mention differently."

"Right."

As I lifted my fist, though, the door pushed open with surprising gusto. A woman exited in a hurry.

At once the three of us recognized each other.

"Delaney? Tom?" Bridget asked.

"Bridget?" Tom and I said simultaneously.

Bridget McBride, one of Tom's old girlfriends, had come through the door, her long blond curls bouncing, her big blue eyes shiny and determined, which was her normal state of being.

"What . . . ?" I began.

A knowing smile spread over Bridget's pretty face. "You are here to see the art."

I nodded. "Yes. You too?"

"Well, I have an open invite." If anyone was good at smug, it was Bridget. But somehow, whenever I witnessed that, I didn't like her any less.

Our friendship was not something anyone could have predicted. She'd held a long grudge over the way Tom had ended their relationship, and things were icy at first, but for whatever reason she and I found a way to get along. We were friends, and it seemed that's what we both wanted. Tom had remained neutral regarding my time with Bridget, but I thought even he was doing okay with it.

For a time, I thought I only wanted us to get along because I sometimes needed her assistance as a local newspaper reporter with access to archived articles. I'd felt guilty about my disingenuousness, but it hadn't been long before I realized I actually liked her. She was a little snotty sometimes, but I'd come to find even that endearing.

"Oh?" I used an inquiring tone. It was clear she was dying to tell us more.

"Well, aye." She nodded back toward the door. "Ryory is an old friend. I did a piece about him years ago. He liked that I was honest, didn't hide his strange ways but didn't make fun of him either. Plus, I gave him final approval of the printed piece, which I rarely do."

"You're very good at what you do," I said after a slightly too long beat. "And that's pretty darn cool."

"Aye," Tom agreed.

Bridget sometimes pretended that she was still angry at Tom, but not today. Today her smile transformed into something humbler, and she nodded. "I agree. He's a lovely man."

But then, as quickly as it had appeared, the smile dropped away. "Particularly when his assistant isn't around. She's up there today, though. Don't expect a lot of . . . fun."

"You know her too?" I stated the obvious.

Bridget shrugged and offered up "Well, not as well as I know Ry."

Ry. I hadn't heard him referred to in that way.

"Oh." I rummaged around in my bag for the invitation as something had occurred to me. I held it up. "Are you responsible for me getting this?"

She shook her head right away. "No, I'm not. I didn't even know you'd applied for an invite, though . . . Oh."

Tom and I shared a look.

"What?" I asked her.

"Ry's assistant is named Ani, with one *n* and one *i*. Though she and I haven't had any deep conversations, I've heard that she loves your bookshop. She probably knew who you were when you applied."

"Ani? I don't think I know the name."

"You might recognize her." She paused and seemed to fall into thought. "And, I think Ry has mentioned the shop a time or two. Maybe. I'm not sure. Anyway, you might have had an in with the bookshop." She shrugged. "Nothing wrong with that."

I nodded, but I didn't mention his times in the shop with Rosie. I might like my friendship with Bridget, but she was still a reporter first, and it wasn't wise to share much of anything with her, especially a secret that could be publicized in one of her articles.

"No, nothing at all," I said.

"Maybe it was just luck of the draw. I don't know how Ani and Ry determined the winners. Ask them. She wasn't thrilled by the idea of doing the showings. She only agreed because Ry wanted it."

"We're just happy to be here," I said. "And very excited to see the studio."

"It's impressive, there's no doubt." She paused. "There's a gentleman up there right now. It wouldn't be like Ani to double-book. What's the time on your invite?"

"Two p.m."

"You're only a few minutes early. Ry was talking to the man like he knew him, sort of. Maybe a friend just stopped by." She fell into thought again. She was always searching for an angle. Her eyes snapped back to mine. "Maybe I'll call you for a quote or something about your time up there."

I nodded immediately. "Of course."

"Well, head on up. I know you'll have a good time. I can't wait to hear about it. Lunch in the next couple weeks?"

"I would love that. Text me."

"I will." She remembered the icy shoulder she liked to extend to Tom and sent him a forced glare. "Just us girls."

"I would never want to interfere," Tom said.

"Right." In a way I had become familiar with, she turned on her toes and walked away toward the road, her long blond curls bouncing as she went. She waved backward over her shoulder. "Later."

"Later, Bridget," I called.

Once she was out of sight, I turned to Tom. "I think she's warming to you."

We laughed.

"Shall we?" He reached for the doorknob just as heavier rain began to fall.

"Let's."

CHAPTER TWO

We stepped into a mostly dark stairway, lit only by a small wall sconce at the top of ten steps. A musty smell tickled my nose, and I held back a sneeze. We heard no noise, voices or otherwise. I didn't feel any moisture on the walls when I touched them, but there was a distinct heaviness of humidity in the air, as if it'd rained inside too.

I smoothed my hair. It was probably a waste of time, but it was a habit I'd had even before moving to Scotland.

"Want me to lead the way?" Tom asked.

"Yes, please."

I took his hand as we climbed the flight of stairs, only to find another flight around a wall at the top. We took it and then two others before we came upon another door.

"We should probably knock on this one." Tom rapped his knuckles in a friendly beat.

I nodded as we waited.

No sound announced that anyone was on the other side before the door swung open.

We were greeted by a woman whose bangs were her focal

point. There was so much natural bright light behind her that I couldn't make out much else.

"Delaney Nichols?" the woman asked.

"That's me. This is my husband, Tom."

She nodded at Tom. "Pleasure. I'm Ani."

"Thanks for the invite." I held it up as I spoke.

"Your name was drawn. We did nothing special for you that we didn't do for all the other winners."

Just saying those words made me think that someone had, indeed, done something above and beyond to ensure I was chosen. I wondered if she'd overheard our conversation with Bridget. I wasn't sure what to say, but Tom was on it.

"Then we feel extremely lucky," he said.

Not many people were immune to my husband's charms, but Ani seemed not to have really looked at either him or me. Her eyes were difficult to see under the long bangs.

My eyes, though, were adjusting quickly to the stark contrast, and I noticed that in the States, at least, Ani could have been a model. Almost six feet tall, reed thin, with high cheekbones, and fabulous shiny, dark hair, I doubted she would have made it two blocks down a New York City thoroughfare without being approached by at least a couple scouts, to which she might have retorted, "Why would I do something like that? I'm Ryory Bennigan's assistant and that's far better." She wouldn't be wrong.

"Come in then. Ry is busy at the moment, but he will join you in a few. You may sit there." She pointed toward two chairs pushed back against the wall right inside the door. "Do you need anything to drink?"

She asked the question with a tone that implied we would decline.

"I'm fine. Thanks."

"No, thank you," Tom added.

"Sit then." With much less bounce, Ani turned just as Bridget had and walked away.

Tom and I shared a look, this one with a conspiratorial smile. We would discuss all of this later.

There would be plenty to talk about, and we hadn't even gotten very far past the front door yet.

Just after Ani disappeared behind an opaque glass wall we were facing, another knock sounded on the door.

Irritation lined her return. Both Tom and I sent her team-player smiles, maybe hoping to let her know we were on her side.

She did not return our smiles, and we couldn't tell if she rolled her eyes. I thought she probably did.

"Delivery," the young man on the other side said when she pulled the door wide.

I leaned forward and peered to see that he was a twenty-something man in a ball cap and a dark jacket with a red stripe around one arm. He was carrying a black vinyl bag with a matching red stripe.

"What kind of delivery?" Ani asked.

"Lunch, I guess."

"Lunch?"

"Yeah. Ordered by"—he lifted the bag and looked at the receipt—"Bennigan."

"Really?"

The man sighed. "Well, I doubt I would just stop by with this big bag of food otherwise. Is there a Bennigan here?"

"You'd be surprised," Ani said as she took the bag. "Were you tipped?"

"I was. A little." He paused. "Hey, you're—"

"Thank you." Ani shut the door and then turned again and disappeared behind the wall, the big bag in her arms, the noise from her footfalls waning as she went.

Tom and I shared more raised eyebrows.

I strained to listen for voices on the other side of the wall, but I sensed that Ani had gone into another room. I heard muted words, but I couldn't understand them, though I could tell that someone was unhappy. Or maybe just surprised?

I looked at Tom, who read my silent question and shook his head. He couldn't hear either.

The voices retreated even farther away, and silence filled the air long enough for me to get a little antsy.

We could see nothing except the wall and a big window, which felt clinical and cold.

"You okay?" Tom nodded toward my now bouncing leg.

I stopped. "I'm fine. Working on my patience, as always."

"Got it." Tom nodded with a half-smile.

Just then, group noises began to build and approach again. As they got closer, it felt like we should stand up, so we did, while attempting to look casual at the same time. I didn't know where to put my hands.

Ani and an older-looking man I didn't recognize came around the wall. He wasn't Ryory Bennigan. The gentleman carried a large, zipped artist's portfolio and was dressed in clothes stereotypical of a university professor, one who'd worn the same sweater all the way through his long career. His gray hair was thick and curly, and his mustache twirled at its ends.

"Oh, hello there," he said to Tom and me. "I'm so sorry

about the time I took. I simply had so much to discuss, and Mr. Bennigan was too gracious to push me along."

"Not a problem." I smiled.

Ani opened the door, but the man was not to be deterred. He walked directly to us instead of toward the door. "Name's Adam Pace. I'm from the States."

I'd suspected as much, considering his accent. "Me too. I'm from Kansas. Delaney, and my husband, Tom."

"Oh." Adam shook both our hands and then gave me his full attention. "I'm from Kansas too!"

"You are?" The small world seemed suspiciously smaller, though I tried not to show my doubt.

"Yes, the University of Kansas in Lawrence."

I hesitated because of the additional world shrinkage. "I . . . uh . . . that's where I went to school."

I was grateful that Adam Pace suddenly seemed as surprised as I did. If this was some sort of setup, he wasn't in on it. "Well, isn't that something?"

"It is."

We studied each other a long moment. He was probably just as baffled by our chance meeting as I was.

He finally spoke. "What are you doing in Scotland? Oh, well, maybe I'm not supposed to ask such a question, but . . . I'm here on business. You?"

"I took a job at a bookshop about two years ago. I met Tom, and . . . just stayed."

"Isn't that delightful!"

"Is your business something to do with the university?" I asked.

"Yes," he said in a way that felt purposefully cryptic. He

continued, "Such a pleasure. Well, I best take my leave, so you may have your time with one of the greatest artists of all time."

"Nice to meet you," Tom and I both said.

Adam hesitated.

"Dr. Pace?" Ani's voice was weighted like a shove out the door.

"Ah. Yes, of course. Goodbye then," he said.

I looked at Ani, who seemed to wish we would all just leave, then turned my attention back to Dr. Pace. "I . . . I work at The Cracked Spine. It's in Grassmarket. Just in case you'd like to stop by and talk about Kansas or something."

"Thank you. That's lovely. I think I will." Finally, he turned and made his way out the door. He thanked Ani too, but she didn't seem to hear.

Once she closed the door, she said, "Follow me."

She turned again, and this time we hurried behind her.

The world on the other side of the wall was vastly different from the one where we'd been.

This side was jam-packed with bright colors and hordes of objects. Tall windows lined the walls, but there was so much stuff in the way that I couldn't see much of a view through any of them.

Ani led the way through the room as I tried to take everything in. I spotted a painting propped on an easel. It reminded me of Picasso's impressionistic style, but only slightly. This painting's subjects were two women with distinct faces, both of their expressions drawn into a pain that I could feel.

"Does Mr. Bennigan paint?" I asked.

"Mr. Bennigan is an artist. He does art," Ani said over her shoulder.

I didn't quite know what to make of that answer, but I decided to hold on to any further questions to ask Mr. Bennigan himself. I knew of his stone carvings, but excitement sparked inside me as I thought about the other art forms we might get to see.

We followed Ani into a long, starkly antiseptic hallway, its uncovered walls a slate gray under dim lights tucked into the ceiling. When we came out on the other side, however, it was as if we'd stepped into a new world.

These walls were also lined with tall windows, but the view here was not blocked, the room surprisingly clear.

Had Tom and I walked farther into the close before entering the third door, we would have seen that a park was in the middle of a square of four-story buildings.

We followed Ani along the perimeter of the room so that we could look out and down to the groomed park lined with benches that begged for contemplation or the reading of a good book.

With the other buildings, the setup felt very *Rear Window*— the old Jimmy Stewart movie—and I could see into lots of other uncovered tall windows.

As I was studying a woman in a black dress directly across the park, Ani said, "You work at The Cracked Spine?" She kept walking.

"I do."

"I love your bookstore."

"Thank you."

Ani's tone remained steady, but this was by far the friendliest thing she'd said.

"Please tell Hamlet that Ani said hello."

"I will."

Briefly, I wondered about Ani and Bridget's relationship. As long as I'd known her, Bridget had been curious about Edwin and the bookshop. I wondered if she'd ever asked Ani or Ryory Bennigan to "spy" for her. Not that Hamlet or Rosie would have given in to any questions they didn't want to answer.

I told myself to stop being suspicious and just enjoy the moment. If Bridget and I were actually going to be friends, maybe I needed to stop thinking she was up to no good.

Ani stopped and turned. "Sit over there. Ryory will be out in a minute." She gestured toward an antique couch, though its white upholstery was pristine. For a moment I wanted to ask if there was a less perfect place we could sit. I didn't want to dirty anything, particularly white furniture.

But there was no other place, unless we wanted to consider the floor and that didn't feel right either.

"Thank you," I said as Ani turned yet again and left down another hallway on the far side of the big room.

We were in a studio, I thought. Other than the couch, it held only one stone, in the middle of the floor atop a large white piece of canvas, a table filled with tools next to it. It felt like the setup for performance art, not a place where the real work was done—the entire area was so vacant and clean—but it was still a beautiful room with an impressive view.

I leaned over to Tom. "Do you know who Jimmy Stewart is?"

"The American actor, aye."

"I used to watch his movies at my grandmother's house. I thought I was going to marry him."

"He'd have been a lucky man."

"Right? Unfortunately, he died when I was just a kid. It was the first time I understood I was watching *old* movies. I cried a little. He was beloved by many."

"Aye, my favorite film of his is *Harvey*," Tom said.

"The one with the rabbit?"

"That's the one."

"You are full of surprises."

"I'm happy to hear that. I'm no Jimmy Stewart but . . ."

"I smiled. Have you seen *Rear Window*?"

"I have." He nodded toward the windows. "I thought the same thing. You can see through so many windows."

"It always surprises me when people don't cover them."

"Aye."

Any further window or Jimmy Stewart contemplation was interrupted.

"Welcome to my studio," a booming voice said from the hallway that Ani had gone down a few moments earlier.

We hurried to stand again.

Ryory Bennigan was in the room. He took my breath away. I tried to look cool, but I doubt my big smile did anything other than make me look a little goofy.

He was quite the sight, and he seemed to know it, though not in an arrogant way.

He was a tall man, seemingly taller in person than via the pictures I'd found. He was a few inches over six feet. He had muscles everywhere.

He wore jeans but no shirt. Tattoos covered his torso, arms, neck, and face. His long red hair was pulled back into a thick but frizzy ponytail. His eyebrows were also thick and red. I realized that it was all a matter of perspective—depending on which of my lenses I used, he could be either a bold artist or a circus performer.

The way he stood today cemented for me that, though he might be reclusive, he wasn't uncomfortable being on display. It seemed a contradiction until I realized that this moment was on his terms, and that might be what was the difference.

After a few beats, he made his way to us and extended his tattoo-covered hand. "Ryory Bennigan. It's a joy to meet you both." His accent was light. Though he was older than Hamlet, he was younger than my one-time landlord, Elias, and that's where his accent seemed to fall, right in the middle of the spectrum.

"Thank you for the invitation," I said enthusiastically as he and I and then he and Tom shook hands.

"Not at all." He put his hands on his hips. "Ani told me you work at The Cracked Spine."

"I do."

"I love that bookshop."

"It's a wonderful place. Do you know my boss, Edwin MacAlister?" I knew they hadn't met, but it seemed like a good moment to lay some groundwork.

"I don't. Not at all."

The answer sounded genuine, but most people in Edinburgh, even if they didn't know Edwin personally, had heard of him.

"He's a big fan of yours." I kept it at that for now, but I vowed silently that I would attempt an invitation for him before we left today.

"That's nice to hear." Ryory nodded gratefully but then brought his attention back to us. He looked at Tom. "And what do you do in our fair city?"

"I own Delaney's Wee Pub in Grassmarket."

"Oh?" He looked back and forth between the two of us.

"It was named that before we met," Tom added.

"Aye?"

"Aye."

"I love a good love story," Ryory said, his big voice somehow working with the sentiment.

"Me too." Tom smiled. "We've been fortunate."

"Excellent! All right, now you must call me Ry. Everyone who knows me does."

"Thank you, Ry." It felt too familiar, but I would work hard to keep from saying Mr. Bennigan.

"I like to begin these short sessions by jumping right in. Would either of you like a try at the chisel and hammer? I will answer questions afterwards, but if you'd like to feel the tools of my life's work in your own hands, I would be more than happy to show you what I do."

Tom and I were both excited for the chance to work with the tools and materials that Ry had used to create so many interesting stones. That's what the slab of granite in the middle of the room was for, of course. It appeared untouched, but we were about to transform it. Even if the end product wasn't good, the artistic process was always fulfilling.

"Come." He signaled us to join him next to the stone. "First, I like to take a long look at any stone I work. For me, it's a sign of respect. I don't turn the stones themselves into something else—carve them into another shape—and I know the Pictish symbols so well that I allow the stone to tell me which symbols to use. This stone, however, felt like one of the blankest slates I've ever used. I didn't feel or see anything. Do either of you?"

Tom and I took his question seriously as we pondered the stone. I knew this wasn't Tom's thing. He had an appreciation for all art, but technique didn't much matter to him. Still, though, I caught his expression as we did as Ry had asked.

In fact, he spoke before I did.

"Animals," he said definitively. "This is a stone for animal symbols." He paused as if maybe he shouldn't have spoken up so quickly. "Aye?"

"That's brilliant," Ry encouraged. "Delaney, how about you?"

I hadn't seen or felt much, but Tom's words had built some impressions in my mind.

"I agree."

"Very good. Then, we're off!"

Ry lifted the hammer and chisel. Tom and I both practiced the best ways to hold the tools before Ry took them back and got to work. He moved slowly at first, pointing out how he angled the chisel blade as well as the pressure with which he hit it with the hammer. Before long, a bird symbol, similar to the one we'd seen on the door downstairs, came to life. This one helped confirm my assumption that he hadn't created the crude one on the door in the close.

He sped up as he continued. Though it was impossible not to be fascinated by his muscled shoulders and arms as they worked, those weren't the most intriguing features to me. I found that watching the concentration in his eyes and the way he kept his tongue between his teeth when he came to a curve was far more captivating. He had a very sharp focus.

"All right, who wants to try the straight line that goes here?" he pointed.

I looked at Tom. "You go first?"

He smiled. "All right."

Ry smiled as he handed him the tools and went over again how to hold them. "I didn't even bother to ask, but have you ever used a hammer and chisel before?"

"Maybe as a lad, but I don't remember it." Tom took them confidently and tested their heft with a couple bounces. "They don't feel completely unfamiliar, though."

"Give it a go. You can't hurt anything except yourself. Go slowly and feel comfortable. Art is all about imperfection."

Tom laughed. "That's good news."

As Tom worked, slowly and methodically going through the motions that Ry had just demonstrated, I stood next to Ry and asked, "The Picts? As much as I've researched you, I couldn't find the reason why you chose them."

"Aye, well, I think maybe they chose me. Does that make sense?"

I nodded. "I think I get that."

"I was a wee lad when we learned about them in school. I was fascinated immediately. I remember the teacher introducing them as the people who made the stones. We were too young to go into their warrior lives, but she showed pictures appropriate for our age, and it all seemed so . . . new but familiar at the same time, like maybe she was speaking directly to me. And, when I learned about their red hair, I felt a kinship that I couldn't deny. I wanted to go out that day and get a tattoo, but, of course, my parents thought that was ridiculous." He laughed. His eyes moved up to my own hair. "How about you? Are you interested in my work for any red-haired reason?"

The intellect has little to do on the road to discovery. There comes a leap in consciousness, call it intuition or what you will, and the solution comes to you and you don't know how or why. All great discoveries are made this way.

The long-winded bookish voice that sounded in my mind caught me off guard. The voices I heard were tricks of my own intuition, made of characters, from books, or real life as I either imagined them to sound or had somehow heard. They usually spoke to me when I was trying to figure something out, maybe thinking too hard when I should just be letting my gut speak to me.

This one was a quote from Einstein, and it was about intuition, or discovery. As usual, it wasn't easy for me to understand what my gut was trying to tell me. Sometimes the meaning became clear later, but most of the time it was much later, a discovery of hindsight, in fact.

"Delaney?"

"Oh, my interest in the Picts is new. I feel the red hair connection but nothing as deeply as you do." I paused as I pushed away the voice and put myself back in the moment. "You know, I was the only redhead in my elementary school class in Kansas. I grew up in a small community. High school opened my world to a few more, but I sure stood out in elementary. I was also odd, a bookworm." I didn't mention that the bookish voices had been with me since then. "At first, my red hair only brought unwanted attention in my direction. It wasn't fun. I only had a tiny knowledge about the Picts until I moved to Scotland. I don't remember ever studying them in my American schools. My boss, Edwin, and I have had some discussions. He's fascinated by all Scottish history." I liked that I managed to slip in another plug for Edwin, but I didn't think Ry was taking the bait.

"I certainly understand being different, though my hair wasn't one of the things that made me stand out as a child. Isn't that interesting, what a mere difference in geography might do to shape a life?"

"It is."

"I'm sorry for your pain."

"Oh." I smiled. "It's been a minute, and I've come to either not think about my hair color or just enjoy having it." I couldn't stop myself from swiping my hand over it like I'd done earlier. "The frizz is annoying."

Ry chuckled. "It's perfect. And, you have opened my eyes a wee bit. I thank you. It's wonderful to see other perspectives, isn't it? I don't go out much." He sent me a wry smile. "This event has given me the chance to talk to people on my terms."

"May I ask why? I mean, why don't you put yourself out there more? Your art would be even more popular if you showed it, I'm sure." I cleared my throat, hoping I wasn't pushing too much.

Though he and I were conversing, Ry was also watching Tom. He didn't appear bothered by my questions. A long moment later, he answered, "I don't do it for others. I create for me."

I'd heard such a thing from other artists, but I'd also heard the opposite—that an artist lived for others' support and opinions, and not even always positive. However, it was the artists who didn't have trust funds or other income that were probably the most enthusiastic about sharing their work. I might have already been a bit too bold; there was no way I was going to ask Ryory Bennigan how he had enough money to live the way he did. I didn't have to. He was kind enough to offer up the answer.

He gave me his full attention. "I have money from my family's shipping fortune. It's old money, though it's a mystery to most where it came from." He leaned closer and lowered his voice conspiratorially. It was all for drama, of course. "The money comes from my stepmother's family. She married my father around the same time I was learning about the Picts; however, he was her second husband, so the money's origins got lost in the changes of her last name. With all the new technology, though, I'm surprised that someone hasn't found the ancestry."

I wanted to ask what name could lead to where the money had come from, but I'd been nosy enough. Again, though, I didn't have to.

"The money comes from Phillut Shipping." He smiled again.

"I won't tell anyone."

"No worries. I've never kept the secret on purpose. It's just not easy to track down." He paused. "Despite all of it, I suppose I'm a wee bit afraid of the outside, groups of people. Agoraphobic, probably."

"You are . . . sensitive?" I asked carefully. I didn't mean it as an insult. In fact, I meant it as a compliment. I liked sensitivity, but some people weren't fond of that word, particularly some men. Lots of artists I'd met, though, were very tuned in to the world around them.

"Overly so. As much as you might think I want attention because of what I've done to my body, that just isn't so. I'm very private. This," he waved his hands in front of his torso, "is a compulsion that I simply can't deny."

I nodded. "I get that."

"Aye." He turned to Tom again. "Oh, lad, you've almost got it. Let me show you one wee thing." Ry made his way to Tom and moved the tools a small inch or so downward.

I took a moment to enjoy watching my handsome husband work on art. He took every task he did seriously and never gave less than one hundred percent of himself to anything. He wasn't overly artistic, but he could focus, and he would make sure he learned as much as he could while we were there.

I also contemplated Ry's sensitivity. "Overly so" helped explain his reclusiveness, particularly if he was agoraphobic or an empath, someone who keyed in on all the emotions around him. I felt some of that, and it wasn't always comfortable. If he was extra tuned in to others, it could be painful.

I was working to understand the man as well as his art. He was so likable, pleasant, and inviting. I had no idea what was truly behind his invitations to his studio, but maybe this really was a way for him to meet others, make friends.

However, it was impossible not to be a little perplexed. He wasn't uncomfortable with us; he wasn't cold like Ani. He seemed to like the company. Knowing this person without having researched him first, I would never have predicted that he kept to himself.

With the instruction, Tom managed the hammer and chisel with the skill of someone who was good with his hands and could follow directions well. He might never be an artist, but given the time, he would probably perfect his stone-carving abilities.

When it was my turn, I allowed Ry to help me with more than just instructions. I let him guide my hands, his over mine. It wasn't uncomfortable or weird. It was fascinating to feel the strength in his hands and the way he moved them along with the tools, the confidence and speed. I was sure he was slowing down from his normal speed, but we moved faster than I ever could have on my own.

Together, we cut out a perfect U. I was sad when he disengaged, and I felt the full weight of the tools minus the inspiration. I wasn't an artist, but I was somewhat sensitive too. I liked the way I'd sensed his talent flowing from his fingers and through mine. It was all probably an illusion, but it was one I would remember forever.

When a bird and a fish symbol were complete, I put the hammer and chisel back on the table and we inspected the work.

"Fabulous!" Ry exclaimed.

Tom cocked his head. "I'm not sure I'd give it that high regard, but I think we did okay."

"We did," I agreed. "That was fun."

"Aye," Tom agreed. He looked at Ry. "Thank you for that."

"My pleasure. Now, would you like to see the room where I keep all the finished art?"

"Absolutely!" Tom and I exclaimed.

As we set off, he spoke about his tattoos, explaining that though the rumor is that he learned how to tattoo himself, he hadn't.

"I could never do that to myself."

"Who is your artist?" Tom asked.

"Oh. It's a secret, lad. I'm sorry."

"I understand."

"Do you have any tattoos? Either of you?"

"No, neither of us," I answered.

"Are you interested?"

"I wouldn't say *interested*, but I might say intrigued and terrified." I laughed.

"Same," Tom added.

"There are some amazing tattooists in this city. If nothing else, I'll make sure Ani sends you a list of those I know are safe and reputable. Just in case."

Tom and I shared raised eyebrows.

"Thank you," I said.

We made our way to the end of the second hallway and into another jam-packed room, but this one was loaded up differently, not with things right next to one another but with a little space in between. It was filled with partially finished stones as well as some paintings and pencil sketches. This was *the* studio, I had no doubt.

"Ry, it seems not much is known about any of your art other than the carvings. It's all incredible."

Ry smiled wryly again. "I've managed to keep everything else a secret. I don't know what will happen now that I've invited so many people to visit."

"We won't say a word, I promise," I said.

Ry shrugged. "We will see if any others do. I didn't even have an assistant before Ani. I did everything myself. I knew I needed someone I could trust completely. Ani fit the bill and she hasn't disappointed me. We'll see what happens next."

My intuition suddenly spoke to me again, though not in the form of a bookish voice. I couldn't help but wonder if Ry's hiring someone to help him and his welcoming visitors might be because he was ill and feeling the need to share before it was too late. He didn't appear to be anything but big and strapping and healthy, yet sometimes those things weren't obvious.

I couldn't bring myself to ask such a question, but thankfully Tom didn't hesitate.

"Ry, are you well?" he said. "You aren't ill or anything?"

Tom wasn't shy, but he was also not nearly as nosy as I was. Maybe it just seemed like the obvious question.

Ry laughed. "I'm right as rain, Tom, Delaney. I think I'm just getting older, and things change when one ages."

"That is true," Tom said. "I'm glad you are well. Thank you for easing our minds."

"Yes, thank you," I added.

"Aye, you aren't the first to ask."

We stood still for a long moment and glanced over all the items in the room.

"They were pirates, you know," Ry said. "The Picts. Ferocious, in fact. Though we have little history, there are accounts from witnesses who saw them attack Roman communities in Britain. Though I know I'm not a vicious man, sometimes I think of all of this as my booty."

"It's all your artwork, though?" I asked.

"Aye"—Ry shrugged—"but sometimes it feels like the contents of a ship's hold in here."

"I see that." There were so many items that I couldn't immediately digest much of anything. I needed to slow my survey.

But before I could scan again, we heard something that sounded like a moan coming from somewhere in the room we were in.

The three of us looked at each other with furrowed eyebrows.

"Did you hear that?" Ry asked.

Tom and I nodded, and then we automatically spread out and tried to listen. The room was more crowded and messier than the others we'd seen—but not so big that we shouldn't be able to find the source of the noise.

"Oh!" Ry exclaimed less than a minute later—though it felt like we were slogging through. "She's here. Come help!"

Tom and I stepped over and around things. I bashed my leg into a jutting, sharp piece of stone but ignored the pain.

We came upon Ry at the same time, both of us over his shoulder as he crouched next to Ani. She was on her side, curled into herself.

"Ani?" Ry asked. "What happened?"

"My stomach. I feel so sick. And I'm dizzy."

I grabbed my phone. It only took a beat to realize this was no simple stomach bug. Considering her positioning, the gray color over her profusely sweating face, and the fact that she was having trouble breathing, something was terribly wrong.

I pushed 999. Thankfully, someone answered immediately. I told the operator where we were and what was going on. As they had the previous times I'd called them, they kept me on the line until emergency responders arrived.

Ani didn't even try to lift herself off the floor. In fact, she seemed to be fading quickly, but the first responders somehow got there and up the stairs quickly. They attended to her with admirable speed and competence. They had her color looking a tiny bit better by the time they loaded her up on a gurney. The stairway was a challenge, but there was no elevator. They maneuvered her down and loaded her into an ambulance.

Later, I would recall the emergency in flashes of color, with commanding voices and talented, life-saving people. Ry, Tom, and I followed them down the stairs and then out of the close to the main street.

As we stood together and watched the ambulance ride away, Ry made a small, choked noise, the first sound he'd made since the EMTs had taken over.

"I'm so sorry, Ry. What can we do?" I asked him.

He shook his head. "Nothing." He swallowed hard. "I wish they'd said she'd be all right."

They hadn't. They'd assured us that they would take care of her but had seemed far from certain that she would be okay.

Ry continued, "I'll head to the hospital as soon as they give me the thumbs-up."

"We could drive you?" Tom offered.

We'd taken public transportation over, but we'd gather the car from Grassmarket and come back if that would help.

"No," said Ry, his attention still on the retreating ambulance before he turned to Tom. "That's a kind offer, but, no, I can get there. I'm so sorry, but I'm afraid our time must be cut short."

Tom and I both shook off his apology, stating that Ani's health was all that mattered. The moments were fraught and awkward, distracted. Even as Ryory Bennigan, famous Scottish artist, hurried back down the close to disappear inside the door with the mark above its knob, Tom and I were unsure which way to turn, what to do next.

Tom recovered before I did. "Lass, she should be fine. We'll follow up. I believe we found her in time."

I nodded. "I do think she'll be fine too, but she was really sick. It wasn't . . . a typical stomachache."

"No, it wasn't, but she's in good hands. The best."

Part of my mind had been focused enough to make the call, but the rest of it was now a swirling mess. Tom's calm words brought me back to a workable level.

I took a deep breath. "Yes, she's going to be fine. Okay, all is well so far. She looked better, right?"

"She did."

"We will find a way to get an update."

"Aye."

I looked down the street one more time, but the ambulance was no longer in sight. I glanced down the close, but Ry was not there either. Finally, I looked at Tom. "I guess we should get back to it then."

"Agreed. Let's head back."

CHAPTER THREE

"Och, that sounds horrible." Rosie's eyes were wide. "I hope the lass is okay."

"I do too." I scratched behind Hector's ears as I held him, the cutest miniature Yorkie in the world, in the crook of my arm. He'd trotted right to me when I entered the bookshop. Though he almost always greeted all of us who worked there, he could tell that I needed some extra attention today.

A moment later, Rosie lowered her voice and said, "At the risk of sounding insensitive, how was everything else?"

"Oh. Well, it was fascinating. An experience I'll never forget."

The bookshop's door burst open, and Edwin came through, a big smile on his face. "Lass, how did it go? Tell me everything."

Rosie and I shared raised eyebrows. She lifted a hand. "Hamlet will be here in a few. Let's wait for him so Delaney might only recount the story one more time."

Just as it appeared Edwin might protest, the landline phone on the corner of Rosie's desk jingled.

"The Cracked Spine," she answered. "Aye. One moment."

She lifted the handset away from her ear and looked at me. "For you, lass."

"Hello," I said.

"Lass, it's Ry Bennigan. Hello."

"Oh! Hello." I braced myself for what felt like possible bad news.

"I just wanted to let you know that Ani will be fine. She's getting better by the moment. They don't know what happened to her yet, but she's going to be okay. They assured me of as much."

"That's great news! Thank you so much for sharing it!" I smiled and sent Rosie a thumbs-up. She smiled in relief too.

"My pleasure. I'm planning on stopping by your shop tomorrow. Ani loves it just as much as I do. I thought I'd come find something for her, and I'd like to thank you in person for keeping your wits about you. You took care of things."

"Oh . . . I'm just glad she's going to be okay. We would love to see you."

"Ta. I'll see you tomorrow around ten."

"That's great. And, Ry, please give Ani our best." I was going to add that she was delightful, but I couldn't bring myself to be disingenuous. She wasn't delightful, but I still didn't wish her anything bad.

"I shall. See you tomorrow."

I hung up the phone.

"What's happening?" Edwin's voice was now lined with concern.

Thankfully, if only so we wouldn't have to further torture Edwin, Hamlet came through the door an instant later.

"What's going on?" he asked as he took us all in.

"Come, sit, everyone. Delaney has a story to tell us," Rosie said.

We found seats around the table in the back. It was tucked behind a half-wall and was where Hamlet did most of his work. He studied old manuscripts and photographs, working to figure out all their particulars. It was a service that the bookshop offered free of charge. Hamlet enjoyed the provenance work, but he wasn't there full-time, so he did things at his pace. Edwin never asked him to rush even though people from far and wide asked for his assistance. Hamlet was talented and his worldwide reputation was only growing.

The retail part of the bookshop was in an old bank building. A stained-glass window on the back wall depicted a scale unequally weighted with stacks of coins. A bit unusual for a bookstore. The rest of the space was filled with packed bookshelves, a rolling ladder along one side. Rosie's desk was at the front where she could greet the customers, or read, or work on one of Edwin's ledgers of accounts. She still wrote them all on paper, using a pencil and a good eraser.

The retail side—which I had deemed "the light side" because it was well lit—was attached to the neighboring building by a pathway at the top of some stairs on the other side of the half-wall. The other side—"the dark side"—only had one exposed lightbulb on the high ceiling, which barely illuminated the stairway. Blacked-out windows along the front and back of that building somehow didn't make the building look abandoned, though they kept the inside shrouded. The dark side used to be Edwin's refuge, where he would spend his time when he worked here, amid his collections in the warehouse. Now, it was my office.

After we got comfortable in the back, I shared the details of the visit to Ry's place. I offered as much detail as I could remember, from the dark stairs to the stark entryway where we waited, and everything we'd done and seen on the way to the room where we'd found Ani. My coworkers were just like me in that they enjoyed the details.

They all wished for a lesson with Ry's hammer and chisel but would never be so bold as to ask him about the possibility. They were fascinated to learn that Ry was an artist of many mediums and wished I'd had an opportunity to snap some pictures on my phone.

"Weirdly, it didn't even occur to me," I said. "I guess I was just so busy taking it all in."

Rosie's favorite thing was that he'd told us to call him Ry, and Edwin was excited for the next day's visit. Everyone was glad to hear that Ani was going to be okay, but Hamlet was, by far, the most relieved.

"I know her from university," he explained. "She and I took a few classes together. She's talented in her own right. When she got the job with Mr. Bennigan, she rang me right off, she was so excited. She asked me not to tell anyone, though." He sent Edwin a sheepish shrug. "Sorry."

"Not to worry, lad. You are a good friend. That's admirable."

On another person, Edwin's words might seem forced or scripted, but he genuinely felt the platitudes he spoke. Though he'd lived an imperfect life when it came to making good choices, he'd grown into his role as the sage older gentleman.

He appreciated Hamlet's loyalty to his friend, and, though he never patted himself on the back, he and Rosie had been instrumental in Hamlet's upbringing. He might not take credit for any of Hamlet's behavior, but he would be pleased that such lessons had been well digested.

"I'd love to hear more about the studio," Hamlet, the most artistic of our Cracked Spine family, requested.

"Interesting. Odd. Messy in some parts, clean in others." The moment I'd run into the stone came back to me. I had an urge to look at my bruise, but I wasn't going to lift the leg of my pants at the moment. As I thought about it, a small pain pulsed through my calf. "It was pretty darn amazing."

"Could you handle the hammer and chisel?" Rosie asked.

"They were heavy but not terrible." I remembered a part I'd forgotten before. "I let Ry guide my hands with his. That was extraordinary. I was sure I could feel his inspiration."

"I imagine so," Edwin said breathily.

Rosie laughed. "Be here tomorrow at ten, Edwin. You will finally get to meet the man."

"I'm very excited."

"I am too," Hamlet added. "If you don't think I'll be too much to add to the mix."

"No! Be here," I said. "He's not what I expected at all, though now I'm not exactly sure what I expected. Maybe an ego, maybe a strangeness that sometimes comes with extremely talented people, but he's none of that. He's quite nice, and found a love, a compulsion, for the Picts. He might be a bit agoraphobic, but he's not shy at all." I shook my head and laughed. "I don't know what to make of him, but I like him. You will too." I remembered something else. "His money comes from his stepmother's fortune from . . . Phillut Shipping, I think? Sound familiar?" I reached for my phone.

Everyone shook their head as I typed in a search on my phone, reading the results aloud.

"It was established in the early seventeen hundreds. It's still around, though now named McBride Shipping." I paused and looked up from the phone. "You don't suppose that's Bridget's family?"

Again, no one had anything to offer.

"I'll ask her. Anyway," I looked at the phone again, "the company specializes in short sea bulk cargo like aggregates, alumina, grain, coal, fertilizers, and steel." I looked up again. "I wonder if stones are ever part of their cargo. I bet no one figures it out simply because of the name change, though Ry did mention that his stepmother had been married before and names got lost on the way."

"Sounds like a fascinating history," Edwin added.

I could tell he might dig even deeper himself. He was all about history.

"Before she worked for Ry, Ani and I had a class together where we studied the Pict symbols," Hamlet interjected. "We were in a group together, and we came up with our own interpretations."

"Which, for all we ken, could be the correct ones," Rosie said. "We don't know for sure what any of them meant. And there are different versions based on regions, aye?"

"Aye," Edwin answered.

Hamlet gave a small shrug. "Well, I doubt they meant the things *we* said they meant. We had fun with the assignment and were consistently silly enough about it all that our professor could tell we actually did the work to create our own world. For example, it is thought that the one that is a disc above the rectangle is a mirror. We decided it should represent a belly and its button."

I laughed. "Clever."

"Maybe not scientific, but there's so little that's known about them, we decided that we'd have some fun. I think it was that assignment that caused her to reach out to Mr. Bennigan in the first place, but she's been cagey about all of that. She's loyal to him."

"How many different interpretations of the symbols are there?" I asked.

Edwin fell into thought. "I'd have to look at all my note-books to be certain, but I think that regarding the . . . belly symbol referenced, there are six different versions, depending on where in Scotland they were used, and probably when. Things were bound to change over time." Edwin shrugged. "I do think you could interpret any of the versions as a stomach and its button." He smiled. "I like it."

"Well, it was a fun assignment," Hamlet repeated. "I'm very glad she's going to be okay."

"Hamlet," I said, "she didn't seem *fun* to me. She was very serious." I didn't want to risk insulting his friend, but I could not imagine the woman we met ever being any sort of fun.

"She was . . . snotty?" He smiled knowingly.

"Well, I don't think I would say that."

"Aye, you would." Rosie put her hand on my arm and looked at Hamlet just like Edwin and I were.

Hamlet nodded. "It's a persona she took on when she started working for Mr. Bennigan. She knew that everyone would want her to get them in to see or talk to him. She's snotty on purpose for work, but in real life, she's sweet."

"Interesting." It was still difficult to believe it was an act, but I didn't speak my thought aloud.

It didn't matter anyway. All that mattered was that she'd be okay.

Edwin stood. "Well, I will see you all tomorrow. I'm off to attend to errands. Does anyone need anything?"

None of us needed anything, though I was curious about his errands. Edwin enjoyed visiting his friends, and he enjoyed grocery shopping, an interest that had come along with his new hobbies of cooking and baking. He'd been trying so many recipes lately that I was surprised he hadn't brought in some cookies for us to sample today. I didn't ask what he was up to, though.

After he left, the store was quiet as Rosie and Hector searched the shelves for a book someone had called in to request, and Hamlet opened the files he'd been working on for about a week now. I announced I was going to spend some time over on the dark side.

It was my space now. I'd organized it and was still cataloging all the items inside. There was so much that I would be busy for a long time. I considered it job security.

After I'd been laid off from my job at a museum in Wichita, I'd been perusing the internet for any possible opportunities. I answered an ad that Edwin had placed. I wondered sometimes if he was looking specifically for me when he wrote of someone who wanted an adventure in Scotland, not to mention who wouldn't be intimidated by working on a desk that had seen the likes of kings and queens. At the time I'd thought he was embellishing the desk, but he hadn't been. It had literally once resided inside the castle on the hill. I didn't know how or when Edwin had acquired it, but he loved it. I did too, although I was much more intimidated by it than he'd probably ever been. I still covered it with sheets of butcher-block paper before I attempted to work upon it.

Other offices—one that Rosie never used and one that Edwin might have only used three times since I'd been there— were located on the upper level. Along with the warehouse, the loo, and a kitchenette (always poorly stocked, probably because of the convenience of the nearby and delicious bakery and coffee shops with fresh treats) were on the dark side.

The warehouse was a tall room, taking up half of the second-level space that the above offices didn't use. The walls were topped off by windows. Edwin had added a temperature and humidity control system to this room only. The rest of the dark side was regulated by a less than reliable thermostat on a side wall at the front. Except for the warehouse, the dark side was usually frigid. Sometimes you could even see your breath.

An old blue key was used to open the warehouse's ornately carved red door. There were only two keys to it, and I kept one. I was worried about the responsibility at first but not so much anymore. Rosie kept the other in her desk on the light side.

It took turning the key a full three times to both lock and release the bolt mechanism. The room was always locked when someone wasn't inside it. I didn't keep it that way anymore when I was inside, but I used to. Along with the top windows, Edwin had installed ceiling lighting that made even tiny details easy to see.

It was only recently that I'd asked about the red door's origin.

Edwin had said that he had no clue, that it had been there when he'd purchased the buildings decades earlier, but he had no idea what business had once been housed on the dark side that required such a door.

It was a mystery I hoped to research someday. But not today.

Today, I decided I would delve into the Picts so I could speak more intelligently to Ry tomorrow. I'd wished for the time to do so before our meeting yesterday, but everything had come about on such short notice.

Once behind the door, I did the typical once-over examination of the entire room. Nothing seemed out of place. It was rare that anything did, but there had been a few times when one of my coworkers had searched the shelves or in some of the files. They usually gave me a heads-up about their visits but not always. They weren't required to let me know. Though I'd claimed the space as mine, it was for the purposes of my work. Everyone at the bookshop was welcome inside.

Its existence used to be a semi-poorly kept secret, but other mysteries and precarious situations had caused Edwin to rethink the need for secrecy. Though we didn't advertise that it was there, we no longer denied it if asked about it.

I'd applied for my job as I'd sat behind my computer in Kansas, answering the advertisement that promised adventure behind the desk of kings and queens. I sat behind it today after I covered it with a fresh strip of butcher-block paper, cutting it to fit perfectly over the top before I gathered my laptop out of a drawer.

Using my old friend Google, I dug in. "The Picts" kicked off the search.

My deep dive first uncovered what I already knew and what

everyone seemed to say—we still don't know much about the Pictish people. Some of the things I read had even been noted as revised with "updated theories," things changing because new archaeological sites had been uncovered or new interpretations had been offered up. What we did know was sprinkled with enough fantasy and mythology that, really, we couldn't be certain of much of anything about them, their lives, or why they suddenly disappeared.

In fact, they didn't even call themselves Picts or Pictish. It was a name that came about later, probably because of the tattoos and pigment they covered themselves with—the *picti*, the painted ones.

I discovered more technical details than even I, someone who loves details, could manage to soak up. And yet each new piece of information was littered with plenty of speculation and disagreement.

I decided I would gather the "facts" that most appealed to me or rang the truest based on the knowledge I already had. I wanted to have some talking points when Ry visited the bookshop.

A new nugget I did glean: What *had* survived over the centuries was something historians called a king list. It presented several different medieval transcriptions, though they all have slightly different information. It appears this list was part of a manuscript that is now lost to time. There were probably seven (maybe more) different Pictish kingdoms in Scotland, and one didn't always get along with the other. However, even that comes into question when the names of the kingdoms are coincidentally the same as the sons of Cruithne—perhaps the founder of the Picts.

This information (the king list) was purportedly discovered at a Pictish monastery (location unknown), later reaching Scottish monks who took some liberties with their own translations, though the list of kings does seem to show up in a lot of different places.

Nevertheless, the list includes some sixty Pictish kings and notes their length of reign as well as their fathers' names, even though it appears that kings might have been chosen down a matriarchal line.

There is nothing definitive about their disappearance. Maybe they were killed off, maybe they melded into other groups. Scottish people as well as all the other people who were around back then weren't known to be shy when it came to conquering and controlling. It was a violent time.

The history of the Picts is gathered mostly from external sources. The Irish annals were a group of texts compiled by Irish monks who took note of historical events in a brief, year-by-year format. At some point before 800 CE, a chronicle that included the Picts was delivered to Ireland, where its information was included in the annals. And despite the historical debates, there is enough data to present a broad (very broad) outline of Pictish history. When reading about the Picts, I frequently came upon the term "pseudo-historical," which only reinforced my doubt about everything else that was noted or highlighted.

Other resources come from early missionary accounts, though the focus of their reports is more about the missionaries, patting themselves on their backs regarding their own miracles or conversions.

Another source I came upon was from an abbot of Saint

Columba's. At least a few Pict kings are discussed in Saint Columba's writings.

As historians look backward at the Picts, even in the Irish annals, there's no indication they were ever their own separate group, different from all the other people living in the areas of Scotland they populated. It seemed the annals didn't want to separate them from others based on their tattoo-covered bodies (some historians even dispute this fact), their flaming red hair, or their strange language that we think was very gibberish-like. Their lands were often invaded by Scots, English, Britons, and Vikings, and they lived in well-traveled areas where lots of folks fought to gain resources or just to survive.

It seems the Picts did fight back when they were challenged, but the final blows must have come around 900 CE, because there's no more information after that.

When they weren't fighting, however, they were farmers. Though cattle and horses were probably reserved for the wealthier, there were lots of sheep and pigs. The Picts grew all kinds of vegetables, including some that aren't as well-known these days, such as skirret, which is a starchy root that has a sweet flavor.

But by far the most interesting findings—and the real reason the Picts are still of such interest—are the stone carvings, more of which continue to be uncovered to this day.

The Picts' history was made of bits and pieces and guesses, along with a heavy helping of imagination and hope. Who wouldn't want stories about a group of people with blue tattoos and fiery red hair? Even though they were probably just going about their daily lives, it's the differences that made them so intriguing.

My phone dinged with a text just as I was going to sketch out my own timeline. It was from Tom.

Lost in research again?

I glanced at the time. Yes, I'd done it again. Hours had passed by in what felt like moments, and Tom was waiting for me to head home to our blue house by the sea.

I responded: I'll be out in a few.

I could stay in the warehouse longer. Tom would have come back to get me or I could jump on a bus. I knew Edinburgh's public transportation system like the back of my hand. But dinner with my husband sounded like the preferable way to end the evening.

Besides, I wanted to be well rested for our visitor the next morning.

I shut down the laptop, made sure everything was locked up, and then hurried through the bookshop, now dark and closed. Rosie had left me a note saying she and Hamlet didn't want to bother me but would see me the next morning.

I relocked the shop's door and hurried up to meet Tom.

CHAPTER FOUR

The next morning, I doubted that any of us had slept well. It wasn't like we hadn't had important visitors to the bookshop before, but Ryory Bennigan seemed somehow next-level.

We all arrived close to 7 a.m., each of us with coffees in hand and some sort of breakfast to share. Even Tom joined in to offer help, which Hamlet took him up on immediately, asking for some assistance with the file drawers in the back.

Hector sat on the floor, watching us with slowish blinks. Even he seemed a little sleepier than normal for our early morning activities.

The shop was never really dirty. We dusted and mopped all the time. I had organized all the bookshelves and was working on an inventory program that would probably only assist us all to find things more easily—well, Hamlet and me. Neither Rosie nor Edwin was fond of any sort of computer. They didn't even use their smartphones for anything other than texting and calling.

Still, though, organization was my thing.

Apparently, we all wanted to make a next-level impression for our next-level guest.

"I hope Mr. Bennigan has a sweet tooth," Rosie noted as she glanced at all the boxes we'd brought in and set on her desk. "I'll wipe down the windows. Delaney, do you want to dry mop the floor? I mopped it well last night, but dust might have gathered. Edwin, how about you attend to the ladder—that third rung is a wee bit loose."

Edwin and I nodded, and we all got to work as Hector walked from spot to spot watching us curiously. Once he approved of the activity in one area, he would trot to the next and take up watch again.

The shop might have never been so squared away, spic-and-span. I was sure Hector approved.

Tom finished up with Hamlet and left to make his way up to the pub just a few minutes before Ryory Bennigan stepped through the doorway, the four of us employees and the cutest dog in the world standing at attention to the side of Rosie's desk.

Hector was first to offer a greeting, with a tiny bark that would make even the sourest of the sour at least twitch with a smile.

Ryory Bennigan wasn't smiling at all, though. And I hadn't thought for a moment that he was a sour person.

Something was wrong. His face was gray and pulled in either desperation or sadness.

He wore a thin brown sweater (he'd call it a jumper), jeans, and tennis shoes (he'd probably call them trainers). Two of his neck tattoos and one at the top of his chest peeked out from the neckline. The ones on his hands were noticeable, but all the others were covered. My dive into research the night before gave me some names of the symbols represented. They were a comb, a horseshoe, and a beast (I'd probably call it a bear).

Suddenly, a thought exploded in my mind. I stepped forward and croaked out one word, "Ani?"

Ry swallowed hard and then shook his head. "No, she's fine."

Both Hamlet and I made funny, relieved noises, but I didn't look at my coworker. I kept my attention on Ry. "What's wrong?"

"A man I recently met was killed. He was . . ." He looked at me and his expression somehow became even more dire. "He was visiting me just yesterday, right before you and your husband arrived."

"The man from Kansas?" I worked to remember his name. It finally came to me. "Dr. Pace?"

"Aye."

Rosie stepped forward and put her hand on Ry's arm. "Och, lad, come sit in the back. We'll get you some fortification."

Robotically, Ryory nodded and allowed Rosie to guide him back.

"Who's Dr. Pace?" Edwin asked me quietly as we let Hamlet and Hector follow Rosie in front of us.

"He was leaving as we arrived. Full name's Adam Pace. I could tell he was American, and we spoke briefly about both of us being from Kansas. He was from the university where I received my degree. I even invited him to the bookshop."

"Oh dear. Well, Mr. Bennigan must have known him well. He's devastated."

"He said *killed*. Do you suppose it was murder?"

"We'll find out," Edwin said.

I nodded but stopped walking. A thought occurred to me. "Go ahead. I'm going to text Inspector Winters and ask if he knows anything."

Edwin, just as innately curious as I was, nodded. "Good idea."

Once the text was off, I plunked the phone into my back pocket, and we hurried to join the others.

Ry was upset, but he also made it clear that he didn't know Adam Pace very well. He liked the man, but I sensed there was more to his reaction than grief or sadness.

"Ry, what was he there for yesterday?" I asked after he repeated that Dr. Pace was dead. I was no longer concerned about being too nosy.

I hadn't had enough time with Dr. Pace to know whether I would like him or not, but, of course, I had felt a connection.

Ry's face fell in what I thought was shame. I was right.

"He had something I wanted."

I nodded him on.

"Well, now I'm sure I'll never get it, which is a selfish view, of course."

"What was it?" Rosie asked.

Ry nodded. "Before I tell you that . . . I shop here." He smiled sadly at Rosie. "I love this bookshop, and Rosie has always been an accommodating companion on my speedy journeys through the shelves. I'm not a lingerer."

"Aye, ta." Rosie nodded.

Ry looked at Hamlet. "I know the connection between you and my Ani. She's been a wonderful assistant, and she's told me about your friendship. Though I knew about this place for years, it was Ani who reminds me how much I enjoy shopping inside it."

"Is she really all right?" Hamlet interjected.

"Aye, lad. Fine. They don't know what happened to her, but she's home. Do you know where she lives?"

"I do."

"She probably wouldn't mind you checking in on her."

Hamlet nodded. "I will."

"Good."

Ry looked at Edwin. "We haven't met. It's a pleasure."

"Same. It's a true thrill to meet you, Mr. Bennigan."

"Ah. Ry, please, Mr. MacAlister. I'm certainly old enough now to be a 'Mister,' but I just can't get used to that."

"All right. And, Edwin, please."

"Ta." Ry sighed. "Anyway, thank you for letting me ease into this. I did want to talk about it, and . . . well, other than Ani, there aren't many people I . . . Goodness, that makes me sound like I want pity. Not at all—"

Rosie put her hand on Ry's arm. "It's all right, lad. You can trust us."

Ry nodded. "I was to have breakfast with Mr. Pace, but when he didn't show up at the restaurant, I sought him out. He was renting a wee house just off the Royal Mile. I knew the address, so I ventured in that direction." He paused, swallowed hard. "The police were there, the building taped off as a crime scene. I didn't want to ask questions, but I overheard all I needed to know—that a body had been found and the name was Adam Pace. They even said 'a gentleman from the States.' I should have let them know I was supposed to meet with him, but I was so shocked that I just walked away and came here."

He looked at Edwin. "I didn't even consider canceling or not telling you about Mr. Pace, but I think maybe I should call the police and tell them what I know about the lad's visit to Edinburgh. It's probably important, particularly if he was murdered. I think the shock has caused me to make some poor decisions."

Even Hector's attention was fully on the artist sitting at the head of the table. Though Ry had mentioned the police, he didn't make a move to call anyone.

"Ry, I can call a police officer friend, ask if he could come here. Would that work?" I offered, noticing that the inspector hadn't texted me back yet.

"Aye," Ry said. "But, may I tell you first about the item that Dr. Pace . . . had?"

We looked at each other, all of us too curious to suggest that he do the right thing and call the police first.

"Of course," Edwin said.

We all nodded along.

"Dr. Pace contacted Ani a few months ago. At first, she ignored him. I used to get a lot of regular mail, and even though my email address isn't publicized, people still somehow find it and so I get plenty of those as well. It's part of the reason I hired Ani, to assist with all of that. Anyway. Ani thought what he had to say was ridiculous, so she didn't tell me at first. But he was persistent, and she finally shared with me what he wanted to show me. I took a meeting . . ."

We waited as he fell into thought.

He continued a moment later. "Even after that first meeting together, I didn't believe him. And, well, he wouldn't show me anything substantial so . . . well," Ry looked up at us, "Dr. Pace claimed to have something that might help us understand the Pictish language."

We digested his words. My thoughts went to the things I'd read the day before. I remembered something specific, though.

"Wasn't it thought that the Pictish language was something like gibberish?" I asked.

Both Ry and Edwin shrugged.

"It's one guess," Ry offered.

"What are the others?" I asked.

Ry nodded at Edwin.

"Well," Edwin began but was interrupted by the bell above the front door announcing that someone was coming inside.

"Excuse me." Rosie stood and made her way to the front.

"Lass, could you call your police friend?" Ry said. "The more I talk about this, the guiltier I feel. I can seek them out myself, but if you do have a friend . . ."

"I do." I reached for my phone.

Inspector Winters answered on the first ring.

"Lass?"

"If you're not busy, would you mind coming over to the bookshop?"

After a moment's pause, he said, "What have you gotten yourself into this time? Never mind, don't answer that yet. I'll be there soon."

CHAPTER FIVE

True to his word, it didn't take long for Inspector Winters to arrive.

Ry greeted him just inside the door, announcing that he'd been at the scene of a possible murder that morning. I was glad that the customers who'd come in just before I'd made the call had finished their shopping by then.

Inspector Winters blinked at Ry, and then, without further hesitation, he turned the sign on the door to Closed. Without knowing anything else, he separated us, directing each of us to a corner. Hamlet was sent to the balcony at the top of the stairway. Ry got the back table. Inspector Winters made the rounds and took initial statements. Of those of us who worked at the bookshop, my statement took the longest. Inspector Winters wanted to get all the details of my and Tom's visit with Ry the day before.

Then finally, in quiet tones, he finished up with the artist in the back. I was in the opposite corner, and even though I strained hard to hear, I couldn't catch the gist of anything.

"Come on back, everyone," Inspector Winters said after he and Ry spoke.

We gathered around the table. I thought maybe Ry would leave after they spoke, but he didn't. In fact, he seemed to settle in.

"All right," Inspector Winters said. "I appreciate you calling me over. I've taken everyone's statement. I also know that Dr. Pace's death is being investigated as a possible murder, but I don't know if anything new has been discovered since earlier this morning. I will stay on top of things. But Mr. Bennigan wanted to share a little more with you all. I'm staying just to make sure nothing gets . . . lost in translation, or if something pertinent that someone might have forgotten to tell me is mentioned."

"Aye?" Rosie said.

I was sure she was thinking the same thing I was. It was odd that we were being further included, but also interesting. Maybe it was as simple as Inspector Winters not wanting to spend more of his time answering any questions I might have. Maybe this would take care of them.

Inspector Winters nodded at Ryory. "Aye. I'll let him tell you."

Ry took a breath. "First of all, I apologize for everything I'm about to share."

When he then hesitated at the surprised looks on our faces, Edwin was the one to speak. "G'on, lad."

"I wasn't quite forthcoming with you all because . . . well, it's all a wee bit messy. Nevertheless, it was all planned."

"What was?" Rosie asked, her tone suspicious.

Inspector Winters jumped in. "Just start from the beginning, Mr. Bennigan. They will understand."

Ry nodded. "What I said earlier wasn't untrue, but there's a wee bit more to all of it. It *was* about three months ago that Dr.

Pace started attempting to get in touch. He is—was—a pale-ontologist, and he was working with some paleontologists and archeologists in Scotland on one of their ongoing Picts projects. He'd been in Edinburgh almost a year by then.

"The research never ends, but Pictish discoveries ride waves of sorts. Just when we think everything that could be found has been, something else is uncovered, and then dissected. Anyway, nothing revolutionarily new has come to the forefront for a long time, so Dr. Pace came to Scotland for . . . well, he called it exploring and relationship-building. He said he wanted to get his eyes on things." Ry paused and took a drink from a cup of water on the table. "One of the many places he decided to visit was Knockfarrel Pictish hill fort, near Strathpeffer—"

"One of Scotland's first archeological excavations," Hamlet added.

"Aye," Ry said.

I didn't know where that was, but Edwin clarified. "North, past Inverness."

I nodded, and we all looked back at Ry.

"Aye. The site is no longer being excavated, but that's where he went, by himself. While he was there . . . well, he found something . . ."

"Aye?" Edwin said.

"A stone, buried near a tree, its top corner barely sticking out. Without considering that what he was doing might be illegal or wrong, he dug it up. It wasn't easy. The stone wasn't what we've come to recognize as a Pictish stone but about half the size. When he first rescued it from the ground, he couldn't make out any details because it was still so covered in the dirt.

But he knew how to clean up such things, so he loaded it into the boot of his rental auto and drove back to Edinburgh."

"He took something from an archeological site?" Edwin asked, though his tone wasn't accusatory. He'd been known to be a little secretive about his own surprise treasures a time or two. "Dug something up?"

"Well, no one has explored it for a long time, but, aye. He . . . well, and I told this to Inspector Winters, he told me that he didn't return the dirt he dug up back to the hole. It was a question I asked him right off when he told me what he'd done, at our first in-person meeting six weeks ago."

Someone could have noticed the hole, and if they cared enough about the integrity of Scottish sites, currently being worked or not, they might report the upturned earth. Even if there were no cameras close by, a curious enough investigator might have been able to track who'd done the digging by asking questions or looking over captured video from routes in and out of the area.

"I think that if he'd just returned the dirt, he might have gotten away with his covert activities." Ry blinked at Inspector Winters. "Though, I'm not saying that's what he should have done."

"He didn't get away with it?" I asked.

Inspector Winters frowned and looked at Ry.

"I'm not sure, but . . . ."

"You think he was killed because of what he found?" I asked.

"I don't know. It's possible."

"Explain the stone, lad," Rosie said.

Ry seemed to think about his response for a moment, but,

finally, he nodded. "Well, he was right in his thinking that he'd come upon something that would be of incredible value, something that someone like me, someone obsessed with the Picts, would want. Anyone would want, really."

"The stone?" I asked.

"Aye, it was a translation."

"Of the language or the symbols?" I asked.

"The language."

I shook my head and we all waited.

"The Pictish language has been lost for centuries." Ry had been sitting with his hands on his lap. Now, he lifted them to the table and sat forward a little.

"Aye?" Edwin broke the new wave of suspense.

"Apparently, there was a monk who thought to do a small translation."

Doubt had begun to weave its way through my entire being, growing with each passing second. Not only did I think that Adam Pace's story had a very good chance of being a lie but I wondered how truthful Ryory Bennigan was being. Were we all being used or mocked? Why?

Maybe this was why Inspector Winters was still here and wanted us all together. Maybe he thought we might be able to poke holes in Ry's story.

"And?" Rosie asked. "What did you think?"

"I never saw it for more than a few moments, and it was only in a picture that Dr. Pace shared with me."

"He didn't show you the stone itself? Why not?" I asked.

Ry sighed. "He wanted money first."

"Aye, of course he did," Rosie said.

"He was going to have me sign a non-disclosure agreement

this morning. I was to pay him a small amount for the privilege of seeing the stone, but I was to sign the agreement first."

"What was the price?" Edwin asked.

"The fee to see it wasn't much, negligible, but he was going to tell me the total cost for the stone today."

Again, doubt tightened my stomach. "Sounds like a setup."

"There must have been more," Edwin said.

"I thought the same." Ry held up his hand. "I was suspicious, though curious enough to play it all out a little further. If the stone was what he said it was, it was one of great importance if it was real."

"Of course. An interpretation of the Picts' language would be invaluable," Hamlet said. "But . . . what language was used in the interpretation? How did someone think to do such a thing? Ry, I'm sorry, but I can't imagine any of it was real."

"Same," Rosie said.

Edwin and I nodded in agreement.

"I don't disagree, but from what I saw, ancient Roman was the language used."

"Well, that might make some sense, but that language was used long before the Picts," Hamlet said.

"Aye. I brought that point up to him, but he kept with the story." Ryory had set his phone on the table. He gathered it and brought it to life, swiping to the photos. He filled his screen with a picture of a sketch. "Again, he wasn't going to let me see the stone until this morning. I barely got a glimpse at a picture of it, but I tried to recreate what I saw. I only captured a wee bit and who knows how accurate it is."

Ry was an artist, and his most well-known subject was the Picts. The sketch was impressive, if scant.

There were no Pictish symbols on the page, but there were some crudely drawn Roman words, written with what I would have called and mistakenly thought, if we really were seeing ancient Roman, were Greek letters.

"What does this mean to you?" Edwin asked.

"Not one thing." His eyes widened eagerly. "It was such a brief glance. Does it mean anything to any of you?"

We all inspected the picture, shaking our heads in turn.

"I'll text it to you, Delaney. If you want, you can look at it on your own time." Ry had my number, and my phone pinged a moment later.

Though what he was saying wasn't overly complicated, it was a lot to digest. The sketch he'd shown us was only a sketch, not proof of anything other than the fact that Ryory Bennigan could make even a crude sketch look interesting.

However, suspicion was only growing, from all of us, I thought—except that Inspector Winters didn't seem to question anything Ry was saying. Why would Ryory Bennigan want to text me this picture? I knew the inspector well enough to have seen many of his expressions, including the neutral one when he didn't give away what he was truly thinking. This was even more relaxed than the poker face I'd become accustomed to. Maybe the answers to my questions were on the way.

"Ry, you said you wanted to apologize to us for what you were going to tell us. I can't figure out why," I said.

"Aye," Ry said. "I have always enjoyed my time here at this bookshop." He nodded at Rosie who returned the gesture. "And Ani and Hamlet are good friends"—he repeated things we'd already talked about. He and Hamlet shared a look before he looked at Edwin. "Though we've never met, and though I said differently when I met Delaney and Tom, I'm more than aware of your fine reputation."

Edwin half-smiled. "Thank you."

"I also know you love your treasures, and you always do things with charity and your country in mind."

"He does," Rosie added.

"Well, when Dr. Pace got ahold of me, you came to mind, and I thought I would consider showing you whatever he brought me. Once I saw the stone itself, I was going to attempt to meet you. When Delaney applied to visit my studio for the festival event . . . well, I saw an opportunity."

"You invited me because I work at the bookshop?" I asked.

"Aye."

"Well, an apology isn't necessary. I'm fine with that, but if you wanted to speak to Edwin, all you had to do was to come into the bookshop and tell Rosie or another one of us."

"Aye, ta, but I liked the idea of getting to know people a little first. I had no idea that Dr. Pace was going to visit me yesterday. It was a surprise. I thought I would meet you, make another bookshop connection." He paused. "It was simple, really. I didn't want to bother any of you if it all turned out to be a fake, so when you applied, I decided to lay some groundwork, and then you and your husband were so delightful. Honestly, I couldn't wait to see the stone and then come talk to you, meet Edwin as soon as possible."

"That's not much of a manipulation, Ry," Rosie said. "I dinnae think that any of us feel used."

"Not at all." I smiled, but it was a sad expression. "Do you really think that Dr. Pace was killed because of what he allegedly found?"

"I would have absolutely no idea." Ry looked at Inspector Winters. "I do know how valuable it would be if it was real."

"That's certainly true." I turned to Inspector Winters. "Have you seen it?"

Inspector Winters shook his head. "No. I didn't investigate the scene, but I messaged the officers who did. They said there was nothing like it in the house."

"So either it's gone missing . . . ," I began.

"Or it never really existed in the first place," Ry finished. He looked at Inspector Winters and then back at me. "The one part that surprised me was that both you and Dr. Pace are from Kansas. I had no idea."

"Yes, that caught me by surprise too . . ." I thought I finally understood what was really going on with us still talking about what had happened. It wasn't about the apology.

"Is there any chance you know anyone at the University of Kansas you might talk to about Dr. Pace?" Inspector Winters asked.

"Yes," I answered immediately. "Is this why . . . you're telling us so much?" I asked both Ry and Inspector Winters.

"It is," Ry said. "Well, I liked you immediately, and I trust . . ." He cast his gaze around the shop. "I guess I trust this world you are a part of."

I nodded. I got it, I really did, but I wasn't sure I could deliver what anyone—Ry or Inspector Winters—might be looking for. I'd do my best.

Ryory looked at Inspector Winters as if he was silently asking for some sort of permission to continue speaking.

Inspector Winters said, "Lass, could you . . . would you mind ringing them? Maybe someone that you know could give you some insight into Adam Pace? The police might appreciate it. I would too, but that's less important."

Rosie chuckled as Edwin and Hamlet raised their eyebrows.

"What?" Ry asked.

Rosie looked at Inspector Winters. "Now you want Delaney's help?" There was no animosity to her tone, though.

Inspector Winters had the grace to nod and say, "I know it goes against my usual feelings, Rosie. I do, however, think a call isn't all that dangerous." He looked at me. "Just a call."

"Absolutely. I'd be happy to."

We went over everything again, just to make sure I was prepared for whatever might come up in the call, but I couldn't wait for this meeting to be over, so I could send a communication to my alma mater.

CHAPTER SIX

As the meeting wrapped up, Ry and Edwin exchanged phone numbers. Hamlet said he was going to stop by Ani's later to check on her, and Inspector Winters and Ry left at the same time.

"I think I need to allow it all to digest a wee bit," Rosie concluded.

"Aye," Edwin agreed before he told us all that he'd see us later. When he left, Hamlet and Rosie attended to customers—who appeared as soon as the sign was flipped back to Open—and I hurried over to the warehouse.

I'd acquired my undergrad and master's degrees from the University of Kansas in Lawrence. Though my favorite place had been the library—I was most happy in the quiet with my head stuck in a book—the Rock Chalk, Jayhawk chant still filled me with pride. Maybe only influenced a little by the fact (one I'd sought out and found) that the chant had been created by one of the school's science clubs on their train ride back from a conference. It had taken some years to come into its current incarnation as a common chant, but I felt the school pride when I heard it in my mind. Not many were interested in the origin story, and it only took being met with a few rolling eyes for me to cease sharing it.

Back in the day, I'd worked close enough with the paleontology department to know the head of the department as well as a few of its esteemed professors, though I had never heard of Dr. Adam Pace.

I decided to begin with the department's secretary, a man named Theo Gupta who'd been a fellow student during my undergrad years. I recalled that he originally wanted to go all the way to his PhD but decided early in the pursuit of his master's that he enjoyed assisting in all arenas instead of specializing. He was an ace at organization, so the department scooped him up. And, as far I knew, he was still there—everyone happy that he was in the position.

An email seemed like the best way to begin, but I was concerned about what the university had learned about Dr. Pace's death. Did they know? I certainly didn't want to be the one to tell them the news. Before I reached out, I texted Inspector Winters again to confirm that the university had been informed, and then I wrote the email.

Hi Theo—I'm so, so sorry for the devastating loss of Dr. Pace. In a twist of events, I'm in Scotland too. I don't want to be indelicate, but is there any chance you and I could take some time to chat, specifically about Dr. Pace's time here in Edinburgh? Could we schedule a Zoom?

Delaney Nichols

It was early in Kansas, about 6 a.m., so I didn't think I'd hear back from Theo any time soon, but only about thirty seconds after I hit send, my email pinged.

Delaney! What in the world are you doing in Scotland? Yes, we are gutted by the loss, but I would love to speak with you about Dr. Pace. Maybe you could help us understand what happened. Do you have time in a few hours? I could be available at ten AM my time.

Theo

I wrote back with a Zoom link. I was a tiny bit concerned that, like Ry and Inspector Winters, Theo would want more from me than I could give him, but there was only one way to find out.

It had been seven years since I'd seen Theo. Even though grief pulled at his features, he looked very close to the same young man I'd known back then. The last time I saw him, he'd just made the decision to end his formal education pursuits and take on the role of assisting. I'd wondered if maybe he'd return to classes down the road, but he'd never looked back. And he was all the better for it, I thought, despite the grief I could see.

"I love what I do," he said, the screen displaying perfectly organized bookshelves in the background. We'd spent the first few minutes of our Zoom just catching up.

"I'm glad you're happy, Theo." I'd blurred my background because there was no place in the warehouse that wouldn't invite a million questions, particularly from someone who worked in antiquity or academia worlds.

"Thank you, Delaney, and your life sounds spectacular."

"It's been fun." I'd given him a rundown about my time in

Scotland. It was difficult to keep it low-key and humble. How do you say "I moved to Scotland to work in an amazing book-shop with the best people ever and married a handsome pub owner who treats me like a queen, not to mention looks great in a kilt" without sounding like you're bragging?

"So, you met Dr. Pace?" he asked.

"I did. Almost accidentally and very briefly. When he told me where he was from, I invited him to the bookshop. He was visiting a local artist, Ryory Bennigan—"

"I've looked him up. He's covered in blue tattoos, right?"

"That's him."

"Such an interesting character."

"And, from what I've witnessed, a nice guy, though I don't know him well either."

"Right. Dr. Pace had tried to reach him for a few months. I know because I was the one sending and monitoring some of the emails. He'd started traveling back and forth between Scot-land and Kansas a few years ago, but he'd been living there for almost a year."

I was surprised to hear that Theo had been the one trying to contact Ry, but I didn't say as much. "Was it difficult to get an audience with Ryory?"

Theo shrugged. "Just non-responsive for a long time. Finally . . . hang on." Theo seemed to look something up on his computer. "His assistant finally wrote back." Theo laughed once. "She was very abrupt, but, ultimately, she invited Dr. Pace to Mr. Bennigan's studio. She threatened him, though, saying that she would have 'angry words' with him if he was lying about who he was or his university-level interest in the Picts." Theo hesitated. "I know that he found something not long ago, but he didn't tell any of us what it was. He was sure that Ryory Bennigan would be interested in it and tasked me with getting the meeting put together."

"Did he tell you anything at all about what he found?"

"No, he didn't want to tell me, or any of us here, the specifics over a call or email. He was going to share everything when he got home again, which of course . . . isn't happening now. All he told me was that he had something that would change the entire study of the Pictish people. His credentials carried the rest, or so he hoped."

So far, Theo's account lined up with what Ryory had said, even with the surprises. However, there was something off about my old friend. Maybe it was just grief, but he was holding something back. Before I could figure out a polite way to ask what that might be, Theo had his own question.

He cleared his throat. "Any chance you'd want to tell me what the thing was? Do you know?"

"Only secondhand, but yes, I know. At least I know the idea of it. It was something to help the world better understand the Picts' language."

Theo's eyebrows furrowed. "Their spoken words? I know about the symbols."

I nodded. "The spoken words. As I'm sure you know, there are varied interpretations of the symbols."

"Of course." Theo leaned back in his chair for a moment and set his chin on his steepled fingers. "How? I mean, there were no recordings, of course."

"No, but something that used the ancient Roman language. I don't know, though, Theo, this is all still unconfirmed, but . . . well, possible. I think, though it's hard to be really sure."

Theo's eyes changed. "Have you seen it?"

"No. And I don't think anyone else has either. I have a police inspector friend, and he said that nothing like that was found in the house where Dr. Pace was staying."

Theo nodded. "That's incredible . . . if it was real." He gave a sad chuckle.

My inner radar beeped again. "Do you think it might not be real?"

Theo's lips pursed a moment. He sat up and leaned closer to the camera again. He lowered his voice even though he was in his office alone as far as I knew. "Perhaps he exaggerated."

"Oh?" I said again.

A long moment later, Theo sighed. "I hate to speak ill of the dead, and I adored Dr. Pace—he was a wonderful man to work for." He took a moment to swallow away what I thought were some genuine tears. "But he . . . he did exaggerate sometimes."

"Scientists really shouldn't exaggerate."

"No. Never." He looked around to the other side, presumably toward the office door before he looked back at me again. "He got in some trouble a while ago. It was that trouble that caused him to change course, and he eventually became enthralled by the Picts."

When he didn't continue again, I said, "What was the trouble?"

Theo nodded. "I'm sure the police will be told, if they ask anyone here, that is, but he falsified some bones."

I didn't interject that this call was prompted by the police, but even as I said, "I don't understand," there was a part of me that thought I might. I'd heard of this sort of thing before.

"Yeah, he was on a site in Wyoming for years, found some dinosaur bones belonging to a Rexy."

"A T-Rex? A Tyrannosaurus Rex?"

"Yes. It wasn't anywhere near a full skeleton, but Dr. Pace must have wanted to make the find even more impressive than it was. The university had just purchased a new 3D printer and . . ."

"Oh no, he made bones?"

"He did, a couple of femurs, without telling anyone." Theo cocked his head. "Are you familiar with what's been going on lately in the world of dinosaur bones?"

"Kind of. I know there's a lot of money in them."

"Yes, it has become outrageous, frankly. I blame it all on the movie *Jurassic Park*, the one from the nineties. We'd have all just remained bone and dirt nerds if that movie hadn't made us look so cool. From there, it's snowballed."

"Outrageous?"

"Fossils are being sold by places like Sotheby's auction house."

"That *is* a big deal."

"Right. In the past couple of years, I know of at least six specimens that have sold for six million dollars each. Or more. Rich people who want to spend their money."

"Okay."

"Anyway, Dr. Pace did more than one thing wrong. He didn't document specimens with the university appropriately, and he found a buyer on his own without acknowledging the fake femurs. He almost got away with it."

"How did he get caught? How did he not get fired?"

"It was all so incredibly stupid, frankly. The night before the auction one of our professors, Dr. Lemmon, visited Dr. Pace at his house. Dr. Pace had the bones out on his dining room table. It was astonishing, apparently. Anyway, he inspected them as Dr. Pace made excuses to him . . . It was a mess and ugly, but Dr. Lemmon also noticed that there was something strange about the femurs. They struck him as just too pristine. It was late into the night by then, but Dr. Lemmon asked specifically about the femurs.

"The jig was up. Dr. Pace couldn't lie when confronted by Dr. Lemmon. But, he tried to say that he hadn't meant for there to be a misunderstanding, that he thought he'd been up-front about the fake femurs to the client, though he couldn't even come up with a good excuse as to why the university wasn't brought into any of it."

"Oh, not good."

"No, let's put aside Dr. Pace keeping the find to himself. There are some nuances there that he tried to use to get him out of trouble with the university. Dr. Lemmon was very forgiving. Anyway, you understand that there are approximately three hundred and eighty bones to a T-Rex. Shoot, even the most famous set of bones in the world is only about eighty percent real. The difference is that Dr. Pace 'forgot' to mention the fake bones to the potential buyer. He said he just got too busy. That didn't fly. Dr. Lemmon ordered Dr. Pace to cancel the auction without explanation."

"How come Dr. Pace wasn't fired?"

Theo laughed again and then sniffed once. "Two reasons, I think. If all the details came to light, the university's reputation would have been tainted—and no one here was shy about stating that. There should have been more checks and balances, there is no doubt. But, honestly, Delaney, I always thought it came down to the fact that everyone just liked him so much. He was mostly forgiven within the department and then we all behaved as if nothing happened. The sale was stopped, the bones were delivered to the university, so we might be in charge of keeping them under wraps. No harm, no foul. Except that Dr. Pace was barred from any further work with dinosaurs, so he needed to find something else to throw himself into. Thus, the Picts, which were a whole ocean away, in theory and practice, came into his life. The department head thought it was a great plan for Dr. Pace to spend some time in Scotland, and out of here, for a while. The politics of academia don't always make sense, but, and you probably know this as well as I do, things get swept under the rug for the 'greater good' sometimes."

"I get that, I guess." I never liked that part of that world, but I felt like I was always removed from it. "But I *am* surprised he wasn't somehow disgraced."

"Only because the auction never happened. If it had and the discovery had been made later, it would not have been good at all." Theo shook his head. "The entire department could have been decimated."

"Close call then?"

"Too close. A lot has changed because of all of it. The Wyoming sites were even shut down until new protocols were in place. For a while, we all walked on eggshells, but the potential buyer of the bones didn't raise a stink, so we all moved on." Theo took a deep breath. "Still, though, Dr. Pace *was* a lovely man, Delaney. Don't misunderstand. Maybe misguided or bored or facing some sort of financial difficulties, but still a nice man."

"Was there ever a real investigation or are you speculating?"

"I think Dr. Lemmon knows the most."

"Any chance he would talk to the Scottish police?"

"Probably only if they insist on it or if there's some sort of legal reason that he must. Other than that, I doubt he wants to ever speak of that time again."

I didn't know what the legalities were, but I would share that part with Inspector Winters and hope Dr. Lemmon wouldn't be too surprised if they called him.

"Would you ask him if he'd talk to me?" I asked.

Theo took a deep breath and let it out with puffed cheeks. "I need to think about that, Delaney. We've only just heard the news, and we're all rattled. Maybe give it a day or two . . . but I wouldn't count on it."

I nodded. "I get it."

"I do suggest that anyone might want to be suspicious of whatever Dr. Pace said he'd found. Though I don't know as much as Dr. Lemmon does, I did think that Dr. Pace enjoyed the limelight. I couldn't see any other reason for him doing what he did, but I could be very wrong. I have no access to his personal life or his finances. I always just thought that the experience with the bones gave him a respect or maybe a small notoriety that most paleontologists don't get to experience. I thought maybe he'd chase that high for . . . well, for the rest of his life."

"That's possible," I said.

I also thought he was a nice man upon first impression, but fraud was not cool. And I had enough distance from the man for my kinder thoughts of him not to get in the way. I might have felt a connection with him, but it wasn't substantial. Though I doubted he deserved to be murdered.

If indeed that's what had happened. We still didn't know if the police had ruled it murder, I silently reminded myself.

"So, we're a mess here," Theo said.

"I'm truly sorry, Theo, and I appreciate you taking the time to talk to me."

"It's always good to see you, Delaney." A noise like a door opening came through. Theo looked toward the door and then back at me, lowering his voice. "I need to go, but I'll let you know anything else I learn if I think it's pertinent. I'll let the police know too."

"I know an inspector who might like to hear from you."

"Okay. Oh! Wait. There is someone who Dr. Pace worked with there in Edinburgh. I don't know if he's heard the news, but . . . well, is there any chance you could deliver it in person? An email sounds horrible."

"At the university?"

"Yes, but not the department you might think. There's a librarian there who Dr. Pace connected with. The guy is brilliant."

My breath caught a little, but I cleared my throat to hide it. I had a feeling I might know who the librarian was. "Who?" I managed to croak out.

"His name is Artair Shannon. I wonder if he's been contacted."

I waited a beat. "Theo, Artair is my father-in-law."

Theo blinked. "No kidding?"

"Not even a little bit."

"Do you get along with him?"

"Very well."

"Well, if that's the case, you might be able to learn more about Dr. Pace from him. He and Artair hit it off grandly.

Though I was under the impression that Dr. Pace didn't tell Artair about his problems with the T-Rex bones, just so you know. I don't think Dr. Pace was forthcoming with anyone about any of that."

"No, I don't suppose he was. I'll talk to Artair." My heart sunk. Artair wasn't a casual friend. He gave himself fully to the people he cared for. He was going to be sad about Adam Pace.

"That's great. Thank you. Will you stay in touch, let me know what he says?"

I nodded. "Of course."

I didn't take the time to explain that my loyalty would always be to Artair, so if he didn't want me to tell someone something, my lips would be sealed.

"Thanks, Delaney." Another noise sounded. "I need to go. Sorry!"

"Bye, Theo. I'll be in touch."

The Zoom call ended, and the screen popped back to the generic sign-in page.

I should be excited about this new lead, but I knew I was about to tell my father-in-law something upsetting.

"Maybe better from me than anyone else, though," I muttered to myself. I hoped I was right.

CHAPTER SEVEN

After the Zoom call with Theo, I made my way to the other side of the bookshop and told Rosie and Hamlet what I'd learned. Neither of them thought I was overreacting in thinking Artair might be upset. They'd both encouraged me to hurry up to the pub and talk to Tom so the two of us might speak to Artair together.

Tom agreed that it would be better to hear the news from us than on the TV or from the police.

"He might know already," Tom added.

"He might."

Tom smiled sadly. "Lass, my da's a tough old guy just as much as he's one with a big heart. He'll be all right. Shall I ring him?"

I nodded. "Okay, call him, but just ask if he'll come over for dinner—if you can leave the pub, that is."

Tom glanced at Rodger who'd been pretending not to listen.

"Go. I'll be fine." Rodger nodded. "Give Artair my best."

"Ta," Tom said.

He called his father, who, even by just listening in, I could tell was in too good of spirits to have heard the news.

"Aye, dinner," Tom said. "Oh, no occasion. We just haven't seen you for a wee bit. Aye? See you then."

He ended the call. "Part one of the mission accomplished."

Artair would meet us at the blue house by the sea for dinner.

Together, Tom and I whipped up Artair's favorite meal, fettucine Alfredo and Caesar salad. We didn't have time to bake his favorite chocolate chip cookies, but there was a small cheesecake in the freezer that I set on the counter to thaw.

I answered the door when Artair arrived and led him to the dining table, a false cheery ring to my voice.

Artair hesitated at the dining room's threshold. "Oh. Something's awry. When you rang, I thought I'd forgotten about something important, but now I see. Something's wrong."

Tom and I both looked at him with wide eyes.

He continued, "It's a weeknight and we're eating in the dining room, you made fettucine—and, lass, as delightful as you are, you're not quite right either. You're too smiley. What happened?"

Tom pulled out one of the chairs. "Delaney and I are fine, Da, but we do have some news to share with you."

"What is it?"

"Will you have a seat first?"

"I need to sit?"

Tom frowned. "Probably."

Artair rubbed his hand over his chin and then nodded. "All

right. But tell me before we eat. I won't be able to swallow anything with a ball of worry in my throat."

"Of course." Tom nodded.

Once we were seated, Tom looked at me with raised eyebrows as if asking who should go first. I nodded. "Artair, you have done some work with a Dr. Adam Pace, right?"

He smiled quickly. "Aye." The smile disappeared. "Oh, dear, has something happened to him?"

I nodded. "It's tragic," I paused, "but, yes, he was found dead in the house he's been staying in. The police are still determining if it was murder."

Artair's face fell. "That is sad news. I'm so sorry to hear it. I liked the lad."

Tom and I gave him a moment.

"I'm so sorry, Artair," I said.

"Aye, Da," Tom added.

Artair looked at us a moment later. "Ta. I'm okay. I *am* sad. Dr. Pace and I worked well together until . . . well, we were friendly for the most part, but, and this doesn't lessen the tragedy, but we only knew each other a short time."

A little relief washed through me. He and Dr. Pace hadn't been close.

"In fact," Artair lifted his eyebrows, "our last meeting was contentious. Again, though, that doesn't lessen the tragedy. I wish I'd just . . . well, no one likes to leave things like that."

I said, "Contentious?"

"Aye. He came to the library a week ago, and I tried to talk him out of doing something he was planning."

Tom and I shared a look.

"Da, would you mind sharing what that was?" Tom asked.

Artair reached for the bowl of fettuccine. "I don't know, lad. It's . . . well, it's not only quite unusual, but I did promise Dr. Pace I wouldnae tell anyone."

"But you and he argued?" Tom urged.

"Aye, but that doesnae mean I can break a promise, even if he's . . . gone, I suppose." Artair spooned some noodles onto his plate.

Tom and I shared another look.

"We met him." I grabbed a breadstick. "Just yesterday. At Ryory Bennigan's studio."

The fork full of noodles and sauce stopped midway toward Artair's mouth. He set the food back on the plate. "Aye?"

I nodded and then told him about my and Tom's time at the studio and my Zoom call with Theo back in Kansas. As Artair enjoyed the fettucine, I told him everything I'd learned about Dr. Pace. He didn't seem surprised by the fraud. His unruffled demeanor wasn't what I expected. Artair didn't have patience for any sort of fraud, or as I might have heard him call such a thing, "tomfoolery."

"I told him about you," Artair said when I'd finished. "That you went to the University of Kansas. He said he didnae know you. I offered an introduction. He hoped to at least stop by the bookshop sometime, but it must have never been the right time." Artair's frown deepened. "He didn't mention that when you met him?"

"No," I said. "It was an unusual situation, though. This was before Ani got sick, and she seemed to want to move him along. Maybe it wasn't the right time for him to mention knowing you."

"Aye. I know he enjoyed many bookshops. Maybe he just didn't put it all together. How is the lass, Ani? Have you heard?"

"We were told she's okay."

Artair nodded. "Well, I might have been fond of the man, but there was something . . . I didnae want to think he was untrustworthy but something about him . . . Your story about what he did with the dinosaur bones only reinforces my gut telling me something was off." He paused and looked at us almost sheepishly. "And, Dr. Pace did tell me what he found near Strathpeffer."

"The stone about the Picts' language?"

"Aye. I didnae believe him, and he wouldnae show it to me."

"Not even a picture?"

"No. Honestly, I thought maybe he was just pulling my leg, aye? I laughed and then got angry when he told me he'd been trying to sell it to Ryory Bennigan. Its verity got lost in our argument. I didnae think he should bother Mr. Bennigan, particularly because I thought he was making it all up. That's why our last meeting was contentious."

I pulled the picture up on my phone. "Here's a sketch that Ry made based on a photo that Dr. Pace shared."

Artair peered at the picture and shook his head. "That doesnae tell me much."

"No, no one who has seen it thinks it's much of anything. Except . . ."

"What, lass?"

"Hope, I guess. Everyone wants to believe in it."

"Aye." Artair nodded.

"I can't imagine Dr. Pace could forge a stone, but what do I know?" I reached for my fork. "It took only a few moments for me and Tom to handle the hammer and chisel."

"But we weren't proficient."

"No," I said. "Perhaps Dr. Pace took to it and created something. Or, maybe a 3D printer was in play. That's how he did the bones."

"That's possible," Artair added. He fell into thought.

"What, Da?" Tom asked.

"There are ways to fake things, I suppose, but it would take a lot of work." Artair took a bite of his dinner. Once he swallowed, he continued, "In fact, to make it all as authentic as possible, it might take the type of skill that Ryory Bennigan has."

I considered what Artair said and made a leap. "You don't think that Ry and Dr. Pace were in cahoots?"

"That they were working together on some sort of scam?" Artair shrugged. "I have no evidence that anything like that happened, but I can't help but wonder now, particularly considering . . . everything?"

"Aye," Tom added.

Artair's eyebrows knitted. "Just last week, he said he was going to use what he'd found to form a bond with the artist and then make the sale."

"He could have been testing the waters, checking if you thought Ry would be or could be interested," Tom said. "Or, I wonder if he wanted you to know his plans. Do you suppose he wanted backup of some sort?"

Artair shrugged. "I dinnae ken. The argument that he and I had . . . It was out of the blue and . . . strange. We'd spent a few dinners discussing the Picts. When we first met, I was the one educating him, and he appreciated everything I shared. But after his trip north, things changed, and he started to behave more secretively. I wasn't bothered, until he finally told me what he found and that he was working to get Bennigan to buy it. It all felt wrong. I was having a hard time believing it. It felt forced, maybe even as if he was challenging me. I couldnae understand it, but you could be right, Tom. Instead of arguing, he might have wanted a trail of his activity. Even with hindsight, I'm not sure. Should I tell the police?"

If I were the police, I would ask Artair about his whereabouts the night before. But I wasn't the police, and besides, Artair wouldn't hurt a fly.

"I don't think there's much there, and the police will probably take a good look at Ry." I paused because I wasn't sure they would. Famous people sometimes didn't get the scrutiny they should. I would talk to Inspector Winters. "However, Artair, if the police come to you, you might not want to be forthcoming about the argument."

Artair's eyebrows rose. "Aye? Oh, of course." He smiled sadly. "I appreciate the advice. It truly might not have occurred to me, but you are right, that might make me look like I had a bone to pick. In fact, I have no alibi. I spend my evenings and early mornings at home, but I also didnae hurt Dr. Pace. I would probably feel guilty if I didnae tell the truth, however, so let's just hope they don't come calling."

"They won't," I said, though I wasn't sure.

Artair wiped his napkin at the corners of his mouth. "While I don't know what went on between him and the artist, I know that Dr. Pace did bother a few other people over his time here. Before he and I had our moment, he told me about some issues. Maybe I should talk to the police, tell them about Dr. Pace's run-ins with the woman who heads up the Natural History Collections at the university, Sara Shoemaker. Dr. Pace and

Ronny Remsen had a real row as well, at least as far as Dr. Pace told me. Ronny's at the Museum of Edinburgh. If I think about it, Dr. Pace never gave me much information regarding either of them, other than that he approached them early on during his time in our fair city. They told him that they didnae want to work with him on anything, and Dr. Pace never shared anything more specific. And their tones werenae polite, if I remember correctly. Perhaps they were clever enough to look into his past at some point. I do think I should have done exactly that."

"I don't know. I don't think his past was made available to everyone. The university wouldn't want his deeds to become public. It would be disgraceful to them. Theo and I are friends, and he trusts me not to publicize what he told me. He didn't ask me to keep it to myself, though."

"Aye."

I sat back in my chair. "How would you feel about me giving the names you just mentioned to Inspector Winters? He might not ask me where I got the information?"

Tom sent me a doubtful eyebrow furrow.

I nodded. "Or he might, but I do think the police should know."

"They might figure it out for themselves," Artair said.

"Maybe. Let's wait and see if they rule Dr. Pace's death a murder. If not, we don't have to do anything," I said.

"Good idea," Artair said, though his tone was now even more doubtful. "No, I'd be okay with you telling the police, particularly Winters. He's a good man. I should ring him too."

He was sad about Pace's death but not in the ways Tom and I expected. Though Artair was softhearted, and he'd liked Pace, they hadn't been as close as we'd assumed. I wondered if Artair was insulted that we hadn't given him enough credit. If he was, he'd never say as much.

"I won't mention you and Dr. Pace argued. You can do that yourself."

"I will. I think I'd like to. If it turns out to be a case, finding a killer is more important than anything." He looked at Tom and me. "Thank you for telling me." He smiled. "And for fixing my favorite dinner. I'm pleased that you thought I might need it." He shrugged. "Maybe I did. It softened the blow, I have no doubt."

We didn't mention Dr. Pace for the rest of the evening. Instead, we talked of things like the plumbing under the kitchen sink and what we might do with a garden in the back— probably not much. Though Artair had always had a full garden, Tom and I weren't as keen on the idea, even if I did come from a family of farmers.

We talked about regular, probably boring, family stuff and decided to let tomorrow take care of itself.

CHAPTER EIGHT

And boy oh boy, did it take care of itself.

The next morning, Tom drove me into Grassmarket. The top news story on the radio announced that "American paleontologist Dr. Adam Pace was found dead yesterday morning. This morning, police officials announced that his death is being ruled and investigated as a murder. Local officials are working in conjunction with officials from the U.S. Consulate General in Edinburgh."

As the announcer moved on to the next story, Tom turned off the radio.

"The American Embassy?" I muttered.

"Aye."

"Should I get ahold of Inspector Winters this morning?"

"Aye, I think so. If I know my da, he'll call him too."

"Yeah," I said, distractedly.

Tom glanced over at me briefly. "Lass?"

"What?"

"I hear the wheels in your head turning."

"I know. It's a shame you know me so well."

Tom laughed. "Not really. It's the best part of my life."

He didn't always say things like that, but I'd stopped being stunned when he did. At first, I thought maybe he was exaggerating or saying things he thought he should. I'd concluded that I was living a real case of imposter syndrome. Now, I just enjoyed all of it and tried to say such amazing things to him every now and then too.

"I'm glad to hear that." I took a moment. "But, yes, the wheels are turning."

"You're going to reach out to the people Artair mentioned?"

"I thought I might. What do you think?"

Tom laughed. "You've tried to trick me with that question a time or two, and I won't fall for it. I think you should be careful. A murder has been committed. I think you should do whatever you want, but always be careful."

"I will. I'm going to work right now. I'm going to regroup with my fellow bookshop people and see what they think about everything."

"That seems well thought out."

"It does?"

"Aye."

Tom parked the car in the space he'd used for years. It happened to be conveniently midway between the pub and the bookshop.

As we'd done a time or two, we gave each other a quick kiss before he went in one direction and I the other.

He was right, though, the wheels in my mind were turning. Fast.

As I'd come to look forward to, Hector trotted to greet me as I came through the door, but today his demeanor was a mix of happy-to-see-me and get-me-out-of-here.

The bookshop did a steady business, but I couldn't remember ever seeing so many people inside it at once. The buzz of conversation was louder than it had ever been as well.

"What's going on?" I whispered to Hector as I held him high.

He wiggled. As Rosie seemed to be giving a speech to about twenty people about the layout of the bookshop, Hamlet hurried around and made his way to me.

"Ryory sent them," he said to me.

"I don't understand."

"This is a group of artists from the Hidden Door Festival. He sent each of them an email saying they should all give their book business to The Cracked Spine."

"And they all came in today? At once?"

"Aye. He made the email sound urgent, apparently. And I think everyone wants to do whatever Ryory says. I don't know. Rosie and I are trying to catch up." Hamlet shrugged.

"Goodness, well, I guess we should help them find a book or two."

"Rosie's telling them where everything is, but, aye, we should jump in and help when she's finished."

The first customer I met was a woman named Willa Brink, a singer from Glasgow, with rainbow-colored hair and a voice that, when she spoke, made me think her singing voice might sound like Stevie Nicks.

"I've always loved Jane Austen," she said to me. "I've read them all, though, time and time again. What could you recommend that's like her?"

"There's the rub," I said. "There is no one like her. I can recommend some classics, but Ms. Austen somehow doesn't read as dated as many of the others of her era do. I can recommend some similar stories, but they will most definitely be more contemporary, which, I think, takes away some of the charm."

"I agree."

"Do you go to movies?"

"I do. I love thrillers."

I nodded. "The mystery or the scariness?"

"The mystery more, but both."

"Have you read Ian Rankin?" It was an easy go-to. Though most readers around Edinburgh knew him and had read his books, every now and then I was able to introduce someone to Rebus, and it was always a thrill.

"I haven't. I've heard of him, though. A local, aye?"

"Yep." I handed her one of his books.

She took it and read the blurb as well as took in the cover art.

As she perused it, I said, "Do you know Mr. Bennigan, or did he just send you an email?"

"Aye. He said to come here this morning." She looked around and then lowered her voice. "He said he would be stopping by if we wanted to meet him."

"Oh! That makes more sense," I said. "Well, when will he be here?"

She glanced at the time on her cellphone. "Soon enough, I predict. He said early."

"He didn't give a time?"

"Not specifically, no."

I nodded. I had a few other questions for the artist, but if Rosie had taught me anything, it was that events needed refreshments. This sounded like an event.

Willa seemed content to browse on her own as I secreted

a message to Hamlet that I was running next door to the bakery.

Thankfully, the young woman behind the bakery's counter, Celia, knew me well enough to understand my need to hurry. She quickly put together a couple boxes of sweets and a few carafes of coffee that we could return later once they were empty.

As she was helping load my arms and hers, a young man hurried in, an exasperated look on his face.

"Pickup," he said to Celia, who was clearly in the middle of gathering the carafes in her arms.

"Aye," she said as she seemed to silently weigh the alternatives. She looked at the young man. "It's bagged, right behind the counter."

"I'm not allowed to go behind the counter."

"Sure you are. I give you permission."

"Can't do it. You need to gather it for me."

It was clear that Celia was working hard not to be rude to the delivery man. Finally, she said, "Okay, then you'll have to wait until I get back from next door."

"Aye?"

"Aye."

The delivery person turned his attention to me. "I know you."

My arms as loaded with things as Celia's were with carafes, I took the moment to truly look at him over the top. "Oh. Sure. You delivered lunch to Ryory Bennigan's studio a couple days ago."

He smiled. "That's right! I knew you looked familiar. Hello again."

"Um. Hello."

The light must have gone off in his head all of a sudden. "Oh. Here, let me help you both with those. Free of charge." He laughed.

Celia sent me a furtive eye roll. "Aye. That would be lovely."

He did lighten the load as we caravanned back to the book-shop. I wasn't too surprised to find even a few more people in the shop. It was sure getting crowded.

"Name's Layton," he announced as we made our way. "I'm the only local Layton on the food apps. You can request me."

"Good to know," Celia said. She was thawing from the ear-lier eye roll. Layton really was a help.

"Thanks, Layton," I added.

After we set everything up on the back table, Rosie reached into her pocket to tip both Celia and Layton. Celia tried to refuse, but Layton took the offered bills and thanked Rosie. Rosie forced the tip into Celia's hands, and then, in a move that shocked us all, Layton handed his tip to Celia too.

"I didn't do the work. You did."

I could tell she didn't want to take any money, but the crowd of hungry and coffee-depleted artists was approach-ing. With a mix of gratitude and irritation, she took the bills and then turned to leave, but stopped when Layton spoke again.

He turned to me. When he spoke, the words were surprising enough to cause Celia to stop and listen. "That artist, Ryory Bennigan. What's going on with him?"

"I don't know what you mean," I said.

"I deliver food all hours, and I see him sneaking around Edinburgh during the evenings and nights a lot. What's he up to?"

It wasn't a terrible question, but it was odd that he was asking me. I figured Ry just liked the privacy of moving around under the cover of night, that there was nothing strange about his activities, but I knew nothing. "I have no idea."

Layton hurried after Celia. "I'll grab my order now."

Rosie sent me a question with her eyes, but I shrugged it off. We would talk later.

Just as the room full of artists was gathering their treats, the front door opened. The noise level in the shop was too high to hear the bell ring, but I saw movement at the corner of my eye.

I turned with a smile, thinking maybe it was Ryory, but it wasn't.

Inspector Winters stood there looking all kinds of uncomfortable. I hurried to him.

"What's up?" I asked.

When everyone else in the bookshop realized it wasn't Ryory who'd come in, they went back to their conversations and bakery treats. Even the fact that Inspector Winters was in uniform didn't seem to spark extra curiosity. They were there to meet Ryory—no one else mattered.

Nevertheless, Inspector Winters lowered his voice as he spoke to me. "I'm here for Mr. Bennigan. He told me he was scheduled to meet people here."

"I'm not sure 'scheduled' is the right word, but he told all these people that they could meet him this morning if they came here."

"Right. Well, he's not going to make it."

"Oh no. Is he . . . okay?"

Inspector Winters nodded and looked around to make certain that no one was really paying us any attention. They weren't. "He's fine, safe. However, officers had to bring him in." Inspector Winters lifted his hand as if he knew the question I was going to ask and didn't feel the need to fight the inevitable. "Aye, he's being questioned in the murder of Adam Pace but not *necessarily* because he's under suspicion, Delaney. We think he might know something that would help."

I nodded. Was now the moment to tell him what Artair had shared? "Do you have a suspect?"

"I can't divulge. But Mr. Bennigan did tell me he was supposed to be here, that people would be waiting. I tried to ring both you and the shop, but no one answered." He paused. "I guess I was a wee bit worried, so I came down myself."

"We probably couldn't hear anything. I'm sorry." My phone was in my bag, and I wasn't even sure where I'd put it down.

I wanted more information about everything but didn't even know where to begin. "So, he's not under arrest?"

"No. He knows he could leave at any time, but he claims to want to be helpful, so he stayed."

"Thank you for coming down here to check in."

"Aye. I might have a wee bit of an ulterior motive. Did you ring the University of Kansas?"

"I did. Zoom call, even. I was going to call you this morning, but I came in to this." I nodded toward the crowd. "You and I need to talk."

A burst of laughter came from somewhere in the crowd.

I continued, "Let me tell everyone about Ryory first."

Inspector Winters lifted his hand. "I'll take care of it. I'm going to jump in and ask some questions about Ryory."

"I'm under the impression that they don't know him, that they were here to meet him."

"Well, if that's the case, it will be quick."

"Okay. Hang on, though." I looked for Rosie and Hamlet in the crowd. I turned back to the inspector. "Give me just one minute so I can let Rosie and Hamlet know."

"Of course."

Rosie and Hamlet were not thrilled about our customers being questioned by the police, even if it was Inspector Winters, and even if they were there for reasons other than shopping. Rosie marched her way to the inspector, and I kept step with her.

"Now?" she asked him.

"Aye, Rosie. I'll be quick and it might be important."

Rosie frowned and then sighed. "Give me a moment." She moved to her desk. "May I have your attention, everyone?"

It always surprised me when my grandmotherly coworker raised her voice to commanding levels, but she was very good at it.

A few seconds later, the crowd silenced and turned their attention her way.

"Aye, weel, we're sorry to report that we have a wee bit of upsetting news. Mr. Bennigan will not be able to join us today—"

The rumble of disappointment sounded around the room, but Rosie cut in again.

"We are all so sorry," she said. "We will schedule another event with Mr. Bennigan, I assure you."

It was a promise that might end up being difficult to keep, but we'd deal with that later. We hadn't scheduled this one in the first place, but she was okay to take the hit, apparently.

"For now, please enjoy the pastries and coffee. We love having you here, and . . ." She looked at Inspector Winters.

He nodded. "This is unconventional, I know, but I have a few questions if you all wouldn't mind."

"About what?" someone called.

"A few things, actually."

"Are we required to answer them?" Willa asked.

"The inspector is a friend of the bookshop," Rosie jumped in quickly. "But, no, you arenae required to answer any of them. Only if you want. Maybe listen to him and then decide."

Her words meant more than his at that moment, and a rumble of agreement spread through the crowd.

"I'll talk to you when I'm done with the others," Inspector Winters said to me before he approached the group.

I watched as he worked the crowd. I tried to assist those who might want to shop while waiting their turn to talk to him. I served pastry and coffee. I tried to smile and ease any discontent, but surprisingly, there wasn't much. Even if people didn't want to talk to the police, many were curious about what might be going on to keep Ry from being there.

True to his word, Inspector Winters was quick and casual with the interviews. As I eavesdropped, I heard a few people say they didn't know Ryory Bennigan and had been surprised by his email.

I did hear Willa Brink tell him that she wasn't willing to answer any questions from the police without an attorney present. She didn't have an attorney, and Inspector Winters would need something more official before she would attempt to hire one.

Inspector Winters thanked her for her time and moved along. Mostly, though, people just said they didn't know Ryory and were really hoping to meet him. When they pushed Inspector Winters about why the artist wasn't there, the inspector avoided answering, though he never seemed rude.

When he was finished and many, but not all, of our surprise visitors had left, he found me. "Could you just come down to the station?"

"Right now?"

"I would like for it to be right now, but I think Rosie might get me fired if I take you away before everyone leaves. Come down when you can. How's that?"

"Good."

I was a combination of excited to talk to him and worried about it. He and I were friends. He'd become close to all my Scottish family. We all knew each other. I'd taken it upon myself to investigate more things than the average bookseller, and I'd even given official statements a time or two. But Willa's protestations rang through my mind, and I knew that it was always a risk to talk to the police without an attorney present.

I'd met a few attorneys over my time in Scotland, but I didn't want to hire one.

I shook off my concerns. "I'll be there as soon as I can."

"See you soon." He turned and made his way to the police cruiser I hadn't noticed until now parked around the corner.

My morning was not going in any of the directions I hoped it would.

There were still people in the store, though. I hurried to help find more books.

CHAPTER NINE

The headliner wasn't going to show, and that disappointment was difficult to overcome. The remaining artists didn't stay much longer, leaving with less-than-happy smiles, which wasn't the way Rosie preferred for customers to remember their time at the bookshop. Today, though, she seemed relieved to watch them go.

"Weel, that was interesting." Rosie picked up Hector as she, Hamlet, and I stood next to her desk.

"I only heard one person refuse to answer questions. A singer named Willa. Did you two notice any others?" I asked.

"Not one," Hamlet said.

Rosie shook her head. "In fact, most of them shrugged and just said they didnae know Ryory Bennigan."

"I wonder if that means that Willa does know him." My gaze went out toward Grassmarket, but I shook off my curiosity.

"Do you know what's going on?" Hamlet asked.

"Ry is being questioned in Adam Pace's murder, though I'm not sure if he's a suspect or if they just think he might have pertinent information. I don't know about any evidence. The police don't like to give up much, even if we are talking about Inspector Winters."

Hamlet nodded.

"Aye," Rosie added doubtfully.

"You think he could be guilty?" I asked Rosie.

"I dinnae ken, but it was odd that Winters came to deliver the message."

"Well, he wanted to hear about my Zoom call with the university. He wants me to go down to the station and talk to him."

"You should go," Rosie said.

I nodded. "I will, but I want to tell you two everything first. You can pass it on to Edwin."

Hamlet and Rosie sent each other raised eyebrows.

"We'd love to hear," Hamlet said.

They were curious, but I wanted to say the words aloud to someone other than the police first. I hadn't interjected myself as much as I'd been pushed into this crime—it was an unusual spot. I would never lie to Inspector Winters, but Artair was now a part of it and I would rather tell a partial truth about something than put Artair under the light of suspicion.

As I told my coworkers what I'd learned since the day before, mostly what Theo and my father-in-law had shared, though, I realized I had more than I thought to tell Inspector Winters. I should have probably called him the night before, even if Dr. Pace's death had just been deemed a murder and it might not be his case, but he was certainly involved. And he had asked me to call the university in the first place.

"Let Artair tell Winters about the argument. Just tell the

police that Artair told you he knew the victim. Everything else is hearsay anyway," Rosie said.

"That's true. Yes, thank you."

The shop was in good condition. Cleaning up wasn't going to be much more than taking the carafes back to the bakery and putting the leftover pastries in the refrigerator. I stepped toward the back table to help with that task, but Rosie and Hamlet protested.

"Go." Rosie motioned me to scoot away.

Hector wouldn't let me go without a quick goodbye, and I was all the better for the brief cuddle and cheek kisses.

I texted Tom as I left the bookshop with what was going on.

He texted back with: **You're official to the investigation.**

Leave it to him to put a good spin on it.

Maybe LOL, I responded.

Ring me if you need backup.

Will do.

I could have walked to the station, but I wanted to get there quickly now, maybe in time to see Ry, so I ran to catch the bus just before it pulled away from the curb. My eyes went back toward the market as the bus turned to head up to the Royal Mile.

I couldn't see any activity inside the bookshop or pub, but there was plenty of foot traffic, as usual. My eyes swung to the bakery, and I realized I hadn't mentioned Layton's observation about Ry's nighttime wanderings to Rosie and Hamlet. They hadn't seemed important, or maybe I just hadn't processed them yet, but now I wondered what Ry was up to at night. I would look for a moment to ask him myself.

As I made my way inside the station at the bottom of the

Royal Mile, the officer behind the front desk did a double take. I recognized her from previous visits and knew she wasn't my biggest fan. I tried to smile as our eyes caught.

"Ah, there she is," the officer said.

"Hello," I said. "I think Inspector Winters is expecting me."

She smiled wryly. "Oh, he's expecting you, all right." She leaned back and crossed her arms in front of herself.

"Delaney?"

My attention darted to Inspector Winters, who was standing off to the side behind the officer at the desk. I waved.

"Come on back," he said.

The female officer sent me a wry and suspicious smile. I couldn't decide if she was seriously bothered by me or if this was all her sense of humor playing out.

I was just going to keep a wide berth for now. If I could.

I made my way to the familiar interview room. There were so many things that had come into my life since I moved to Scotland, most of them so surprising that I sometimes had to pinch myself.

One of the less-than-awesome things was that I was familiar with a police interview room because I'd spent so much time inside it talking to Inspector Winters or answering his questions. What had at first been scary had probably become too comfortable.

He met me as he came around the other side of the table. "Coffee?"

"No thanks."

We sat inside, me in the same spot as always. Even the chair in here felt familiar.

"Okay, so, let's start with your call to Kansas." Inspector

Winters grabbed his notebook and pen from his pocket. "Who did you contact and what did they say?"

Yet again, I replayed my conversations with Theo, and then Artair. I shared the details from Theo but kept Artair's part as simple as Rosie had suggested, mentioning that he told me that he knew the victim and said he'd probably call Inspector Winters. He hadn't yet.

"Are you saying that faking dinosaur bones, or artifacts for that matter, is a thing these days?" Inspector Winters asked.

"No, but I don't know that for sure. What I do know is that dinosaur bones are a big business, really big, and 3D printing has . . . given us all a chance to see or create things that were impossible before."

"That does makes sense." Inspector Winters thought a moment. "I'll get in touch with Artair."

"I think he might expect that. Last night, we didn't know it was murder yet."

"Aye."

"What made the police determine that Dr. Pace was killed?"

"He was poisoned."

"Oh!" I leaned forward, my arms sliding on the table. "Isn't it mostly women who kill with poison?"

"It is."

"What kind of poison?"

"We aren't sharing that yet," he said.

"Someone came by his flat yesterday morning and poisoned him? Or was it the day before? Was it a fast-acting poison?" My earlier hesitation and concern that I might overtalk was gone, replaced now by that familiar curiosity that had put me in this chair a few times before.

Inspector Winters hesitated as if wondering what to tell me. "Good questions. It will be in the news soon anyway, but according to the medical examiner, the poison was administered about an hour before he died."

"Have you checked nearby cameras to see who stopped by?"

Inspector Winters frowned. "Gosh, we didn't think of that."

I sat back. "Sorry. Of course."

"He didn't have any visitors. There is a security camera in the front doorbell."

"So, how was he poisoned?"

"Well, he didn't have any visitors at the front door. We have no view of the back of the house he was renting."

"Did someone break in?"

Inspector Winters squinted at me. "We're not releasing that information to the public quite yet, lass, but we might soon. Stay tuned."

"I will." My mind was already going in a million different directions. Then, something else occurred to me. It was a tenuous connection but maybe not. "Inspector Winters, did you know about Ani, Ryory Bennigan's assistant?"

"What about her?"

"She was sick and was in the hospital the night before Dr. Pace died. I don't know what was wrong with her, but it sure seemed like it could be some kind of poisoning. There was a guy who delivered food too—"

"Really?" Inspector Winters grabbed his notebook again and added more lines to the pages.

I nodded. "And they were all at Ryory's studio for a while." I paused. "Is Ry still here?"

Inspector Winters closed his notebook again and stood. "I need to go, Delaney. Can you show yourself out?"

He didn't wait for my answer, but I thought his rush to leave told me what I was most curious about. Ryory was probably still in the building. I wished I could follow Inspector Winters, but I would probably be arrested if I started wandering around the police station unescorted. The receptionist probably wished for the day such a thing would happen. I would not give her the satisfaction. Well, at least not today.

I considered other possibilities that might keep me in the building, but nothing came to me that didn't seem like unwanted loitering, but the questions were done. For now.

I sent the receptionist a quick nod as I made my way out the front door instead.

CHAPTER TEN

I couldn't believe I had never visited the Museum of Edinburgh. I loved history, but my museum time was usually taken up touring the National Museum, where my good friend Joshua worked. He and I would stroll through exhibits together, sometimes even in the middle of the night, using Joshua's key to get in after hours. Tom had joined us once, but museums weren't his thing, and I thought he was probably glad I had Joshua in my life for such outings.

The Museum of Edinburgh was housed in a historic, and mostly yellow, building named Huntly House located on the Royal Mile. It did, indeed, look more like a house than a museum. After speaking with Inspector Winters, I could have taken the bus back to the bookshop, but since I was at the bottom of the Royal Mile anyway, I decided to walk back up and stop by the museum along the way.

I peered into the front windows. The inside wasn't quite jam-packed but was fairly crowded with objects I was sure to find interesting.

The intuitive mind is a sacred gift and the rational mind is a faithful servant.

I pulled back from the windows as the bookish voice sounded in my mind.

"Hello again, Mr. Einstein," I muttered quietly. Then I looked around to make sure no one was listening to me. They weren't.

I pondered the words and decided the genius was right on track. I was following my gut by coming here. I hoped he was also telling me I was on to something good.

Time would tell, I supposed.

I made my way to the red door—nothing like the warehouse's. This was just a door. I pushed through and entered the homey place, immediately deciding I was a fool for not having visited before. I didn't have time to really look around today, though, so I hoped Ronny Remsen wouldn't be put out that a stranger needed to speak with him about a man who'd been murdered. "Welcome," a gentleman said as he walked toward me, a smile on his face, a kilt around his waist.

Oh, I did love a good kilt.

"Thank you," I said. "You look fantastic."

"This old thing?" He waved off the compliment. "Thank you."

I noticed the recommended fee posted on a sign above a donation box. I grabbed a few bills and slipped them through a slot on the box.

"Thanks again. Look around all you want. We close at five today, but that's hours from now. Can I point you towards any of the exhibits?"

I hadn't made a plan beyond searching for Mr. Remsen, but an idea came to me. "Have anything on the Picts?"

"Follow me." He turned and waved over his shoulder.

I followed the man into the depths, up some stairs, and to a corner that was lit mostly by an adorable paned window that looked out onto the Royal Mile.

The exhibit was made up mostly of informational posters on the wall next to the window, as well as small sculptures in a case.

"Okay, so nothing here is authentic, though we have had a stone or two before. Some of those move from museum to museum throughout Scotland, and it won't be our turn again for a little while. However, we have worked hard to recreate things and give as much information as possible." He chuckled once. "Those of us interested in the Picts here at the museum have spent hours arguing about the validity of what we know and our interpretations of the symbols. We can't be sure of much when it comes the Picts."

"I've heard that." I peered into the top case. A tableau had been created beneath the glass and was more than just a representation of a stone or two. Someone had spent a great deal of time making the scene.

A castle stood atop a green hill surrounded by Highland mountains. Two stones sat on the green grounds. The stones were too small to see, but some handouts had been left to the side of the sculpture to show blown-up representations of them.

"This is an interpretation from a site near Inverness. Some people involved with the Picts can become a wee bit obsessive. We have a few patrons who even like to contribute. This is from one of them."

"It's fantastic!"

"Thank you."

I stood up straight again and extended my hand. "My name

is Delaney Nichols. I work at The Cracked Spine bookshop in Grassmarket."

"I've always loved that place." Like many, he gushed a bit on the word "love."

"So do I."

"You're from the States?"

"I am. Kansas. I came here for the job and stayed. Well, then I met a delightful Scot, and we got married. Sometimes he thinks it was his kilt that turned my head."

He smiled. "Nice to meet you, Delaney. I'm Ronny."

A stroke of luck, I thought as we shook. I sent a silent nod to Mr. Einstein for whatever help he'd just imparted.

"Nice to meet you too," I said. I could have tried to talk around the real reason I was there, but I thought the longer I put it off, the sneakier I might sound. "Ronny, may I be up-front with you?"

Ronny's smile faded and he hesitated at my suddenly serious tone. "I don't know. What's up?"

I nodded. "I got your name from my father-in-law, Artair Fraser. Do you know him?"

"Of course. He's at the university library." A hint of Ronny's smile came back. "Your husband is Tom?"

"He is! You know him too?"

"I do." Ronny laughed, but there was an ironic tone to it. "He dated my sister."

"Oh dear." I knew some of the stories regarding the broken hearts Tom had left in his wake. "Should I say, 'I'm sorry'?"

Ronny shook his head. "No. Jane broke up with him."

"Oh!" I cleared my throat. "Good. I think. Yes, that is good for me."

"Well, she thought he was about to break up with her, so she ripped off the Band-Aid first, if you know what I mean. She was a wee bit heartbroken, but she found the real love of her life soon afterwards. Happy now, with a wee bairn."

"That's wonderful." I filed the name Jane Remsen, although she might have a different last name now, to the back of my mind. I doubted I would bring up Jane to Tom, but you never knew when you might run into someone. Edinburgh didn't feel like the huge city it was. "Ronny, I'm here mostly to talk to you."

"Okay." His eyes moved to the display case and then back to me. "About the Picts?"

"Kind of. A lot of strange things have happened over the last few days, and the latest one led me to you."

"That's certainly intriguing." He paused. "Look, I'm not here alone. Let me track down the other docent, Bea, to let her know she'll need to take care of our visitors for a while. Cup of tea in the break room?"

"That would be great," I said. "Thanks."

I wasn't a fan of tea, but I could manage it if I had to.

Ronny excused himself, and I turned my attention to the Picts' posters on the wall, intrigued by the drawn figures covered in blue tattoos and topped off with red hair. Ryory really had the look down.

I skimmed the words, not surprised by anything I read, until I came upon a list of the materials that had been allegedly used to carve the stones: fine punches, mallets, and smoothing stones.

Not chisels? Did they not *have* chisels? Was Ry's work less authentic because he wasn't using the same tools the Picts had used?

I didn't know what a "fine punch" was, but I thought it was made with a point, not the line of a blade. I made a mental note to research my questions.

The moments in Ryory's studio came back to me. It had been a fun experience, and one that I suddenly wished to repeat. I wondered if I would be better with the tools the second time around.

"Lass?" Ronny appeared again.

I turned and smiled. "Yes?"

"Come, let's have a cuppa and you can ask me your mysterious questions."

I nodded and followed Ronny to the basement break room. Even the break rooms in Old Town were charming.

We sat at one of the small, round wood tables with matching folding chairs. A white refrigerator was rounded at the edges and adorned with an extra-large stainless-steel handle. The countertops were simple but matched the red polka-dotted linoleum.

There was no coffee, but I took the cup of tea graciously and then dumped in some sugar. I wanted to dive in and ask Ronny about Dr. Pace, but there was something about the young man that told me I should go a little slower. Tea was poured and a few sips taken first to grease the wheels.

Once that was accomplished, Ronny said, "All right, Ms. Nichols, what's up?"

"Did you hear about Dr. Adam Pace?"

A twitch played at his eye. "No."

I nodded. "It's tragic news, and I apologize for dropping it on you like this."

"I'm listening," he said. His tone had changed completely.

He was no longer as friendly or as curious as he'd been. He was professional and succinct.

"Mr. Pace is dead. The police are investigating his death as a murder."

"What?" He sat up straight. "No, that doesn't make sense."

Ronny found his phone in the sporran that was belted around his waist. He scrolled through quickly and found the news about Dr. Pace. He looked up at me briefly with disbelieving eyes before he reread the news. Finally, he put the phone on the table.

"That is terrible." He'd turned a little green as he reached for the mug in front of him again. I let him take a sip before I spoke again.

"You knew him?"

"I met him once in person, talked to him a couple times over the phone. He was . . . well, he and I didn't get along, really, but goodness, I wouldn't wish that on anyone."

I nodded and waited another moment before I pushed on. "What happened?"

He'd fallen into thought, his eyes had unfocused, but they snapped back to me. "Oh, it doesn't matter."

I tried to keep the cringe from showing, but it did a little bit anyway.

"What?" he said.

"Well, the police might want to talk to you about your relationship with Dr. Pace. I, uh, Artair told me that Dr. Pace brought up your name to him. Artair is going to speak to the police, and he might mention you." I hoped I wasn't making a huge mistake by forewarning him, but the words came out of me before I could even fully grasp that Ronny might be a potential suspect.

"And how is that relevant to Dr. Pace's murder?"

"I don't know," I admitted. "It's just that . . . well, I think the police might want to talk to everyone who worked with Dr. Pace, particularly if they didn't get along with him."

"Of course, well, I didn't work with him. I sent him away long before much could really happen."

"Ronny, I'm not anyone official, but I met Dr. Pace briefly and he worked at the university in Kansas that I attended. We know, knew, some of the same people. By my own doing, I've become enmeshed in the tragedy, and I'm simply curious. May I ask why you sent him away?"

Ronny frowned for a moment. "Mostly, I didn't like what he said, and I didn't get a good vibe from him."

I nodded. "I get that. You listened to your gut, your intuition. But since you are, were, in the same world as him, and Artair might let the police know he mentioned you, they might show up with questions." I tried a smile. "At least you'll be ready."

"Aye. Good point," Ronny said a moment later. "That's fine. I'm happy to tell them about our brief interactions."

I nodded again and then took a sip of the tea. "Any chance you'd tell me?"

Ronny's eyes lit as if he suddenly understood my curiosity and didn't mind feeding it a little. "Well, you came in interested about the Picts. Was that because you thought Dr. Pace came in to talk about them?"

I nodded.

"Interesting. Well, his time here had little to do with the Picts. You know he was a paleontologist?"

"I do."

Ronny fell into thought again and gave a small laugh. "Honestly, Delaney, he was a piece of work. He tried to sell us some bones. Bones that weren't his to sell, I'm sure."

"Dinosaur bones?"

"Aye." Ronny took a big swig of his tea as if the mere thought made him need fortification.

"Was this recently?"

"A month ago, or so."

"He claimed he had *authentic* dinosaur bones he wanted to sell you?"

Ronny chuckled once. "Aye. I never looked at them, though. We told him we weren't authorized to make such a purchase, that he needed to go through the appropriate channels, which is true. But I didn't feel like I could trust him anyway. He was . . . *shifty* might be the right word. And he didn't want to follow proper procedures. He kept ringing me, lowering the price, hoping I'd get the museum to take him up on it. It was . . . uncouth."

"It sounds it. Did he tell you anything about how he acquired the bones?"

"He said he dug them up himself in Wyoming in the States." He looked at me as if confirming I knew where he was talking about. I nodded. "He said he had a full skeleton of the smallest dinosaur on record—"

I was shocked to hear that Ronny wasn't talking about the T-Rex bones I'd already heard about. I jumped in with another question. "Which is?"

"*Oculudentavis*. I'm sure I'm not pronouncing it correctly. It's just over a centimeter and, oh, I'm not a paleontologist, so forgive me for any possible inaccuracies, but he said it was a bird. I believe he even said that the name means eye-tooth bird. It had some wicked-looking teeth or something like that."

"He dug it up in Wyoming?"

"So he said."

"Could it have been true? I mean, did you research any of it?"

"Only a little bit. I found that Oculudentavis is a documented dinosaur. If he truly had a skeleton, it would have been the first one found in Wyoming, though."

"He didn't show you any pictures?"

"No. We sent him away, told him he needed to do things the right way. Don't get me wrong, Delaney, even though we thought he was less than trustworthy, we were excited about the possibility of Scottish museums having such an item. However, it felt wrong to continue the conversation when there was simply nothing we could do unless he followed proper protocol. And . . . well, the longer it went on, the more he lowered the price, like someone on the telly trying to sell something, it sure seemed like things weren't on the up-and-up."

"I'd feel the same way, I'm sure."

Ronny fell into thought a moment. He looked at his phone and then back at me. "I don't pay attention to the news much. I guess it's a good thing you came to talk to me. You're a better surprise than the police, but it is definitely unsettling to hear about his death, even if I didn't like the man. It . . . in an uncomfortable way, it only reinforces our wariness, though. We weren't the only ones he was trying to scam, if, indeed, that's what was going on. And I do think that's what was happening."

"Did he mention any others when he was talking to you?"

"No, not one."

"Did Dr. Pace *ever* talk to you about the Picts?"

"No, but . . . well, he did look at the exhibit I showed you." Ronny cocked his head. "Oddly, my meeting him went somewhat similar to ours, though I found him at the exhibit. Then he said he had something else he wanted to talk to me about. Why are the Picts involved?"

I thought about dinner the night before. I was sure Artair thought Dr. Pace had met some animosity from this museum, as well as the university's Natural History Collections, because of something he'd inquired about or approached them with regarding the Picts. Here at least, he'd still been peddling dinosaur bones—or so he'd said. I wondered if the University of Kansas knew he had them, again. I suspected the university knew very little about anything that Dr. Pace did here in Scotland. If he'd truly taken bones from a site, I couldn't help but wonder about those checks and balances. Maybe the smallest dinosaur wouldn't be difficult to travel with, but anything from a T-Rex would be nearly impossible. I didn't really believe that he had taken them, though—I knew enough about excavations to understand some of the methods—they were extreme and precise. Could Dr. Pace have made a whole bird dinosaur skeleton from a 3D printer? I would guess he could have. I needed to talk to Theo again.

"That's what I knew about Dr. Pace. That he was interested in the Picts," I finally answered.

"He barely brought them up with me. He didn't even have much to say about the exhibit." Ronny paused again. "I could tell there was something else on your mind, just like I could tell there was something else on his mind."

"I'm not stealthy."

"Neither was Dr. Pace, really. I've done this for years. If it has taught me anything at all, it's how to read people. It's my favorite part of the job."

"I'm sorry if it seems I was trying to trick you—"

"Oh, no, it doesn't. Not to worry." Ronny looked at me for a long moment and sighed. "Should I ring the police? Tell them about Dr. Pace trying to sell us some dinosaur bones?"

I nodded. "I think you should. It might also help with any sort of surprise visit here and at the museum, which is always alarming."

"That's true. I will ring them."

As I'd become accustomed to doing, I offered up Inspector Winters's name and number.

"Brilliant. Thank you," Ronny said.

We were interrupted by the appearance of a young woman who seemed to be in a rush.

"There you are," she said to Ronny and me.

Ronny stood, so I did too. "Can I help you?" he said.

She held up a brown paper bag. "Lunch delivery. No one was up front. I've been looking for someone for a few minutes. I gotta drop this and go, so I hope I can leave this with one of you."

"Of course." Ronny took the bag from her. She was back out through the doorway before he could finish thanking her. He looked at me. "This is Bea's. I should track her down. I'll ring your inspector in a few minutes. May I walk you to the door?"

"Thanks, that would be great. Thanks for your time too."

"My pleasure." He paused. "How is it that I'm saddened by that man's death? I didn't even like him."

"You're human."

"Well, sure, but, and this isn't a description many people enjoy having directed at them, but he was . . . pathetic. Now I'm wondering if I should have been more patient with him, heard him out better. I could have taken him out for a pint. Maybe we could have just talked."

"That's not on you, Ronny."

"No, but if there is a next time, I'm going to do better."

We wove our way back up to the lobby where a woman waited, peering out the front window.

"Hey, Bea, are you looking for this?" Ronny said as he held up the bag.

The woman was petite and yet seemed regal with her steely gray hair pulled back into a flawless bun. She wore a simple black dress and sensible black shoes.

"There it is!" She reached for the bag. "I ran to the ATM around the corner for approximately two minutes because I forgot to add a tip to the delivery. It appears it was all for naught. Thank you, Ronny." She smiled at me.

"Ah, this is Delaney Nichols from The Cracked Spine bookshop. Delaney, Bea."

"Aye? It's a lovely bookshop. I've been a time or two." She moved the bag to her left arm as she reached to shake my hand with her right one. As she did, her sleeve came off her wrist, displaying a blue tattoo.

As we shook, I clumsily tried to look at the tattoo. "A Pict symbol?"

"Oh aye." Gently she pulled her hand away and held up her arm so I could see the entire three inch or so mark. "It's the beast. You know the Picts?"

Ronny and I shared a look.

"Not as well as I'd like, but I'm learning," I said.

"They're a fascinating group."

"Do you know Ryory Bennigan?" I asked, realizing I'd never asked Ronny that question. I looked back and forth between the two of them.

"I've heard of him, of course, but I've never met him," Bea said.

"Same," Ronny added. "Do you know him?"

"I had the opportunity to meet him recently." I nodded at Bea. "Your tattoo made me think of him and all of his."

Bea smiled. "Aye. You know he doesna do any of his own tattooing."

"I heard that."

She leaned a little closer to me, though it was just the three of us. "I know who his artist is, though. Want to know?"

"I do!" Though I felt a little guilty for agreeing. Hadn't Ry wanted to keep it a secret?

"Her name is Willa Brink. She did mine too."

I froze as the information from the last few days jumbled around in my head. "I think I met her. Is she also in a band?"

"Aye."

I knew Edinburgh was a "small world," but this connection seemed so random, except that my intuition had told me I was onto something by coming here today, hadn't it?

The bookish voices weren't magical, but they were often mysterious.

"Huh," I said.

"Delaney?" Ronny asked.

I looked at him and Bea. "Willa came into the bookshop

just this morning. I didn't know she was a tattoo artist, though. Where's her shop?"

Bea pulled back, her mouth making a stern, straight line. "Oh. I don't think I'm supposed to tell."

"Her tattoo business is a secret?"

Bea looked at Ronny who shrugged. "This is all news to me," he said. "I've noticed Bea's tattoo before, but I never even thought about it being Pictish. Of course it is."

Bea turned back to me. "Don't tell her I told you."

"I won't."

"She's in Old Town, in a place above another bookshop on Victoria."

"I know the bookshop."

"Then you know the stairway that leads up to the Royal Mile."

"Of course."

"Her door is unmarked, though there's a small carved-out symbol above the knob."

I didn't mention that Ry's door was marked with a symbol as well, but the memory of it crossed my mind. Along with the memory of Willa's refusal to talk to Inspector Winters.

"Do you just knock on it? Is there a secret code or anything?"

Bea was becoming increasingly uncomfortable as I became bolder in my questions.

"Aye," she said sheepishly. "If she's there, she'll answer, but don't tell her where you got her name. She likes to keep her tie to Mr. Bennigan a secret, but she's so good at tattoos, she would have a thriving business even without him as a customer."

"I won't tell her, but thanks, Bea."

"What's up, Delaney?" Ronny asked.

"I have absolutely no idea, but you know when it seems like a bunch of random things are trying to tell you something? Maybe in code or something?"

"I guess."

"I'm perplexed. I think there are things that tie together, but I'm just not sure how."

Ronny laughed. "You're invested in this mystery?"

"I am. I often put myself into the middle of things, but this feels more like I'm supposed to . . . that sounds silly."

"Listen to your gut, lass." Bea bit her bottom lip. "Nice to meet you, but I'm off to lunch." She turned and made her way toward the stairway that would lead to the break room. "Come back and see us sometime. I'd like to hear what you figure out," she called over her shoulder.

"I will. Thank you," I called to her retreating figure.

Ronny said, "Does Ryory Bennigan have something to do with Dr. Pace? Do you think Ryory Bennigan is . . . a killer?"

"I hope not, and, no, I don't think he is, but . . . I do think you should let the police know about Dr. Pace trying to sell you the bones. And, Ronny, we might have only just met, but I can tell you were most likely quite lovely to Dr. Pace. Don't beat yourself up."

He nodded. "Thanks, and I will ring your inspector right away. And thanks for the heads-up, Delaney. It is a pleasure to meet you. I hope to see you at the bookshop someday."

"Thanks for your time. Come see us. My coworkers would love to meet you."

I slipped more bills into the donation box as I made my way outside. Ronny closed the door behind me.

I stood on the cobblestone road outside the museum and wondered what to do next. Originally, I'd wanted to talk to Ronny and then find Sara Shoemaker in the Natural History Collections at the university, but now I knew that Willa Brink was a tattoo artist. It had to be the same Willa Brink, didn't it?

However, there was something else entirely that directed my next move. The lunch delivery. I wondered if Ani was back at work and feeling better, and I wondered if Inspector Winters had found any tie with her illness and Dr. Pace's death.

And because of Bea's lunch, I remembered again the delivery at Ry's studio. Could there be some sort of tie there to a poison?

Gosh, I hoped not. But still.

I jumped onto a bus that would take me to Ry's studio. And I hoped I wouldn't be turned away.

CHAPTER ELEVEN

Without hesitation, I turned the third door's knob, the one with the carving above it. I made my way up the dimly lit stairway and then stopped at the door at the top. I'd been bold, until that very moment. Now, I felt like I was doing something I shouldn't.

"Okay," I muttered to myself. In fact, I thought I might have heard from Ry by now, but I hadn't. Was he still with the police? Where was Ani?

I knocked.

For a long few seconds, I didn't hear anything, but then I thought footfalls might be headed this way. I was so surprised that someone might be coming to the door that I put my ear against it, and I was about propelled inside when it swung open.

Ani answered. She seemed pale and even thinner than she'd been before, but she was upright and didn't seem wobbly. "Delaney Nichols?" she said with a small, forced smile.

"Hi, Ani. How are you?"

"I'm fine." She frowned.

I didn't know what she knew about the morning's activities at the bookshop or Ry's being questioned by the police, but I was glad to confirm that she was out of the hospital.

I gave her a moment, as it seemed she was gathering something to say, but before she could speak again, Ry called out from behind the opaque wall. "Ani? Who's here?"

"It's Delaney Nichols." She looked at me again and lowered her voice. "He's working. You weren't expected. Don't stay long."

"Okay." I nodded.

"Aye?" More footsteps came this way. Ry appeared from around the wall. He was covered in dust, but I didn't see anything that might indicate he'd been questioned by the police, even if I didn't know what those signs might be.

"Come in, lass." His tone was neither regretful nor welcoming.

"I don't want to disturb," I said.

"You are not a disturbance. Come in. Did you speak with your colleague in Kansas?"

"I did."

"I can't wait to hear. Ani, would you grab us some tea?"

I didn't need the tea, but I wasn't about to decline. I sent Ani a stiff but hopeful smile. I had thought I might have an in with Ry, considering he was the one who'd asked me to reach out to the university. I was happy to see he'd been released by the police as well as still curious about Dr. Pace and the University of Kansas.

Ani did not return the expression. "Come in, Delaney. Always good to see you."

As I stepped inside, I said, "I'm really glad you're okay. Did the doctors figure out what happened?"

"It was food poisoning."

I nodded. "That bag of food that was delivered? Was it maybe from that?"

"Oh. No, I didn't eat anything from that bag. It's a mystery where I picked it up."

Well, there went that theory out the window. I tried not to appear too disappointed.

"Come along." Ry signaled that we should follow him.

On our first trip there, Tom and I hadn't made it to Ry's living spaces. Today, we walked through the rooms we'd seen before, passing by the stone I suspected he'd been working on, though I didn't have time to inspect it. We finally came to a large warehouse-style living space, surrounded on two walls by floor-to-ceiling windows. It was sparsely furnished with a modern but cushiony couch and chairs and a "televator," which was something I'd recently learned was a television on a lift. I wouldn't have noticed it if Ani hadn't grabbed a remote as we entered, switching the TV off and sending it downward into a storage cabinet.

The old building's wood trim and paned windows some-how mixed perfectly with the contemporary furniture.

A large island separated the living room from white cabi-nets and stainless-steel appliances. Ry guided me to a stainless-steel stool attached to the island. He sat next to me and we swiveled to face each other.

Ani went about gathering the tea, but my attention was now solidly on Ry.

A cloud of dust seemed to hover around him, but, again, I couldn't spot any stress.

"I'm sorry to disturb your work, Ry," I said.

"I needed a break anyway. I was hoping you were the police, in fact. I was with them this morning, you know. You are a pleasant surprise. I didn't want to disturb you again. Tell me how your call went."

I nodded. "Absolutely, but how did the questioning go?"

"Oh, fine. They know I swung by the bookshop, but they are waiting on some things before officially clearing me. They do think Dr. Pace was murdered the morning I came to visit him, but if the medical examiner further determines that it occurred the night before, they might want to talk to me again. The hospital didn't want me visiting Ani, so I was home alone all evening. I've seen enough on the telly," he nodded in the direction of the cabinet, "about weak alibis to know that they might want to talk to me again." He took the mug that Ani slid in his direction. "Thank you," he said to her.

"You don't seem concerned," I said as Ani put a mug in front of me. I thanked her too as I noticed that most of her hands, except for the tips of her fingers, were covered by her long sleeves. I'd thought it was warm in the studio, but I'd already noticed she was pale. Maybe she was cold too. Or maybe she still felt ill but wanted to put on a brave face. She remained silent as she stood on the other side of the island, her arms crossed in front of herself.

"No, not concerned," Ry said.

"Ani, would you like to sit?" I asked, though it was not my place to do such a thing. I couldn't ignore that she didn't seem a hundred percent.

Ani jolted a little at the question. "No, I'm fine."

Ry didn't appear to notice the brief exchange. He looked at me. "Who did you speak to in Kansas?"

"A friend. His name is Theo," I said. "I'm afraid he didn't have much to offer, Ry. The university had heard of Dr. Pace's murder, and they're upset. He was liked."

"Did they know about the stone he said he had? Was it real?"

I shook my head. "No, all they know is that he was here studying the Picts. That's it. They knew of no stone. I'm sorry. There might be more to come, but Theo didn't have much."

I decided not to tell Ry about the dinosaur bones. I had a loyalty to the University of Kansas as well as to Theo that was more important than what Dr. Pace had done—at least for now. I'd told the police, but I didn't want to add hearsay to Dr. Pace's already sullied reputation with Ry if I didn't have to.

Ry nodded. "Well, the fact that they didn't know about it tells me enough. I do think that if it was legitimate, Pace would have talked to them about it."

I nodded too. "Probably."

"Right. Thank you for looking into it, Delaney. I did wrangle you and your fellow bookshop corps into this mess, and I'm sorry for that."

"No need to be," I said. "It's a pleasure to know you. We all feel the same."

"Ta. Well, I didn't kill the lad, Delaney. I'm not concerned about that. I'm more than happy to help the police in any way, though perhaps with an attorney if there is a next time." He held his mug between his hands on the island. "What I am is regretful because I wasn't as friendly to Dr. Pace during our last meeting, no matter the legitimacy of the purported artifact."

I turned my attention to Ry again as I tried the tea. It tasted just like all the other awful teas I'd attempted, but no one offered sugar, cream, or anything that might help make it more palatable. I could do this, I told myself.

Ry's words seemed genuine. His confidence as well. I also didn't want to tell him yet about the bones that Dr. Pace had tried to sell to the Museum of Edinburgh. Though that news might ease his regrets because it illustrated how Dr. Pace was probably behaving badly with a few people, I knew I might have already shared too much with Ronny. I was sure curious about Ry's regrets, though.

I set the mug on the island. "You didn't really believe at all what he was saying about what he'd found?"

Ry shook his head. "No. I wanted to at first. But the more I thought about it all, the more doubtful I became. I told him I wouldn't give any money at least until I saw the item in person and was able to authenticate it."

"What do you think he was up to?"

Ry shook his head. "I don't know, but he just wanted money probably. He thought I was an easy mark because of my reputation regarding the Picts." Ry shrugged. "I am, but I'm also not stupid. The police told me there was no stone inside the house, nothing that looked like what Dr. Pace described, nothing that looked like the sketch I made. I speculated that if he ever did have something like that, maybe someone wanted it, so they killed him to get it. It's an idea."

"What did they think of that?"

"They didn't let on what they thought about anything."

I took another sip. "Maybe it never existed."

"That's possible too."

"Or maybe he had another place where he was storing stuff," I added.

Ry nodded. "Anything is possible. I wish I had more to offer the police, though. I had absolutely nothing except that I was irritated by Dr. Pace during that last visit, and I wished I hadn't been. I was up-front about that but also clear that I wasn't bothered enough to be murderous, similar to what it seems others have said."

"Do you know if they found anything like a 3D printer in the house?"

Ry blinked at me. "I have no idea. I didn't ask and they didn't offer that up. They ignored any question I had. They made it clear who was in charge."

"He was poisoned, so was Ani the night before," I said, leaving it there to see what they might say.

"I thought the same thing!" Ry said. "Towards the end of the questioning Inspector Winters came back into the room and asked for more details of that specifically. He said he was going to be in touch with Ani, ask her for permission to her medical records, but I don't think he has yet, and I don't think food poisoning is the same as killing someone with poison. They are just covering all bases, perhaps."

"I haven't heard from them yet. I'm happy to give the police any access." Ani turned so her back was toward us as she cleaned up the tea things.

It felt like a purposeful move, like she didn't want us to see her face, but I might have been reading way too much into it.

Ry continued with a half-smile. "They put me in my place, you know."

"How?" I asked.

"Oh, you know, played the role of the cops well. Ignored my questions and then were firm with me that they were the ones to ask them. I've seen enough shows to know the routine, but it was still intimidating when you're the one in the middle of it. I behaved. Mostly." He paused. "And they let up as time went on. I truly don't think I'm a suspect. I don't think they have much of anything to go on, though. I genuinely wish I could help, but, as I already mentioned, I won't speak to them again without an attorney present. I think that's only wise."

"I agree," I said.

"Why do you ask about a 3D printer? Do you think he . . . made things?" Ry asked.

"You can print on stone, right?"

"Aye, you can. It's very possible and used widely. Architecture, education . . ."

"It is?" I realized I'd assumed what I knew without researching any of it. To be fair, I hadn't had time to do much of anything beyond trying to keep up.

"Sure. I've been approached by sellers of such things, but they were on the up-and-up about it. No, it's not a world I want to be a part of, but, alas, it's probably the way of the future. Everything can be duplicated."

"Like artificial intelligence seems to threaten. That would take the artist out of the art."

"Well, aye, but you have to be pretty clever with computer design as well. Right, Ani?" He glanced at his assistant.

She turned to face us again, appearing no different than she had before. "Aye."

"Ani's a computer whiz," Ry said.

"Not really," she said quickly. "I just grew up with them. Ry didn't."

"Aye. She's young, but I now have legitimate records of my art, my money, everything! Before Ani, I just went about my days without thinking much about such things. She keeps me aware of my finances. It's the first time in my life I've paid attention."

I watched Ani sip her tea. Ry had lived the curse of the rich. If I understood correctly, he'd have had no need to pay attention to things like bank account balances because the accounts were always full. Suddenly, I had nosy questions regarding how much money he really had and how his money might have been left to or given to him—funds, annuities, those sorts of boring things, but those questions were far too personal, even for me.

However, I realized with a ping of clarity that Ani knew more about Ry than probably anyone else. Even if he had money managers, they didn't know the real man. Ani knew Ry as well as his bank account balances.

"I'm curious now, though," Ry said. "Delaney, how can we find out whether there was a printer in the house or not?"

I shook my head. "I did ask the police, and they said there wasn't."

"Which might lend more weight to the idea that Dr. Pace was also using another space to work on things. I wonder if he leased something else out in his name and if the police might be able to find that place," Ry said.

I nodded. "Are there any studios anywhere that you know of that rent out space?"

Ry and Ani shared a look. They both shook their heads.

"No, but I'll ask around," Ry said.

I nodded as a question that didn't seem too personal came to me. "Ry, may I ask . . . why is your tattoo artist a secret?"

"Oh." He looked surprised and then at Ani again. She shook her head. "I don't think I'm allowed to say."

"They don't want the publicity?"

Ry squinted and looked out toward the wall of windows. "That's not really it. It's both sides. We like keeping it to ourselves."

I nodded, took another sip of horrible tea. Though it didn't fortify me, I pressed on. "Is it Willa Brink?"

Without missing a beat, he and Ani looked at each other again.

"I just can't say, Delaney. I'm sorry," Ry said.

I couldn't tell if I'd hit upon anything or not. I couldn't tell if they even knew someone named Willa Brink, and I didn't want to push their kind hospitality. Well, I wanted to, but like asking about money, I couldn't bring myself to.

"I understand." I took a fake sip of tea. "I appreciate your time, and I really did want to see how Ani was doing." I looked at her. "You appear to be okay." Not great, I thought, but okay, enough probably.

"I'm absolutely fine."

"Well," Ry interjected. "She was very, very sick and her vitals weren't going in the right direction. Thank goodness for the medical professionals who came to her rescue. She could have died. I give you credit for your clear-headedness and quick thinking, Delaney."

"Oh. No—"

"Well, Ry, I don't know . . . ," Ani began.

"That's what the doctor said."

She reached over the island and put her hand over his. "I'm okay."

They were friends, family in the way I was family with my coworkers. Their fondness for each other was genuine and very father/daughterly.

Ry continued as Ani took her hand back, "Your question about Willa, though . . . I all but forgot about the artists, and I know she was one there. I did appreciate the police bringing over the message that I wouldn't be there. I will need to try to do that again. I'm so sorry for the way that went."

"We would love to have you all back at any time."

"Thank you," Ry said. "Ani and I will put something together."

I heard a tone of dismissal in his voice. I slid off the stool, and Ry stood as Ani came back around the island.

"Thank you both for letting me interrupt your work today," I said.

"It was a pleasure to see you, Delaney. You and your husband are friends now. Please come by anytime. We have canceled the rest of the personal visits for now, but you, your husband, and everyone from The Cracked Spine will always be welcomed."

Ani blanched as she stood next to me. I could tell the last thing she wanted was for me to take Ry up on that invitation.

"I appreciate that. I promise we won't make a habit out of it."

"Not at all. I look forward to our next visit. Ani, will you see our guest out?"

"Aye."

We left Ry in the living room as I followed Ani's quick steps through the building. I tried to look at everything again. There was so much to digest along the way. There was not enough time. We'd only begun our explorations when Ani had fallen sick, and now she was moving too quickly for me to fully take in my surroundings.

As I followed her into the entryway, she pulled the front door wide. "Delaney, Ry is a busy man."

Ry hadn't seemed bothered by my company, but I heard what she was saying. "I appreciate that, Ani."

"If you do, you'll let him work."

"Of course."

I stepped toward the doorway as Ani made a move like she was going to grab my arm, but she stopped short and pulled her arm back.

"What?" I stopped.

Ani was stone-still for a long few seconds. Finally, she said, "Nothing. Nothing."

"Are you sure?"

"Goodbye, Delaney."

I looked at her, but she didn't seem to want to say anything else, so I made my way through the doorway and then turned to look back at her just in case there was more she wanted to tell me.

Ani shut the door, decisively and firmly.

What had just happened? Had there been something she wanted to tell me? Was Ani scared—and, if so, about what?

I couldn't understand those few moments, but I was sure that Ani wasn't going to tell me anything more.

I needed to get to the bookshop anyway.

CHAPTER TWELVE

It was already late afternoon when I hurried off the bus and toward the bookshop's door.

Rosie sat at the desk as she went through the mail. She looked up and peered at me over her brightpink reading glasses. "Lass? You all right?"

Hector stood from the cushion on the floor next to the desk and trotted toward me. We met halfway and I lifted him to my cheek.

"I'm fine. Why?"

Rosie chuckled. "Your cheeks betray you. They pinken a little when you're onto something. What have you found?"

"I don't know if I've learned anything helpful, but I do have more information."

"What's going on?" Rosie asked. "How did it go with Inspector Winters?"

"Good." I glanced at the mail on her desk. "If you don't have anything urgent, let's go back and I'll tell you everything."

"Aye. The mail can wait."

As I told her all that had happened and who I'd visited with,

I remembered that the day had started with a packed bookshop as well. There was no sign of the gathering.

"You *have* been busy," Rosie commented.

"I have, and I'm sorry I wasn't here to help you clean up."

"Not to worry. Hamlet and I took care of it quickly. What did you think of the museum? I havnae been for years."

"It was great, but I didn't see much. I liked Ronny, and I thought Bea was interesting."

"And she said that the lass that was here this morning, Willa, was a tattoo artist?"

"You sound doubtful."

"I doubt everything," she said, which was also true. "She was the only one who didnae want to speak to Inspector Winters, aye?"

"She was the only one I saw."

"Something's strange about her being here to 'meet' Ry, do you think?"

"I do, but I can't pin down anything, really. It could have just happened that way."

"I think the same."

"I'd like to talk to her. I know where her studio is. I might try to visit."

"Aye. Just not alone, lass."

"Okay."

Rosie sighed. "It's been a day. We'll try it all again tomorrow."

There was much more I'd intended to do with my day, but it was time to turn the sign to Closed.

"Let me finish up tonight, Rosie. You guys took care of this morning so well, I'll make sure we're squared away tonight. You and Hector head home."

Rosie considered my offer for a moment and then shrugged. "Aye, ta lass. That doesnae sound like an offer I want to refuse."

Rosie gathered her things, and I walked her and Hector to the door. I closed it behind them and watched as they made their way to the bus stop. Once they'd boarded, I locked the door and turned off the lights.

I faced the almost spotless bookshop and went through the closing checklist in my mind. It wouldn't take long.

I gathered my phone and texted Tom.

How late do you need to work?

I can be done in an hour or so. You?

About the same. I have a plan for this evening.

LOL. Well, I can't wait to hear it. See you in an hour?

See you then.

I grabbed the cash from the small register that Rosie used and crossed over to the dark side, where I put it into the safe inside Edwin's office. A deposit would need to be made in the morning. Inside the warehouse, I did a quick check of my email, finding nothing urgent. I put the laptop away again and locked up. I checked that the coffee machine was off and unplugged in the kitchenette. I glanced at the leftover pastries in the fridge and wondered if Tom and I would grab dinner or if we should just have a pastry or two. I ended up closing the door with the boring idea of vegetables on my mind. I flipped off all the lights.

Back on the retail side, I took a feather duster to the shelves and then wiped down the back table and chairs with a dusting spray, though I could tell it had all been done just hours earlier. Rosie's desk was spotless, but I wiped it down too. I remembered that Hamlet liked to make sure his file drawers were locked before he left for the day.

All of the drawers but one were locked. I was going to grab

the key from the hiding place, but the drawer had come open as I'd checked it. There was something inside that captured my attention.

It was a printed article about, of all things, 3D printing using stone. I retrieved the three stapled pages and started to read.

While the subject matter was one I might normally find fascinating simply because learning new things was my jam, this article wasn't written compellingly enough for even a data nerd to get into. Still, I tried to digest the methods and explanations that were lined out.

Once I got through the whole thing, I noticed a note in Hamlet's handwriting was next to it. "For Ani?"

Why was it on top of everything? What was going on between Hamlet and Ani that this article was where I'd found it, now? Coincidence?

There were no dots of information to connect, but it was another piece of a strange puzzle that sure kept pointing at the famous artist's assistant. I put the article back in the drawer and locked it.

A text from Tom popped onto the screen.

I'm ready.

I'll be there in a few.

One last once-over glance of the bookshop before I left, locking the door behind me and changing gears mentally so I might be able to convince my husband of an adventure he was sure to find . . . not as exciting as I might.

"Well, no, lass, I really don't want one," Tom said after I enthusiastically shared what was on my mind.

"Would you care if I got one?"

He chuckled once. Though it was a reaction I was used to, this time it was done with much less humor. "It's your body to do with what you want."

"What if I got your name over my heart?"

His eyebrows rose at that one. "That sounds intriguing, but . . . may I think about it a wee bit?"

"Sure. You have until we climb the stairway up to the Royal Mile."

Tom's eyebrows furrowed. "In that case, I'd better get to thinking."

Like I had done with the bookshop, Tom went through some closing steps at the pub, even though it wasn't closing quite yet. Rodger, Tom's longtime employee, would finish up the evening, but that never stopped Tom from running over his own checklist. All was in order.

The late May evening was chilly, verging on too windy to walk outside. We had two different sets of winterwear—milder winter and not-so-mild. Tonight was just right for our milder winterwear, even with the slight mist in the air. My hair would frizz, but I was used to that.

As we made our way up Victoria Street, I quickly told Tom all the same things I'd told Rosie but ended with what Bea had said about Willa being Ry's tattoo artist as well as hers, and Ry and Ani's non-answer to the question I'd posed.

"And you just happened to meet Bea today?"

"I just met Willa and Bea today, but it wasn't something they did, it just happened. Though my intuition told me that visiting the museum was the right thing to do."

"Your . . . intuition?"

"Yes, that one." I hooked my arm though his as we made our way.

I'd told Tom about my bookish voices. He hadn't reacted in any way except perfectly, with positive acceptance. He hadn't asked me to explain them in detail. He hadn't doubted me.

"That's interesting," he said.

"I agree. Anyway, I believed Willa this morning, though, when she said she was there to meet him, but there was no reason for her to think I'd figure out who she was. Ry and Ani are tightlipped about it. There must be some sort of NDA or privacy agreement or something."

"Aye."

"You sound suspicious. What are you seeing that I'm not?"

"I don't think I'm seeing anything you aren't, but I have many questions, even if I don't know where to begin. If you go see Ry again, though, would you take someone with you? Please."

I nodded. "Because you're concerned about Ry or Ani?"

Tom shrugged. "I'm concerned about you and bothered by everyone else. A murder has been committed and you didn't know the people involved until now. Just please be aware."

"I hear you and I won't go alone again."

"Ta."

We climbed the hidden stairway, coming out and onto an alcove just off the Royal Mile. I'd been at that exact spot more times than I could remember, but I'd never noticed the doors on the buildings on either side. Now that I really looked, I saw three: two on one side, one on the other.

Neither of the two on the one side held any sort of carving or decoration, but the one on the other side did.

"Huh," I said. "I'm actually surprised it's here. Until this moment . . . well, I guess this just makes it more real."

"Bea didn't lie."

"She did not. All right then." I knocked a friendly three raps.

Only a few seconds later, the door opened as a wave of patchouli greeted us before we could even make out the person who'd opened the door. The light inside was dim, and my first thought was how in the world could anyone see to create tattoos.

"Hi, Willa, remember—"

"Oh. Delaney, right?" she said.

"And this is my husband, Tom."

"Well, it's nice to meet you, Tom." She put her hands on her hips. She was backlit enough that I couldn't quite see her face, but her next words sounded like she was frowning. "Why do I feel like I've been caught at something? Why are you here? How did you know I was here?"

"I was told you were Ryory Bennigan's tattoo artist," I confessed.

"By whom?"

I cringed. "I'm not supposed to say, but I will add that it wasn't Ry."

"Huh," she said, but I thought I saw a shift. She wasn't quite as put out. "Okay, do you want a tattoo?"

I glanced at Tom and then back at Willa. "I thought about it, but I don't think so, not tonight. I just wondered if you have some time to chat?"

"Chat? About if I'm Ryory Bennigan's tattooist?"

"I know it's weird that we're here . . ."

"That's putting it mildly, but you have also piqued my curiosity, so come in. I have an appointment in half an hour, though. You'll have to go then."

"Thanks, I promise we won't be that long."

Willa nodded and stepped back to pull the door open wider. She still wasn't thrilled about our visit, but she was definitely more curious than angry.

Once we were through, the dim light gave way to something much brighter coming from a room down a short hallway to our right. We followed Willa as she led us that way. She grabbed her cellphone from a counter right inside the room. She turned off the background music that had been playing as Tom and I looked around.

Led Zeppelin had been rocking through some speakers attached to two ceiling corners. The rest of the place gave off the same sort of rock-and-roll vibe. Though the light was bright, the walls and décor were dark—black walls and floors and a black leather chair for customers.

There were rock group posters on the black walls. Pink Floyd, The Who, The Rolling Stones, and others joined who must have been Willa's favorite—Robert Plant and the rest of Led Zeppelin.

Willa's long, curly hair and her flowing clothes were more bohemian than rock, and her voice really did remind me of Stevie Nicks.

"Aren't you in a band?" I asked.

"I am."

"Rock?"

"A little bit of everything."

"Which do you do more, sing or tattoo?" I asked.

"Oh. Tattooing is my job, the band is my hobby, though if we received a big recording contract, I could be persuaded to switch."

I nodded and couldn't help but think about how I loved my "job" so much, it didn't seem right to call it just a job. But this wasn't about me.

"This is such a great place," Tom admired. "Almost makes me want to get a tattoo. Almost." Though a mild-mannered Scot who looked fabulous in a kilt and gave the impression that he might only listen to bagpipe music, Tom loved rock and roll, even headbanging sometimes. It was the thing I'd found most surprising about him. I wasn't quite the fan he was, but I enjoyed him enjoying it.

"Thanks." Willa nodded.

"Do you have any tattoos?" I asked her, noticing her bare forearms sticking out from her blousy sleeves.

She smiled. "Not one. I can't make such a commitment. My taste changes so much that I think I would regret using a space on my body for something I didn't like as much a year or so later."

"Huh, and that sells your work well?"

"I should be humbler, but I don't have to do much to sell my work. My art is popular by people who feel like they *can* make a lifetime commitment." She gathered a notebook. "Would you like to see some of it?"

Tom and I nodded eagerly.

Willa rolled a table like you might find in a hospital room toward us. She set the notebook on it and opened it, letting us thumb through.

Any artist was a mystery to me. My mind doesn't "see"

things the ways theirs does. Those who were brave enough to create art on skin were beyond my comprehension. I wasn't a visual person, and the idea of such responsibility frightened and awed me.

Not surprisingly, looking at the notebook made me think of Ry's tattoos, but there weren't many Pictish tattoos inside the pages of the notebook. In fact, I didn't spot any I'd seen on Ry, which would track with the secrecy of his artist. I was working up a way to ask Willa again, see if she would tell, but I wasn't there quite yet.

"Wow, Willa, is this all original?"

"It is. People bring in pictures sometimes, but I always add my own touch."

We saw trees, dragons, cats, dogs, superheroes, flowers, birds—all kinds of plants and animals.

"These are wonderful," Tom offered.

"Thank you."

Though we were still going through the book, Willa continued, "So, what do you *really* want to talk to me about?"

I looked up at her. "Are you Ryory Bennigan's tattoo artist?"

Her expression didn't give up anything. "I see. Well, what I can tell you is that I am aware of the fact that Mr. Bennigan's artist is a secret. If I am that person, I cannot confirm. If I'm not, I can't tell you who it might be, even if I know." She cocked her head. "Why does it even matter?"

Tom and I shared a look before I turned back to her. "I don't know."

Willa laughed. "You don't even know why you're asking the question?"

Well, because if she was his artist, she'd lied about knowing Ry. However, maybe that lie was in place because of some legal NDA. I was speculating.

"I don't. I just wondered," I said.

"Ah, well, I have no information for you." She paused. "Actually, I do. There is something I can tell you."

She had our full attention—and she seemed to relish it for a moment.

"I know Mr. Bennigan's assistant, and I've done a tattoo for her. It wasn't all that long ago."

"Oh!" I said, wondering if that was her way of telling us that she was, in fact, Ry's artist. As I inspected her, though, I couldn't uncover anything more to what she said. "Ani?"

"Aye."

Willa reached for the book on the table and flipped to a page toward the end. She pointed. "This one."

It looked like a hummingbird with teeth. It was oddly horrifying. "Is that . . . ?" I couldn't remember the name of the dinosaur.

"It's an Oculudentavis," Willa said confidently.

I nodded. "Right. The world's smallest dinosaur."

I was working hard to hide two things: my surprise and my brain's machinations as it tried to understand the connections. I would have to ruminate on it later so I didn't make Willa suspicious. Tom kept it cool too, but I was sure he was wondering the same things since I'd already told him about the meeting with Ronny and Bea.

"You know about dinosaurs?"

"Some." I left it at that.

"Impressive. It was very small. The tattoo was done in about double what's been estimated as its actual size," Willa said.

"It's wicked," Tom added.

"I improvised a wee bit because we don't know everything about it, like we don't know the exact colors, of course, but Ani wanted the red eyes."

"It's an incredible work of art," I said. "Where on her body did she get it done?"

"The back of her upper arm. She's shown it around quite a bit. I've had a few others come in for the same thing."

I watched Willa closely, but she didn't give up anything else at all. She talked about the tattoo proudly but also as if it was just another day at the office.

"I hope to see it in person," I said.

"I love it," Tom added. "May I snap a picture of it? It almost makes me want to get my own tattoo."

I was silently proud of his quick thinking.

"Aye, of course."

Tom took a quick picture. "Ta."

A knock sounded from the shop's front door.

"That's my customer. I'll see you out."

I was disappointed to leave but also anxious to think through the new information.

We followed Willa to the door, where she bid us a hurried goodbye as the lion's share of her attention shifted to the young woman who was entering.

I wished we could watch the process, but that felt like the wrong thing to ask, though I did wonder about the privacy of it all. Did people ask to watch?

Once outside, Tom said, "Well, I'm glad we didn't have to go under the needle, but that was certainly interesting."

I nodded. "Thanks for getting a picture. That was quick thinking."

"What's running through your head?"

"I'm thinking that Ani's Oculudentavis tattoo makes it seem like she and Dr. Pace discussed the prehistoric animal but didn't tell Ry."

"Or Ry didn't admit to being a part of that. They aren't required to tell you anything. They are, however, not supposed to lie to the police. Maybe they did tell Winters even if they didn't tell you, aye?"

"There's that, I suppose. I thought I was onto something regarding the food delivery, but that wasn't it."

"Seems like it could have been something, though. If there is a connection, it's to a killer. Dr. Pace claimed to have a skeleton of the Oculudentavis. He was trying to sell it to the Museum of Edinburgh, but how does that connect to Ani? And why does she have a tattoo of the very same dinosaur? I don't know. Like you said, that's not the way things are done. You don't just walk into a museum and sell them something. There are procedures, at least in Scotland."

"In the States too, I'm sure. Dr. Pace would have known that, but he didn't care."

"Desperate for money."

"I just don't know."

Tom put his hand on my wrist. "Lass, I have an idea."

"Okay?"

He smiled. "Ice cream."

"Ice cream?"

"Aye. I think we need to stop thinking about this for a wee bit. Ice cream is a wonderful way to forget about murder, don't you think?"

I smiled, pushing away those annoying thoughts about vegetables. "Well, butter pecan is."

"I would argue that chocolate chip might do the trick too. Some of each. Aye?"

I took a deep breath and let it out. "Oh, yes, I think that's perfect."

CHAPTER THIRTEEN

"Yes, I meant to send it to her," Hamlet said as he held the printed article.

I felt like I might have crossed a line, but the drawer wasn't something that was meant to be off limits to anyone. Hamlet hadn't seemed bothered by my accidental snooping.

"Why?"

"She'd mentioned stone 3D printing to me offhandedly a couple months ago maybe. Neither of us knew much about it, but when I saw the article, I thought I'd send it to her. I forgot all about it, I'm afraid."

"I thought it might be something like that. Did she, by chance, mention other names, Dr. Pace, or anyone, at that time?"

"No, Delaney. Nothing. I rang her last night to see how she was feeling, but we didn't talk about much of anything other than she was fine and she was home."

Though we hadn't been in as early as the day before, Rosie, Hector, Hamlet, and I had all arrived around eight, ready for—and probably hoping for—a normal day at the bookshop. No one had heard from Edwin yet.

We all stood near Rosie's desk. Hector had decided he wanted Hamlet to hold him. He relaxed contentedly in the crook of Hamlet's arm.

Hamlet continued, "Our conversation was brief, but she sounded fine. I wanted to ask her more questions, but it didn't feel like the right moment. She didn't seem to want to talk about her time at the hospital."

"Hmm," Rosie said.

I looked at her. "What?"

"Something about her . . ."

"Do you suspect she might have faked it, somehow?"

Rosie frowned. "Maybe. No, I don't know, but I wonder if she wasn't quite as ill as you might have thought. She *might* have faked it, or some of it."

"I guess that's possible, but why?"

Rosie shrugged. "Get you out of there. End the party. Didn't like you. I don't know."

I looked at Hamlet.

"I don't know either," he said. "She's usually pretty quiet, doesn't seem to want extra attention sent in her direction. Pretending to be sick sounds like it would garner more attention than she would normally like."

I wondered about Rosie's suspicion, but she hadn't been there. She hadn't seen how sick Ani seemed.

"Och, let's get to work," Rosie said. "We've plenty to do."

They didn't need my help on the retail side, so I headed to the warehouse.

Though the ice cream had been a welcome distraction the night before, my brain hadn't stopped turning over all the information. I tried to keep it all on a back burner until I could write it down and give it proper attention.

That was going to be my first task, maybe mostly so I could then concentrate on other things.

Once I made sure nothing had been disturbed in the warehouse, I grabbed my laptop and pulled up my email, surprised to find something from Edwin that he'd sent this morning. Just what I needed, I thought, something to offer even more distraction.

> Lass—I have a favor to ask. I was contacted by a fellow bookseller who requested help with an item found in his mother's attic. It's not one thing to do with Ryory Bennigan or the Picts, but if you have the time today, would you stop by his shop and see if you might be able to help him? It's George's shop. I think you know where it is.
>
> Thanks, Edwin

It wasn't unusual for Edwin to send a request via email, but this one didn't mention what type of item he was talking about, which was more cryptic than usual. But I did know George's place. It was a fabulous bookshop on the edge of Old Town. Overflowing with books and cats, every time I visited the tight space, I decided that Edwin's purchase of the two buildings was a great idea. We could keep the retail side to books only and spread out on this side when needed.

From what I could tell, the proprietor, George, spent most of his time hunched next to an old cash register as he worked on stacks of wrinkled and messy paperwork. As much as I loved his shop, it most definitely felt claustrophobic inside, which, some thought, was the charm of the store.

I texted Edwin asking if this afternoon would work or if he wanted me to go that morning.

He replied that the afternoon would be fine.

Further diverted, I spent a couple hours doing my regular job, which today entailed answering emails about items that people thought Edwin might want to purchase, and an invitation for both Edwin and me to attend a dinner party at the house of a local writer. I sent Edwin a copy of the email and asked for his input but didn't hear back immediately.

I started cataloguing some small sculptures created by an eighteenth-century Scottish artist that I'd found on one of the shelves in the warehouse when an image of Dr. Pace came to my mind and wouldn't leave. I sighed and gave in to the moment, expecting a bookish voice but not hearing one. Instead, an idea came to me. I grabbed my phone and called from my contact list.

"Delaney?" Joshua answered after two rings.

Joshua and I had become fast friends when I'd first moved to Edinburgh and found my museum soulmate in the supersmart young PhD who worked at the National Museum. He and Hamlet were also close friends, and Tom, Rosie, and Edwin adored him too.

"Hey," I said. "What am I interrupting?"

"Nothing. Really. What's going on?"

"Do you know Ryory Bennigan?"

"The artist?"

"Yes."

"I've met him. We spoke with him a while ago, asking if we

could display his work. He declined. Apparently, we try to convince him every couple years or so."

"That doesn't surprise me. I won't go into the details right now, but the real reason I'm calling isn't about Ryory but someone he knew. What do you do if people approach you about buying something for the museum?"

"Oh, well, we look at it. We present it to the board if we like it. The board then decides if we should purchase it, or 'rent' it, as sometimes happens."

"As director of the Treasure Trove, do you have some say?"

"No, that's different. But my position with the museum keeps me in the loop and the board listens to my opinions. Why?"

"Did you hear about the man from America who was killed?"

"I don't . . . oh, a moment." It sounded as if Joshua was opening a desk drawer. "I did hear, but I didn't put it all together. What was his name?"

"Dr. Adam Pace."

"That's right! Here it is. He came to the museum, asking if we wanted to buy something. I've been so busy that I didn't pay much attention. Goodness. What happened to him? Do you know?"

"Poisoned."

"What kind of poison?"

"I don't know. It hasn't been announced. At least, I haven't heard. What did he try to sell the museum?"

"Some fake dinosaur bones." Irritation lined his voice.

"You were quick to say, 'fake.'"

"Aye, I spotted his scam right away. I've seen a bone or two. He was up to no good."

"You saw actual bones?"

"Yes, he brought them in."

"How did you know they were fake?"

"Coloring, texture, so many reasons. I'm sorry he was killed, but he wasn't the brightest of bulbs, you know. Hang on, did you say that Ryory Bennigan knew Dr. Pace? What was that about?"

"I don't have that whole story either, but something about a Pictish stone Dr. Pace found."

"Well, that was surely another fake item. Unless he dug up a stone somewhere, which would be against Scottish law, by the way. Considering what I saw of him, I wouldn't be surprised by any measure he took, though."

I didn't offer what I knew about where the stone might have come from. "Right. Do you think Dr. Pace 3D printed the bones?"

"That's a good guess, Delaney, and that's exactly what I think he did. You know, it's something that's done in our world to fill in missing bones, maybe, but we don't mislead anyone as to what's real and what isn't. That's a big no-no."

"Of course."

"There's more, though. The bones he brought us to look at were part of a creature that never actually existed."

"I don't understand."

"Right. Well, he showed us something named Oculudentavis. It was once considered the world's smallest dinosaur, at least of what we know."

"Once? Not anymore?"

"Well, it held the position for a long time. We all thought it was a bird-shaped dinosaur, which has been proven untrue. An examination of a more complete specimen was found in 2020, and it was then classified as a small lizard instead."

"Not a hummingbird shape with teeth?"

Joshua laughed. "That's exactly how it used to be described based on what we knew until 2020. Not anymore. No, it wasn't a bird. It was a lizard-like animal."

"How could such a mistake be made?"

"Originally only a skull was found, and it certainly looked like a bird's head, though with teeth on the beak, but now the larger specimen has been discovered. Scales and body shape determined it was a lizard. In fact, not even a dinosaur."

"Wouldn't everyone in the paleontological scientific community know that?" I managed the tangle of words only because I spoke them slowly.

"They should, but some people are arrogant enough to think that maybe we, in the museum community, wouldn't know, that we didn't stay up on things. He wasn't completely wrong, but *I* read everything, Delaney, you know that."

I did know. I thought about Ronny and Bea. Their story was so different, but maybe they *didn't* read everything.

"I do know that. Did you report him?"

"To whom? There are no real legal authorities who would care enough. It was fraud, yes, but people do try to sell fake bones as fake bones. Dr. Pace probably would have just changed his story if someone had questioned him officially and said he'd never claimed they were authentic. If his university cared in the least, they should have prevented him from trying to peddle his wares."

I thought about Theo and how the University of Kansas staff had liked Adam Pace enough not to reprimand him too drastically over the T-Rex bones. The university probably should have done more, but I didn't have the whole story, of course. I would bet some of Rosie's shortbread that the university didn't know a thing about all that Dr. Pace had been doing in Scotland. Out of sight, out of mind.

"They might not have known?" I said, working not to sound too defensive of my alma mater.

"They should have. He was affiliated with them. I know it's not easy to know what all your people are doing, but they still should have."

"You're not wrong."

"Anyway, he wasn't on the up-and-up at all. We sent him away and stopped answering his messages and emails, etc. He didn't give up, but we have enough security here to make sure he wasn't welcomed back inside. He only tried to come back once as far as I know."

"Joshua, how widespread do you think his attempts at fraud—that's what I'm going to call it because I don't have any other words for it at the moment—were?"

"In Edinburgh? A city that prioritized the preservation of its history? He might have angered more people than the police will ever be able to investigate."

There had to be something that would narrow down the suspect list, but it had only been growing at every turn.

I didn't envy the police and their jobs on this one.

However, maybe they did have some sort of evidence to get to the meat of the matter. Nevertheless, I hadn't heard about any arrests.

Joshua sighed. "Gosh, I'm sorry for sounding bitter. That's not the right way to be when someone dies, particularly if they're murdered. I am sorry for the loss of life, but my experience with the man was not positive."

"It's okay, if you can't be bitter with friends, who can you be bitter with?" That probably wasn't a real saying, but it fit.

Joshua laughed. "When are you coming back in for a night tour?"

Joshua and I could spend hours touring the museum, particularly when it was closed, but it had been a while.

"We need to do that. Next week maybe?"

"That works. Text me with a night, and we'll do it."

We ended the call after I told him he'd hear from me soon.

"How do they ever figure out anything?"

My question was regarding the police, probably Inspector Winters specifically. He might share some things with me but never everything. Of course, the answers had to be in all those things the police kept to themselves.

I answered my own question the best way I could think. "One bite at a time."

I started putting things away so I might run Edwin's errand when I heard the noises of a ruckus outside the warehouse door.

For a few seconds, I was still as I listened. Was something wrong or had I misheard? No, there were noises, voices.

I stood from the desk and went to the door. Even if Rosie had just dropped a glass in the kitchenette, she didn't need to clean it up by herself.

I stopped in my tracks as pounding sounded on the door. It was made of thick wood, but a male voice came through.

"Open up, Delaney!"

"What?" I uttered quietly, still frozen in place. I knew the voice didn't belong to Tom, Edwin, or Hamlet, but it sounded slightly familiar.

I wasn't inclined to follow the order, but I was worried about my coworkers and the state they were in on the other side. Did they need my help?

There was no other way out of the building. The windows were too high to reach, even if I could climb the shelves.

I'd never been concerned about my safety in the warehouse before, but my wild imagination conjured up something horrific.

I turned to reach for my phone to call for help just as the bolts on the door began to give way.

CHAPTER FOURTEEN

"Och, lass, I'm sorry," Rosie said from somewhere behind Ryory Bennigan as he came through the warehouse doorway. Rosie hurried to follow him in, making the room quite crowded.

Ry sent her a quick look before he turned back to me. "It's urgent . . ."

"He took the key from my hand when I told him where you were," Rosie said. "I'm so sorry."

"It's fine, Rosie," I said. "Is everyone all right?"

"Aye, but . . ." She sent Ry an unhappy frown before she looked at me again. "I'm sorry."

I made my way around Ry and pulled Rosie into a hug. "I'm okay if you're okay."

My heart still pounded in my chest. Or was that Rosie's I was feeling? I pulled away and looked at her. She was fine, the glimmer in her eye there not because she wasn't well, but because she was angry at Ry's behavior.

I turned and looked at Ry. "Why?"

His shoulders fell. "I'm sorry. I . . . didn't think. I'm not used to asking. I just do. That was wrong." He looked at Rosie. "I'm sorry, Rosie. You told me where Delaney was and gathered the key from the desk. I just reacted. I needed to talk to Delaney and Hamlet urgently. I should have slowed down. I'm so sorry."

Rosie's eyes softened but not completely. Her lips pursed, she nodded at Ry and then turned to me. "Hamlet is out, but he'll be back in a bit."

"What did you need to see us about?" I asked.

"Ani's been taken in for questioning in the murder of Dr. Pace."

"Oh, I'm sorry." I paused. "Do they have proof?"

I thought about the logistics and wondered how she might have managed to pull off a murder if there were witnesses that she'd still been in the hospital, one witness being Ry himself.

"I don't know. I need your help."

"To do what?"

"I was hoping you and Hamlet would help me break into Ani's flat."

"Och," Rosie said. "You and Ani are both *baurmie*."

Ry's eyebrows lifted. "You might be right, Rosie, but it's something that I think needs to be done, if only to save our sweet Ani."

Sweet?

I sighed. "Let's go back over to the other side. I'll grab coffees and pastries and we'll wait for Hamlet. I'm sure he'll want to hear your reasons for needing to break into Ani's flat too."

Ry blinked. "Aye, but we could be running out of time."

"For what?" I asked.

"For the police to find the evidence."

For an instant, the idea of calling Inspector Winters flashed through my mind. Considering the look Rosie and I shared, I assumed she was thinking the same thing. However, I could not deny that I sure wanted to know what the evidence might be before I called the police.

I turned back to Ry. "Head on over. I'll be there with refreshments in a minute."

Ry lifted the hat he wore and ran his hand over his pulled-back hair. I suddenly realized that he was dressed to hide, with clothing covering all the tattoos and a hat mostly hiding his red hair. Of course, those who knew him would recognize him easily, but he'd been going for furtive.

Shoot, I thought, even those who didn't know him well would probably suspect it was him. He made a big impression.

"Ry?" I said.

"Aye, Delaney, you are right. Aye." Ry looked at Rosie, and the corner of his eyes pulled tight. "Oh, Rosie, I'm so sorry I scared you."

"Aye. Apology accepted. Let's go back over. Hamlet will be here soon, and Delaney will join us shortly."

Rosie was always quick to forgive. I'd tried to learn by example, but I was going to be irritated at Ry for at least a little longer.

Seemingly genuinely humbled, Ry let Rosie lead the way back over to the light side. Once they were out of sight, I put my hand to my chest. My heart rate was coming down, but I'd been completely rattled.

The treats in the kitchen would give me a moment to get

my wits about me. In fact, once I took another deep breath, everything I'd been feeling transformed into a little excitement.

There was evidence?

Shortly, we were sitting at the back table. Hamlet had returned from his bank errand, and I had the tray of day-old, but still delicious, pastries set in the middle. No one had reached for one before Rosie asked, "What's the evidence?"

Ry nodded. He'd composed himself too. "Shortly after you left this morning, Delaney, Ani confessed something to me. She told me that she was holding something for Dr. Pace—a 3D printer."

"Holding onto a printer? What does that mean?"

"I asked the same question, but she kept it vague, telling me that he brought one to her flat last week—in a box. She didn't open the box. She wasn't sure if it had been used or not. You can buy them so easily now."

"You can?" I asked.

Hamlet jumped in. "Aye. There are larger, more advanced ones used at universities and such, but you can buy one for home use that can do most anything, if maybe more slowly and on a smaller scale than the bigger ones."

"I was under the impression that this is a smaller one."

"Okay," I said. "The police will definitely want to know about a 3D printer given to Ani by Dr. Pace. Do you think that's the evidence they used to take her in?"

"I have no idea, but if it isn't, I thought I could hide it."

"Ry, we can't break into Ani's house and take anything from there," I said. "You know this. Don't you?"

"Aye," Rosie added. "We willnae stop you, but you cannae ask this sort of thing of anyone."

"I think that's becoming clearer to me, Rosie. I panicked. Shortly after she told me about the printer, the police came and got her. Put handcuffs on and everything. My initial reaction was to save my friend. I . . . did what I thought might be the best way to accomplish that."

"I'm sorry," I said.

"Me too," Hamlet said.

Ry looked up at my sympathetic coworker. "I suppose I thought you might help because you are close. She told me about your friendship."

"Well, we are friends, and, honestly, I don't think that she killed Dr. Pace, but what you are asking. It's . . ."

"Ridiculous?" Ry said.

"Aye," Rosie said.

Ry sighed. "You are right, and I'm sorry. I . . . I don't get out much, and I think I need some guidance on how to behave better. In fact, Ani has been working with me on such things."

Rosie, Hamlet, and I smiled, but just a little. He was a grown man who'd lived an unquestionably odd life. Yes, I felt a little sorry for him, but now I also wanted to tell him what my mother once said to me when things weren't going well and I was somehow panicking and making bad decisions.

Shape up and just keep doing better. You'll get where you want to go.

"How did you and Ani find each other?" I asked instead.

"I was informed by my banker that I needed to get organized. I didn't even try to put things in order myself before I sought out help."

"Was there something wrong with your money?" Rosie asked.

"No, but I was neglecting things, the signing of papers and such. My banker told me I needed to hire someone, so I found Ani."

"How did you find her?"

"I placed an ad on a job website, asking for someone who was smart and creative and could keep secrets well."

A real smile pulled at my lips now. Ry's ad had been similar enough to the one Edwin had placed that I felt a kinship of sorts deepen a little. Answering that ad had changed everything. Perhaps Ani's experience was the same.

"That sounds like the Ani I know," Hamlet said. "She's a lovely person and would be loyal to the end."

"I know, that's why I want to break into her flat and take out any possible evidence that might not have been gathered."

"What if she killed Dr. Pace?" Rosie asked.

Ry shrugged. "Then he deserved it."

I knew unconditional loyalty to a friend, but I still wasn't going to break into her place.

"Did she confess to anything other than the printer?" Rosie asked.

"Not to me. The police took her out of there quickly."

"Ry, I think you're just going to have to hope for the best. Maybe you could hire an attorney for her," I offered.

"That's not a bad idea, but I still don't think she killed Dr. Pace."

"I don't either," Hamlet said. "I'd bet my life on it. Ani couldn't."

I wasn't as convinced, but I kept my thoughts to myself. I

wondered if Ry knew about Ani's tattoo of the creature whose bones Dr. Pace tried to sell, the creature that turned out not to be real at all. I wondered lots of things, but I wasn't going to vocalize them now.

"Lad, why didn't you just go break in on your own?" Rosie asked. "I might if it were my close friend on the hook."

"Look at me, Rosie. I don't hide well. Even in the dark, I'm recognized and photographed, my face all over social media. I know it might be difficult to understand that Ani and I are alike in that we are introverts. I didn't expect my choices to turn me into some sort of freak show, but here I am. I could never get away with it."

"You're not a freak show," I said. "You're interesting."

"You think?"

I shrugged. "Yes, absolutely, Ry."

Ry ran his hand over his hair again. "The worst thing I've done is bring you all in on my problems. That is unforgiveable."

Hamlet laughed. "No, it's interesting too. We are capable enough of saying no. Don't worry about it, Ry. I appreciate your loyalty to Ani."

"Aye?"

"Yes, definitely."

For an instant, it looked like Ry considered asking again if we would help him, but he thought better of it. He might have learned and grown some as we'd spoken. I took it as a good sign of improvement, but he sure had a long way to go.

When Ry left the bookstore, I watched out the window—it took less than half a minute for someone to give him a double take and then pull out their phone to snap pictures. I'd offered to drive him home, but he'd declined, saying he'd parked a car around the corner.

"That doesn't look fun," Hamlet said over my shoulder.

"No, it doesn't."

"I can't believe he asked us for help."

"He was desperate. Desperate people do desperate things."

"I suppose. Do you think he'll break in on his own?"

"I don't know. I doubt it. I just hope he makes it home without incident."

"Yeah."

I still had plenty to do. I turned away from the window and thought about which thing to tackle next.

CHAPTER FIFTEEN

I had to admit to myself that though I would never have agreed to break into Ani's flat, I was sure curious about what was inside it. I asked Hamlet if he could remember seeing anything like a printer in a box or something that might not have seemed to belong in there. He said he hadn't, but that he hadn't been there in a while.

He was concerned about her, but though they were friends, they weren't that close. I could tell that he wasn't quite sure what he was supposed to feel about her being questioned, but he couldn't deny his worry. Rosie patted him on the shoulder and told him it would all work out fine.

None of us were sure what to do, but I had some things I wanted to explore, and Ry had sparked another idea.

I told Rosie and Hamlet my plans. They wished me good luck as I left the bookshop. I texted Tom with the same information and set out.

I hurried to the bus stop and looked out the window just as Tom was peering out of the pub's front window. He waved and blew me a kiss. I returned the gesture, sending more gratitude out to the universe.

My first stop took me to yet another lovely, historical neighborhood in Edinburgh. Dr. Pace had been staying in a townhouse one block from the coast. It was far from my and Tom's blue house by the sea, but the view from the second floor of the townhouse was probably just as breathtaking.

Crime-scene tape was still strung back and forth across the front door. A short gate that led up to the house's landing had been padlocked. If someone wanted to badly enough, they could easily leap over the short, wrought-iron fence.

I saw the doorbell camera that Inspector Winters had said caught no one coming or going from the place other than Dr. Pace. I couldn't tell if it was still recording—I couldn't spot an indicator light—but I nodded toward it just in case someone was watching. I wasn't trying to be covert.

Well, not at that moment, at least.

I took in the narrow home's architecture. Though built with stone blocks, it was pristine in the same way many rental homes were now—until parties trashed them, that was. There was no outward sign that Dr. Pace had done more than live peacefully inside the townhouse. There was a tall, paned window on each side of the front door. Both windows were covered with curtains, but I would have liked to make my way up to the porch and try to peek in. I didn't attempt the maneuver.

The townhouse was the second one from a corner. I made my way up to the corner and then around it, checking to see if there was a way to look at the back of the house, where there wasn't a camera. Or there hadn't been, according to Inspector Winters.

I was surprised to find a path wide enough for a single car to travel. Small garages had been set on the properties behind the townhouses, though how anyone managed to park a car in any of them, considering the tight space, was beyond me. Maybe scooters and bikes were stored, and cars were parked on the street out front.

A wood fence and gate covered the expanse of the back garden that wasn't taken up by the garage. Though the front of the home looked great, the garage and fence could have used a new coat of paint as well as the pulling of some tall weeds tangled with the slats.

I hesitated but only for a moment until I stepped into the weeds, reached for the top of the fence and pulled myself up. On the very tip of my toes, I could just barely see over, but I quickly determined that there wasn't much to see anyway.

The small backyard was cobblestoned and held two chairs and a table, perfect for a morning coffee if it wasn't raining. It wasn't currently, but the clouds above looked threatening.

The back windows were covered with closed blinds, so I couldn't see inside from there either.

For a brief moment I considered climbing over to see if I could look through the windows behind the sides of the blinds, but I thought better of it. Many people would be disappointed in me if I did such a thing.

I lowered myself back to the ground in a less-than-graceful move, twisting my ankle on something solid in the weeds.

"Ouch." I lifted my leg, but the pain subsided quickly and I was able to set it down only a few seconds later.

My eyes searched the spot in the weeds where my foot had landed, but it was so choked with weeds that I couldn't see what I'd stepped on. It might have been a rock, but who knew what manner of creature was hiding in those weeds?

If we knew what we were doing, it wouldn't be called research, would it?

It was Mr. Einstein again. Though the words I heard in my head didn't literally tell me to reach into the weeds, that's probably what they were telling me anyway.

"Oh, all right," I said as I reached.

My ankle was less twingy now, so I used my toe to rummage first. It took only a few seconds to find the item and I kicked it free from the mostly dead greenery.

I glanced up and down the alleyway, but no one was watching. In fact, I realized that if I'd truly hurt myself, I'd be stuck back here until I could reach someone to come get me.

However, I could have used my phone or the one that I'd just kicked from the weeds to track someone down. It was a flip phone, though it didn't look all that old. It was a little dirty but in good shape.

I didn't even think about the fact that I was picking up an item behind the home of where a murder had been committed, and that was on me. It was as if my curiosity pushed away my common sense. It wasn't the first time.

I flipped up the top, the tiny screen inside lighting with one tiny bar of power.

"Huh."

Again, I didn't even think about the fact that I was now covering the buttons with my own fingerprints in an effort to see what I could find. It had been a minute since I'd had a flip phone, but they still seemed to work like they used to. The button pushing led to an outgoing call list, the top number assigned a name that I had become familiar with. Ani.

"Oh, hello, Ani."

In what must have only been excited clumsiness, I dropped the phone.

"No!" I crouched and reached for it again but then pulled my hand back and just looked at it.

It wasn't broken, but the screen was no longer lit. I debated whether to pick the phone back up or cordon it off for the police to come gather it. I realized quickly that I'd done enough damage to compromise any evidence that might be found. But, it wasn't covered in blood or anything.

I grabbed my own phone from my back pocket and called Inspector Winters.

"Delaney?"

"Hi. I, uh, have something."

Moments later, I was back on the bus, flip phone in my bag, and headed to the police station.

I admitted that I'd already touched the phone, so he told me to bring it in. On the way, I opened the call list again and took pictures on my own phone just as it died completely.

I met Inspector Winters in the interview room and handed it over.

"I was just looking in the back," I said. "I didn't think I was doing anything wrong. I didn't climb a fence or peek in any windows."

"No, lass, you weren't, technically, but I'm not sure peering from an alley at a house where a murder recently occurred was wise."

"I didn't jump over the front gate to try to look in the windows."

Inspector Winters bit his bottom lip and seemed to work not to laugh. "That crossed your mind, though?"

"Only fleetingly."

"You made the right choice." He sat forward in the chair. "And, lass, this phone might be a lead, so I thank you for ringing me right away. It was found in the weeds *outside* the house, so it could belong to anyone, but we'll sure look at it."

I nodded. "I took some pictures before the battery died," I admitted.

"Show me."

I texted him the pictures. Ani was the only name on the call list, the rest were just numbers. I didn't know Ani's number or if it was the same Ani, but the unique spelling made it seem likely.

"I guess we shouldn't assume, though?" I voiced, trying not to jump to conclusions.

"We will track it all down."

"Is Ani still being held?"

Inspector Winters's eyebrows lifted as if he was surprised that I knew. They lowered again. "I can't share that with you, lass."

I nodded. "I have a little more to share, unless Joshua has already called."

Inspector Winters nodded. "He did. I talked to him just a couple hours ago. It appears that Dr. Pace was a busy man. He talked to a fair number of museums throughout not just Edinburgh but all of Scotland. We have barely scratched the surface, I'm afraid."

"Oh dear." I paused. "Did anyone pay him for anything?"

"Not that we've found, but we're looking for that too. If someone discovered they purchased a fake item, of course it might be possible they were angry enough to commit murder.

I doubt anyone was murderous enough to want to kill him just for trying, but, again, we'll leave no stone unturned, no pun intended."

"Seems reasonable."

"This potential list is long."

"I was thinking that." I looked at the phone that he'd put into a plastic bag on the table. "Maybe that will narrow it down."

"If it belonged to Dr. Pace, I think it could."

"It's a burner, right?"

"If I were to bet, I would say that, though flip phones are back in style with some folks, younger people actually. The anti-technology group and all."

"That's a younger crowd?"

"Mostly."

"Ani's age."

He shrugged. "Maybe."

Of course, they'd find my fingerprints too, but Inspector Winters knew I'd handled the phone and he hadn't seemed angry.

I debated telling him about Ani's tattoo that Willa had said was bird-like, but that Joshua had told me wouldn't be an accurate representation. But the police had brought her in. There was a point when I needed to let them do their jobs, even if I *might* have something to offer. Such an idea had backfired too—I'd mentioned things that had led the police on a wild goose chase. If they had questions for me, they'd ask.

And, the phone seemed like a good, solid lead.

Inspector Winters saw me to the door, telling me to be careful but also thanking me for calling him when I did. He suggested strongly that I shouldn't explore the townhouse without him or another officer with me.

"You'll take me inside?" I asked.

"No, I won't, but I will look at it from the outside with you." He paused. "Thanks for calling me, lass."

"You're welcome."

I left the station and took off up the Royal Mile. It was getting late and cold, but I didn't want to wait for another bus. I pulled my shirt collar closed and picked up the pace.

It was time to find Tom. Dinner with my husband sounded like the best way to end the day. Maybe we could have ice cream again.

CHAPTER SIXTEEN

Edwin was in the bookshop when I got there the next morning, along with Hamlet, Rosie, and Hector.

I smiled and picked up Hector as I made my way toward Rosie's desk, where they all were gathered. "How is everyone?"

"Fine," Hamlet and Rosie said.

"How are you, lass?" Rosie asked.

I laughed. "My mind is whirring, but I'm fine."

"Edwin's been working on the case too," Rosie said as if it was perfectly acceptable for a bunch of people who worked in a bookshop in Scotland to also be working on a murder case.

"I've been researching, asking around, looking into Ryory Bennigan." Edwin frowned. "I just heard about his visit yesterday."

"It's fine," Rosie said to him. She sent me a look as if to say she might wish she hadn't given our boss all the details of Ry's bursting his way in.

"What have you learned?" I asked him quickly as Hector wiggled into the crook of my elbow.

Edwin turned his attention to me and shrugged. "Everyone

describes him as a recluse, but when he does go out in public, he's kind but odd. He doesn't always know how to behave, which tracks with what happened yesterday."

I nodded. "He doesn't get out much. He could use some better social skills, I guess, and he did apologize."

"I did speak with someone once who witnessed his deep displeasure," Edwin said.

"Oh?"

Before Edwin could share the details, my phone dinged so loudly with a text that I felt the need to apologize.

"Go ahead, lass," Edwin said. "It might be something important."

Because I was still holding Hector, I grabbed the phone from my bag with one hand. "Oh. It's a text from Theo. He's the one I spoke with at the university in Kansas. He's hoping for another Zoom in fifteen minutes."

"He must have something," Rosie said.

I texted Theo that I was available. "Do you guys want to come to the warehouse with me?"

They all shook their heads, but not before taking a moment to consider the question.

"No, lass, you go, but come back and tell us all about it," Rosie said.

"Tell me about the displeasure from Ry first," I said to Edwin.

"The contention occurred with the organizer of the Hidden Door Festival. Her name is Shelby Clayton. Ry wanted to do his private showings in conjunction with the festival, but Shelby told him that 'private' wasn't how they did things. The emails she received from Ry were . . . she said, 'biting' and much fiercer than she thought Ry could be. Shelby gave in to him, but she didn't want to."

"The email could have been from Ani, not Ry," Rosie said.

"I bet it was Ani," I said.

Edwin shrugged. "I don't know, but that was it."

"Okay, I'll let you know how the Zoom goes."

I handed Hector to Rosie and then hurried over to the dark side to get everything set up properly. Directly after I opened my laptop and accepted the Zoom invite, the ringtone sounded.

"Hi, Theo," I said as he came into view.

"Hey, Delaney." His expression was a mix of sad and confused.

"Are you okay?"

Theo nodded. "Oh, I'm fine, but we've . . . the authorities from Scotland notified us and asked us a whole bunch of questions."

"Was it rough? I'm sorry."

"It's okay. It just made it all so real. I had little to tell them, but as a department we're certainly down in the dumps." He sighed. "I'd like to share something with you, but I need to keep it between us for the time being, and I'm telling you because I have a favor to ask. Is that okay?"

I nodded immediately. "Sure."

"Okay. After the conversations with the police, we opened Dr. Pace's office here, broke locks on his file drawers."

"That was a big step."

"It was, but then it was . . . well, it was pretty awful. I can't go into all the details, but Delaney, Dr. Pace was up to no good in many ways."

"Oh, Theo, I'm so sorry. And you don't want the authorities to know?"

"Not yet."

"I'm so, so sorry," I said again when he seemed to fall into melancholy.

Theo nodded and waved away my apology. "No, no, not your fault. The favor, though . . ."

"Anything. What do you need?"

"I . . . we were all so fond of him."

"I get that. It's always disappointing to find out someone wasn't who you thought they were."

"That's true, but there's more to this than you and I discussed."

"I'm listening."

"I overheard something that I can't let go of. I knew I shouldn't eavesdrop, but I couldn't help myself."

"I know the feeling," I said with a small smile.

"The head of the department, Dr. Uhman, was on the phone to Dr. Pace's bank. The Scottish authorities told us they were going to do a forensic investigation of Dr. Pace's accounts. The bank called Dr. Uhman to confirm Dr. Pace's years of employment, etc."

"That makes sense."

"Dr. Uhman was curious enough to ask a few of his own questions regarding dollar amounts, but, of course, the bank didn't share. However, they did say one thing—even though I don't think they were supposed to. I think it's important, at least." Theo paused. "If I understood what I overheard, money was leaving Dr. Pace's account on a consistent basis and going into another account."

"Savings?"

"I don't think so. I think it was an account in Scotland, not Dr. Pace's, from what I could gather."

"A lot of money?"

"Hard to know. I'm not sure Dr. Pace ever had a lot of money, but it was relatively new activity."

"No dollar amounts talked about?"

"No, but the bank representative also asked Dr. Uhman if he would know why Dr. Pace kept sending an identical amount of money to a Scottish account. Dr. Uhman didn't know, of course."

"No name, I bet?"

"No, and I don't think I'm supposed to know as much as I think I do."

"I won't tell."

Theo nodded, his brow furrowed. "What if someone was blackmailing him, Delaney?"

I might have thought that eventually, but I hadn't gotten there yet. It seemed like a quick leap, but possible. "I guess that might make sense, but why?"

"The obvious reason would be because they found out about his lies."

That part rang with true possibility. "I don't know, Theo."

"I don't either."

"What can I do?"

"First of all, I was hoping you might tell me if my idea has legs. You're there. Has there been anything like blackmail talked about in the news? Is Dr. Pace's murder news at all?"

"Dr. Pace's murder has been in the news, but no blackmail. I am looking and asking around. I haven't come upon anything like that, but I also haven't been thinking that way. Maybe if I switch my perspective, I will find something."

Theo nodded. "That's what I was hoping for. That's the

favor—could you ask some people? Do you have any connections? It feels so far away, and . . . well, maybe the answers will clear Dr. Pace's name."

"Of course. I understand. I will tell you whatever I find."

"Thank you. It sure is disappointing when someone turns out to be somehow so different than you thought."

"Well, we don't know the whole story yet, Theo. He could still have been the man you thought. People can get desperate. Many times, people are put in situations they couldn't have predicted and don't know how to handle. They do the best they can."

"Thanks, Delaney. That does help me feel better. I'm sad and disappointed at the same time, but I'm working through it. We all are."

"Hang in there."

"You'll stay in touch?"

"Absolutely."

I could tell Theo didn't want to end the call. He liked having the company, but there was nothing else to discuss, so we finally disconnected.

I closed my laptop and sat back in the chair. This was a whole new twist.

Something came to me, but it was so vague and unconnected to anything else that I only paid attention to it for a moment. Hadn't Ry said he'd hired Ani because his bank manager told him he needed someone to get him organized or something like that? Maybe there was more to it. Maybe there were money issues . . . somewhere. My leap was bigger than Theo's. I shook my head.

I made my way back to the other side of the shop, where

everyone was still waiting, their attention fully on me as I came down the stairs. There were no customers in sight.

"Theo told me that he received word that a consistent amount of money was leaving Dr. Pace's account and going to another one, one in Scotland. He wonders if maybe Dr. Pace was being blackmailed," I said.

"Any names?" Edwin asked.

"No."

My coworkers looked at each other with furrowed brows. They couldn't spot an obvious blackmailer either, but it was, unquestionably, a new idea.

I said, "I have something else. I've already given it to Inspector Winters, and I meant to research it myself this morning, but Theo's call set me off track. Come on, let's go to Hamlet's laptop."

Out of habit, we all looked toward the front window to make sure someone wasn't on their way in before we headed to the back table.

I pulled up the pictures on my phone. "I went to have a look at Dr. Pace's rental house. In the back I came upon a flip phone. I took pictures of the outgoing call list before the battery died."

"That's interesting," Hamlet said as he pulled out his own phone to check the number next to Ani's name against the one he had stored. "It's hers."

"I wondered."

Ani's name and number took up five of the calls.

"Numbers aren't that easy to track down anymore, but let's see what we can figure out." Hamlet typed the first mystery number in to the search engine on his phone.

"Museum of Edinburgh," Hamlet said. "That came up quickly."

I didn't think I'd shared with everyone what had happened. I summarized, "I met Ronny Remsen over there. He told me that Dr. Pace was trying to sell some bones to him, but he just turned him away and told him to go through the proper channels."

"I haven't been to that museum for ages," Hamlet said.

"I can't remember my last time," Edwin said.

"It's been a while," Rosie said.

"This makes me think that the phone did belong to Dr. Pace, though we can't be sure."

"Let's assume for now but keep an open mind. All right, let's try another number." Hamlet typed into the search engine again.

We went with the idea that it was Dr. Pace's phone. Ultimately, what we uncovered was that he had called Ani five times. Dr. Pace had also called the Museum of Edinburgh twice. Of the remaining six calls, we could identify five.

Three calls were to a takeaway restaurant near the house he'd been staying at and two were to another bookshop in town.

"Oh, Edwin," I said. The number belonged to a bookshop, but it wasn't George's. "Your errand! I got so off track yesterday. I'm so sorry!"

"It's all right. It's not urgent."

"Ry's visit set everything off," Rosie added.

I felt hot shame. No matter what, I had been hired for a job and I should never neglect whatever Edwin wanted me to do. I felt terrible. "I'm so sorry," I repeated.

"No worries, truly."

"I'll do it today."

"If this was his phone, the bookshop that Dr. Pace contacted is called Turn," Hamlet said.

"Turn is a lovely shop," Rosie added.

Hamlet couldn't track down to whom or what the last number belonged.

"Turn is Mary Katherine's shop," Edwin said when Hamlet came up empty on the last number. "She's fond of paleontology and always carries a big selection of what I call 'dinosaur books.'"

"Maybe I'll visit that shop too," I said.

"Wouldn't hurt," Edwin added. "She's lovely. She's also smart as a whip and wouldn't put up with any nonsense. I'd like to hear about any meetings she might have had with Dr. Pace."

"I guess I could ask Inspector Winters about the number we can't identify, but he might not feel the need to answer me," I said.

"Or he wouldn't because he doesn't want you snooping wherever it goes," Hamlet added, but he sounded disappointed.

"It might be the only way, though," Rosie chimed in.

"I wish I still had reliable contacts amid the police force, but I fear my people in law enforcement are retired or dying off." Edwin smiled sadly. "It was a fun run while it lasted, though."

Though in my eyes, Edwin was perfect, I'd learned about his somewhat checkered past. Well, I'd learned about *some* of it. Certainly not all, according to what Rosie had said—or *not* said in certain moments.

I wrote down the unidentified number and told myself to

keep my eyes open for whatever or whomever it might be attached to.

"We could just ring it," Hamlet offered.

"Can you block your number?" Rosie asked him.

"Aye." Hamlet did exactly that before he put his phone on speaker and dialed the number. A recorded message answered telling us it was an out-of-service number.

"What do you suppose that means?" Rosie asked.

"Other than it's not working, I don't know," Hamlet said.

"Maybe Inspector Winters can find out where it used to be attached," I said. "I'll see if there's a moment I can ask him."

Hector, having been set on a chair, put his paws on the table. He barked once in agreement and lightened the moment enough for us all to laugh a little.

"Aye, good idea," Rosie said.

With the list in my pocket, I announced that I was heading out to the bookshops. I promised Edwin I would take care of his assigned task, but, again, he didn't seem bothered that I hadn't.

There were far worse duties than spending time in bookshops, and I could see the others consider joining me, but they decided to keep on their own tasks. Another day.

I gathered my things and took off for Mary Katherine's place first, excited to visit a bookshop as well as meet another Edinburgh bookshop owner.

CHAPTER SEVENTEEN

Turn was located only three blocks from The Cracked
Spine. There were two other bookshops even closer, but I
didn't pass either one of them on the way. Bookshops in Edinburgh, though plentiful in number, never seemed to be in com-
petition with each other. There was a distinct sense that we
were all in this together.

Those of us at The Cracked Spine would call several other
bookshops to help a customer find a book if we didn't have it
on hand. And we'd taken similar calls from the other stores
ourselves.

I'd made it a goal to visit every bookshop in the city, but somehow still hadn't managed the task. But as I peered through Turn's
front floor-to-ceiling windows, I decided I would ask Tom to
spend a day visiting them all with me. He'd enjoy the task just as
much as I would.

I pushed through the front door and walked into the bright
space.

There were no books on this main level, just a switch-back
ramp that went up to the next level. I didn't understand the
strange layout, but I took the ramp upward, nonetheless.

I quickly spotted a glass display case on the left side of the next level that held a cash register and a cardboard display stand. Everything seemed perfectly neat. The glass of the display case shined, nary a fingerprint marring it anywhere.

It wasn't that we weren't tidy at The Cracked Spine, but we were in very old buildings that Edwin had never wanted to remodel so that we would maintain the original character. Turn had been around a long time, but from what I could tell, it had been completely gutted at some point and made to look and smell modern.

I loved the scent of books, but there was no doubt there was a difference between the scent in this bookshop and the one where I worked. This place felt . . . not only more of this century but classier too.

"Welcome. Can I help you?" A woman appeared from behind some shiny, light wood shelves next to the glass case.

"Are you Mary Katherine?"

She pushed up her very large, round-framed glasses. "I am."

"I'm Delaney Nichols. I work at The Cracked Spine." I approached her.

A smile brightened Mary Katherine's expression. "Edwin's place? How is that lad? Come on up."

I finished the journey up the ramp, where I found that the world of books extended so far back that I couldn't quite make out where the shop ended.

"Holy moly, you have a big place," I exclaimed.

Mary Katherine came into full view. I hadn't noticed the wheelchair before. I tried not to look surprised, but I was, a little.

I also realized that the bookshop extended back maybe

three times that of The Cracked Spine's space, and all the shelves were low enough for someone in a wheelchair to reach.

"It is big. Keeps my guns in shape." Mary Katherine flexed her arms.

"I bet."

"So, I haven't seen Edwin in over a year. Did he send you here to look for something?"

"No, I'm here for a whole other reason."

"Hmm. That sounds mysterious."

"Well, it is a mystery, and I'm very nosy, so it's become natural for me to ask questions even if maybe it's not my place."

Mary Katherine rubbed her hands together. "Oh, this is sounding better and better. Have a seat and tell me what you're being nosy about."

I followed as she led me to the middle of the shop, where a gathering of comfortable chairs made a circle. On the way, she called out to a couple other customers to let them know where she'd be if they needed help.

I took one of the cushioned chairs as Mary Katherine stopped where we could face each other. She was probably in her fifties, and she dressed like Rosie, in bright colors that somehow seemed to work together—though if I'd tried to pull off the same thing, I would have looked ridiculous.

"Is Edwin well?" Mary Katherine asked.

"Very. He's doing great."

"How are Rosie and Hamlet? And I can't believe I haven't met you. It's a pleasure."

"It's nice to meet you, and Rosie and Hamlet are fine, great too."

"The wee dog?"

"Hector is perfect too. Everyone sends their best."

"All right then, Ms. Delaney Nichols, tell me about the mystery."

I nodded and leaned forward. The customers weren't close by, but I didn't want anyone to hear. Mary Katherine leaned closer to me too.

"A man was killed recently. He was from the same place I was in America—Kansas. His name was Adam Pace, and he was a paleontologist."

"Oh!" she said. "Yes, Dr. P. I knew him. His death was so tragic. You knew him?"

"Kind of."

She nodded, eager for me to continue.

As I told her how I'd met him briefly and some highlights about what I'd learned, she listened intently. She wasn't emotional at all, despite the nickname she'd given him implying they might have been friends.

"So, the police are investigating it as a murder, I heard," she said.

"Yes."

"Well, that's just plain awful . . ."

When she didn't continue, I tried not to push but I couldn't help myself. "I hear a 'but' in there."

She shook her head. "No but. He was just . . . interesting, I guess."

"Did you like him?"

"I didn't dislike him. He was nice enough to me. He spent a lot of time and money in this bookshop. I felt a little guilty about all the money he spent. I told him he was welcome to just look through the books here in the shop if he didn't want to keep buying them." She laughed. "I'm not a good bookseller, am I?"

"On the contrary, that's the only way to do it."

"Aye, Edwin feels the same way, I do know that. Most of us in the bookshop biz do, but, well, Dr. Pace probably bought thirty books over the last couple months or so. And they were expensive books, things for the smart people." She laughed and backed up the wheelchair. She turned to the right. "Come on, I'll show you the section."

As I followed behind her again, she spoke over her shoulder. "Though lots of people like to look through the books in my dinosaur section, very few buy any of them. They are educational material, so I mail many copies throughout the world. Even though I'm not the only place to get them, I've acquired a bit of a reputation for having even the most obscure tomes."

Most stores would have designated the section of three packed shelves as paleontology, but Mary Katherine had placed a sign on the end of the first shelf that said Dinos Galore!

She noticed me smiling at it.

"Well, you've got to have a little fun sometimes," she said.

"I agree."

"Anyway, Dr. Pace was working his way through all these books, buying most of them. Honestly, I find it all kind of boring, but about ten years ago I supplied some professors in Ireland with some books, and all of a sudden I was the place to call if someone needed something on dinosaurs."

"It's good to be the place people go."

"It is. It has been . . . good for business. I'm not saying it's the service that pays all my bills, but it's been a nice thing to have. A good help."

"I think The Cracked Spine is mostly known for Edwin and Rosie and, over the last few years, Hamlet's ability to figure out the provenance of old documents."

"You are one hundred percent correct, Delaney. The Cracked Spine is known for all of those things, but you too, the redhead from America." She smiled at me.

"I was included in an article a few months back. It's been weird to be recognized."

She patted the arm of her wheelchair. "I'm a wee bit known for being the book lady in the chair, and even though I have dino books, I think most people seek out this shop for the vast number of biographies I keep in stock."

"I love biographies and autobiographies."

Mary Katherine laughed. "I do too!"

"We have that in common."

"True. Anyway, though Dr. Pace spent lots of time and way too much money in this section . . ."

She veered the chair around me, and I trailed behind again. She stopped in another aisle. "The last book he bought was this one." She gathered a larger sized, brown-covered book.

"*The Picts*," she recited the title.

I'd looked through this same book myself. "The last one he bought?"

"Aye. I asked him if he was tired of dinosaurs."

"Was he?"

"He didn't answer, just shrugged and left the shop."

"Mary Katherine, I . . . uh, well, I think that Dr. Pace called you a few days before his demise. Do you remember what the call was about?"

Her mouth quirked. "You are a curious one, aren't you?"

"Way too curious."

"I understand." She shook her head again. "I don't remember a phone conversation with him, but that doesn't mean he didn't talk to one of my employees. I'm the only one here right now, but I'm happy to ask them and get back to you."

"That would be above and beyond the call of duty."

"My pleasure. I love mysteries, even if I don't sell many of that genre." She laughed. "I need to come visit you all. I haven't been in The Cracked Spine for too long."

"We would look forward to it."

"And I'll ring you if I learn anything new about the phone call."

"Thanks, Mary Katherine."

"Aye. A pleasure."

I headed toward the ramp in the front, but another thought came to me. I turned back around.

"Mary Katherine, did you and Dr. Pace *talk* much about dinosaurs, other than just selling him the books?"

"Only a wee bit, why?"

"Did he ever bring up the Oculudentavis?" I hoped I'd said it correctly.

"Oh, aye, maybe." She fell into thought. "Can you give me more context?"

"It's the world's smallest dinosaur."

"Aye, the bird creature! He found something about it in one of the books and showed it to me. It was wicked."

"Yes, that's true, but . . . well, it turns out it wasn't a bird at all. Did you two ever talk about that or look at a lizard-type creature that wasn't a dinosaur in a book?"

"No, just the bird creature. How was it not correct?"

"Well, the head looked like a bird, but a bigger specimen was found in 2020, and it proved that it was a lizard instead."

"Interesting. No, we never had such a conversation. That's . . . well, interesting. I wonder if I have an up-to-date book about it. I need to research that."

"I didn't mean to make more work for you."

"Not at all." She hesitated. "I just like to make sure I have accurately stocked shelves. Things change so quickly that I miss a lot, but you've done me a favor. I will make sure that *I'm* educated."

There was something about her that suddenly seemed different, maybe her coloring.

I took a step back in her direction. "Mary Katherine, are you okay?"

Her eyes were unfocused. They snapped back up to mine sharply, and she smiled, seeming the same as she had before. "Oh, I'm fine, lass. Absolutely."

I nodded. I wanted to ask if she was sure, but that felt almost impertinent. I just smiled too. "Okay. Great. Well, really nice to meet you."

"Same."

"Come see us soon. I know everyone at The Cracked Spine will look forward to your visit."

"Aye. See you soon." She still smiled.

I couldn't think of what else to say. Had I upset her? I hoped not.

I left Turn and made my way the short distance to George's, my mind working though my time with Mary Katherine. At what moment had she seemed to change? I was pretty sure it was when I shared that the Oculudentavis wasn't a bird. Did it matter?

I regretted not asking her more about Dr. Pace's interest in the Pict book, but it was difficult to discern which avenue was more important when it came to his murder—the Picts or the dinosaurs. He'd been dabbling in fraud on both fronts.

The sun was out, and the chill was light. I took a deep breath to clear my overthinking mind as I spotted George's just up ahead.

Once inside the shop, which was seemingly even more cozy after my visit to Turn, I was greeted with the scents of books—more familiar to the scents from The Cracked Spine. I also thought I smelled pipe smoke. Given the obvious dangers of mixing fire and objects made mostly of paper—as well as Edinburgh's law prohibiting indoor smoking—I couldn't believe someone was smoking a pipe. And it smelled like the old-fashioned kind, not the e-pipes of today.

"I'll be right there," a voice called from the back.

I saw only one cat today—an orange-and-yellow tabby who didn't come to me when I tried to coax it in my direction. George appeared a few moments later.

"Aye?" he said with a big smile as he pulled the ornately carved pipe from between his lips. "Delaney, lass, I've been waiting to see you for days."

"I'm sorry. Edwin told me about it yesterday, but I was so busy."

"Aye." He waved me closer. "Come here then. I cannae wait to give it to you."

"Okay."

The pathway was narrow because of some packed floor shelves I had to maneuver through, but I made my way to the counter and met George there. The cash register sat atop, as well as the messy stack of papers. I had wondered if he kept the papers there just to look busy or if he was actually studying them. He'd always been so friendly when I'd come in that I didn't think he used them to hide from customers. He set the pipe onto a small metal ashtray and then bent over to retrieve something from under the counter.

With a content smile on his face, he lifted an eight-and-a-half-by-eleven cardboard box and set it on the counter in between us. Dramatically, he placed his hands on the sides of the box.

"It was by accident that Edwin discovered this amazing find. Well, he called it fate." George shrugged. "I don't know if I can argue with that, but whatever it was, here it is and he wanted you to have it."

"Edwin discovered it? I don't understand. I thought I was supposed to pick it up for him."

"Well, he wanted someone other than Hamlet to authenticate. Before your Hamlet became so good at his job, Edwin sent many things to me."

"Goodness, I'm intrigued."

"Aye. Are you ready?"

I returned George's playful smile and peered at the box, more than ready for unveiling. His happy mood was infectious.

He lifted the lid.

Immediately, I knew what was inside the box. A book, but it was no ordinary book.

"Oooh," I said.

George reached into the box and lifted out the book as well as the tissue paper it had been placed upon.

"Is it a . . . ," I began.

"It is a first edition, lass, as well as a signed copy."

"No!"

"Aye. And it's yours, a gift from Edwin." He scooted the book closer to me.

There were a number of reasons why I could recognize this book immediately, the main one being that I now worked in the world of rare and valuable books. Another was that I'd dedicated myself to ancient things as a lover of history. Though this book wasn't ancient, just old, so maybe the most credible reason I knew all about it was because I was from Kansas. And so, of course, was Dorothy.

"*The Wonderful World of Oz*, by L. Frank Baum," I breathed the words.

The green and red design on the front cover was familiar. The first edition's cover hadn't been illustrated with Dorothy or Kansas, or even Oz. It highlighted the lion, a king that seemed apprehensive and wore glasses.

"Isn't it something?" George said.

"It's in incredible shape. Where did he find it? Should I ask him?"

"One of your regular customer's grandmothers passed, rest her soul. There were other books there too, but this was the special one."

"George, there aren't many like this one."

"No, there aren't. Open it. The illustrations are magnificent."

I'd seen a first edition of this book a few times, but none had been in this shape. And, I'd never seen a signed copy.

"I'm afraid to touch it," I said.

"Aye, I understand, but it's in good shape. It will be fine."

I lifted the book, and though my intention wasn't to confirm its status, I'd been trained to look for certain markers, the first one being some words on the base of the spine. If the Hill imprint wasn't there, it wasn't a first. But it was there.

Just as I turned the book to open the cover, the shop's bell above its front door jingled, sounding exactly like The Cracked Spine's bell. I was used to looking that way immediately to greet whoever was entering.

I was discombobulated for many reasons, heady from the book, but I realized immediately that I knew the person coming inside.

Layton, the food delivery guy.

"Ta, lad," George said as he came around the counter and took the bag of food that Layton extended.

"You're welcome," Layton said.

When he looked in my direction, Layton did a double take. "Hey, I know you," he said like he had once before.

"Hi, Layton." I nodded. "I'm Delaney."

"That's right." He seemed perplexed. "Didn't I see you at a different bookshop? And at that artist's studio?"

"You did."

"You get around." He laughed.

I smiled. "So do you."

George watched the exchange and then handed Layton a few bills.

"This is my area, I guess." Layton held up the money and looked at George. "Thank you, kindly."

"You are welcome."

"See you around, Mr. George and Delaney," he said before he turned to leave.

We waved our goodbyes.

George carried his lunch back around the register and stored it under the counter and away from the book.

"Well, what do you think?" he asked.

"I'm too stunned to think much of anything, except that Edwin really shouldn't have."

Only a few months ago, I'd heard about a signed first-edition *Oz* selling for over a hundred thousand dollars at auction in the States.

George waved away my concern. "Edwin has so much money, he needs to spend it on something, and he likes spending it on the people he most cares for. You are one of those people."

Suddenly, my throat tightened, and tears burned at the back of my eyes. "I . . ." I told myself to get a grip. I was often in emotional awe about the way my life had gone, but this wasn't the time.

I didn't mind a few tears every now and then, and though I wouldn't trade my life in Scotland for anything, I often missed my family back in Kansas. This book brought those feelings to the forefront.

It was complicated.

"It's okay, lass, I understand." George paused. "And just so you know, everyone was pleased with the transactions. The customer, Edwin, and me. It was all very fair, though not outrageous."

I nodded and cleared my throat. "That's good to hear."

"Aye. Well, now, may I interest you in half a sandwich?"

"No, thank you, George. I think I need to track down my boss."

"I understand."

I repackaged the book and lifted the box, holding it close to my chest.

I told George thank you again and made my way out of the bookshop.

I really needed to find Edwin.

CHAPTER EIGHTEEN

I'd been to Edwin's mansion in the country a few times, for some special occasions. But he wasn't one to host lots of parties. Well, he used to when he was, in his words, "younger and even more foolish," but not so much over the last decade or so.

I'd often wished to have known him when he was younger and more foolish. He'd never been anything other than proper and respectable around me.

After leaving George's, I hurried back to the pub to show Tom the gift and let him know I was taking the car out to Edwin's. Tom couldn't quite believe what I'd been given either, but he agreed that an in-person thank-you was needed.

I also called Rosie to ask if she'd covertly ensure he was home. She agreed without question, and my trip went off without a hitch.

On my way, I passed a few old, turreted manor houses throughout the countryside. Sometimes mistaken for castles, the style was actually called Scots Baronial. Though Edwin's house was not Scots Baronial, it was still a big house on a beautiful expanse of groomed property.

Every time I visited I wondered about the complete lack of security. There was no gate at the bottom of the long driveway, no security guards. There was a perfect place for a small shack at the bottom of the hill right next to where you turn in for the driveway, where a big guy with a surly attitude could stop and ask folks what their business was with Mr. MacAlister.

Its architecture was a close cousin to Scots Baronial. Three greystone stories with white-paned windows sat comfortably atop a small hill. The driveway extended to the side of the house where the garage was located. Edwin had owned only an old Citroën since I'd known him, but the garage could have held at least three other vehicles.

Just before the downhill slope toward the garage, there was a parking area that could hold four or maybe five additional cars. I pulled Tom's car into a spot closest to the front door and parked.

I'd gotten better and better at driving on the left side of the road. As I reached for the box with the book, I realized I hadn't felt any extra anxiety on the drive. Rosie had told me I'd get used to Scottish driving eventually.

Still carefully holding the book, I exited the car. I pushed the button to ring the doorbell, noticing that Edwin still hadn't put in a front door camera.

He didn't even ask who was on the other side before he pulled the door wide.

"Ah, lass, hello!" He wore his typical dress slacks and button-down shirt. Even though he currently wore slippers instead of his normal dress shoes, he was still as dapper as ever. Upon seeing my face full of emotion, his smile disappeared. "Is everything okay?"

I stepped into the house and pulled him into a hug, him on one side of me as I held the box with the book on my other side. He was caught off guard but returned the hug a moment later.

"Everything is amazing." I laughed, my eyes crinkling in an attempt to stop from welling up.

"Ah. Oh, I think I know what this is about. You visited George?"

I liberated him from my grasp. I sniffed and wiped my watery eyes. "I did. And . . . Edwin, it's too much."

"Nonsense." He waved away my concern. "Come through and join me for some coffee."

I followed him down the long hallway that led to the kitchen. On the wall to our right, we passed one of my favorite paintings. It was a Scottish Highland landscape, and I admired it every time I saw it. Though my eyes were still a little teary, I couldn't help but glance at it.

We passed the stairway to the second floor. A well-lived-in parlor was to our left followed by a small loo. The kitchen, a large island, and two dining areas took up the entire back of the house, with windows displaying green, hilly countryside as far as the eye could see.

The dining area closest to the appliances held a casual table and chairs. The farthest dining area was set with a formal table that I'd never seen Edwin use. Whenever I'd been there and a meal had been served, Edwin had been the one to cook it, and those of us in attendance had sat at the casual table.

Though the setup might be unusual, it worked, and the decked-out kitchen was the star of the show anyway. With top-of-the-line, oversized stainless-steel appliances, light wood shelves, and white marble countertops, the space was not only aesthetically pleasing but also a joy to work in.

I knew Edwin had a weekly housekeeper, but for the most part he cleaned the kitchen. He said it was his Zen.

Edwin poured me a mug as I sat on a stool at the island. He slid the mug as well as a tray with creamer and sugar in my direction.

"I've been enjoying this flavored creamer lately. I look forward to hearing what you think," Edwin said.

I reached for the silver pitcher of creamer, which smelled slightly nutty as I poured it into my coffee. I stirred and looked up at my boss. "Edwin, you really shouldn't have gotten me that gift. It's far too much."

"Delaney, it is not too much for me, you know that." He paused. "And though I went through a long phase of being comfortable about talking about my money, I have become more and more hesitant. Please don't make me speak of it again."

I quirked a smile at him. "Nice try, but I do need to talk about it. Please."

Edwin sighed. "Fine, but let's make it quick so we can move onto a more productive conversation, like what might be going on in the investigation of Dr. Pace's murder."

I expressed my protests about it being too much, and even though it sounded like what people often feel obligated to say after receiving such a large gift, I really was genuine. When I finished and Edwin opened his mouth to protest, I lifted my hand.

"Wait," I said.

Edwin nodded and took a sip of coffee.

I thought long and hard about how my protests had made me feel, and how they might have made Edwin feel—not unappreciated really, but not fully appreciated either.

Finally, I looked back up at my boss and said, "Edwin, it's the most incredible gift I've ever received. I'm honored that you would trust me with something so . . . stunning. Maybe I should just say thank you."

Edwin smiled. "Aye. That's perfect. And you are welcome."

"I do sometimes feel like Dorothy, but this time she found her home in Scotland. It's so good to be here, but it's because of the people, not the place. If it weren't for you, Rosie, Hamlet, Hector, and Tom, Edinburgh would be a beautiful place to visit but not quite a home."

Edwin put his hand over mine. "Lass, we all feel the same. You have given us an adventure we didn't even know we needed. Ta for that. Now, tell me how your other bookshop visits went."

"All right. First, may I have a refill? That creamer is delicious."

"Of course." He poured.

"Edwin, I think I made Mary Katherine uncomfortable," I said. "I'm pretty sure it was when I told her that the Oculudentavis wasn't a bird."

"Why would that make her uncomfortable?"

"I don't know, but I've been replaying the moments in my head and I can't remember anything else that seemed to bother her."

Edwin nodded. "She said she'd come visit the store soon?"

"Yes."

"Let's all be on the lookout and see if we can understand what that might have been about. I can't imagine Mary Katherine being upset about anything."

"Upset," I repeated the word, my forehead furrowed in thought.

"Aye?" he said to my tone.

"She wasn't upset." I paused and looked at my boss. "Could she have been afraid? Oh, that seems silly."

"Afraid?"

I thought about it another long moment. "No, I must be wrong. Ignore me. I'm overthinking."

"All right. Now, I rang a friend up north. Ian Fallmuth, an old friend who also happens to be an archeologist."

"Oh, that sounds interesting."

"Aye. He was near enough to Knockfarrel to take a look in person when I told him about someone digging there without authorization. I told him to look near a tree. He did explore indeed. And while I probably shouldn't have asked him to do it, he seemed curious enough to do some investigating on his own either way." Edwin paused and then cupped his hand, turning it palm side down on the counter. "The site at one time was an old fort. It's now a hill, a mound of sorts. While there are some trees not far away, on or right by the mound itself, there are very few."

"That seems a lot like the miniature display I saw in the Museum of Edinburgh."

"Could have been a representation."

"Did he see any sign of the earth being disturbed?"

Edwin shook his head. "He said that he didn't see any signs of that, particularly not near any trees. Of course, he can't be one hundred percent sure that he was looking at the right things, but he's a thorough man if there ever was one."

"What was Dr. Pace up to?"

"I don't know, lass."

"Theo mentioned blackmail, that his bank account was draining. Maybe he was trying to fill it again. But the more important discovery would be to whose bank account the money was going."

"I guess that sounds reasonable, but *what* was he being blackmailed about?"

"Maybe the original dinosaur bones he tried to sell back in Kansas?"

"That might explain why he'd come to Edinburgh, or at least left Kansas. He needed to get away from his past, go somewhere with new people he might be able to trick into giving him money for fake things. But what is there to blackmail? The truth came out, aye?"

I nodded. "Well, maybe there's more. If that's the case, then the person doing the blackmailing might be here in Edinburgh, which . . . well, I guess I don't know what that might mean." I fell into thought another moment. "Or . . ."

"I'm listening."

"Maybe it's even simpler than that, Edwin. Maybe he chose Scotland simply because of the Picts. There is so much mystery surrounding them, it seems like the perfect subject to make things up about. I think Ry and I discussed this. He was trying to make money by selling the new discovery, so he could pay a blackmailer."

"You have a point, but we still don't know why."

"Yes, my *point* doesn't lead anywhere." I laughed.

"Oh, I disagree. I think it leads right to a killer. It's just finding the right fork in the road to take. I asked Ian if he or any of his archeologist friends had heard of Dr. Pace. He asked around and got back to me, saying that none of them had spoken to Dr. Pace,

but one had known about him. They'd corresponded years earlier about something he couldn't remember, couldn't find in his
email right off, but would keep checking and get back with me."

"Maybe there's something there?"

"There's something somewhere, I'm sure. We, or more
properly the police, just need to find it."

"Probably the police."

"But you're not ready to give up, I'm guessing."

I smiled. "Not yet. In fact, I have wanted to talk to someone
else for a few days, but other things got in the way."

"Who?"

"Sara Shoemaker at the university. She heads up the Natural History Collections."

"I know Sara!"

"I thought you might." I smiled.

"Would you like some company to visit her?"

"I would love some."

"Give me a few minutes to get myself put together." He
stood up, dusting non-existent crumbs off his already impec-
cably dressed self.

"Sounds like a plan."

CHAPTER NINETEEN

The Natural History Collections were housed in a part of the University of Edinburgh campus called King's Buildings, inside a two-story brownstone on a corner. The building extended down both streets. A short five stairs led up to beautiful wood double doors with brass knockers and sunray-paned windows on their top halves. The doors were under a carved Zoology sign. Above that was a carved crest with 19 on one side and 28 on the other.

"Even the doors are spectacular," I said as Edwin reached for one of the knockers to use it as a handle.

"Aye." He smiled.

One of the things he said he liked about having me around was that I gave him new eyes, a new view on his "old" world. He'd mentioned he'd probably feel the same way about the expanse of my parents' farm in Kansas if he were ever to visit it. The two did not seem the same to me, but I know my parents would love for him to test out his theory.

There were still so many places in Edinburgh I hadn't seen yet. I couldn't wait to visit them all.

I stopped just inside the front doors to take in the displays. I loved being overcome by waves of science. Though the place didn't smell of anything but clean, fresh air, my olfactory imagination took me right back to my high school and college science labs.

And though my real passion was words, I had come to be fond of all labs, discovering a special love for those with beakers atop flames, their insides boiling and steaming.

There were no beakers in sight either, but as I spotted the lines of polished, light wood cabinets and sliding glass doors, I had the sense that I'd stepped into the greatest scientific laboratory of all.

"This is spectacular!" I said.

Edwin smiled. "It is."

My tribe was made of nerds. And I loved them all the more for it.

An elderly man came around the corner. "Ah, good morning. May I help you?"

His accent was as thick as my previous landlord, Elias's, but I could tune my ears quickly now.

"Aye, Edwin MacAlister and Delaney Nichols here to see Ms. Shoemaker."

"Aye? Is she expecting you?" He stopped by a short podium and reached for an old-fashioned phone just like the one on Rosie's desk, lifting it to the top of the stand and grabbing the handset.

"I rang her a wee bit ago," Edwin said.

"Aye."

I hadn't known about the call, but I wasn't surprised. I mouthed "Thank you" as our arrival was announced.

When he hung up the phone, the man said, "Apparently you know your way up?"

"I do," Edwin responded.

"You are welcome to make your way." The man smiled and continued through to another hallway.

I followed Edwin down another hallway. As we made our way, my eyes drank in the vast array of display cases. There were lots of fossils, of course, but I was especially intrigued by the skeletons, most of them wired to their proper form.

Over his shoulder, Edwin noted, "The collection includes specimens and objects that represent invertebrates and vertebrates. I believe some of the items have been dated back three hundred years."

"So cool."

"I know. Maybe we'll take some time to look around when we're done."

"Other than the gentleman who greeted us, it's just us in here."

"It's not open as a museum, but people are welcome to look around if an appointment is made. The collections are for the students."

I should have known that. This time I said the words aloud, "Thanks for making the call."

"You are welcome."

We turned and took some stairs up to the next level, coming out and into a wide hallway that held lots of closed doors. We made our way to the end, and Edwin knew exactly which door we were to knock on. He rapped a few friendly times.

"Come in, Edwin," a voice called from inside.

As we pushed through, a woman stood from behind her

very messy desk. In fact, the entire space was messy to the point of claustrophobic. She made no apologies.

"Ah, this must be Delaney, the lass you spoke about. I'm Sara." She extended her hand over the desk. She wore big, round glasses, a severe bun, and not a stitch of makeup touched her skin. She was tall and very thin. Even with her thick sweater tucked into some brown dress pants, everything looked a bit too large on her frame. Her smile lit up the whole office and I liked her immediately.

We shook. "A pleasure. Thanks for your time."

"Sit. Throw the papers on the floor." She gestured.

Edwin held the stack of papers that had been on the chair on his lap. I set my stack on a ledge under a window—well, on top of some other papers that were already on the ledge.

Once we were all situated, Sara continued. "I have no secretary here, and I have no idea how to manage coffee or tea. I do, however, have bottles of water in my desk. May I interest either of you in some H_2O?"

"No thank you," Edwin and I both said.

I suddenly hoped she spoke in chemical formulas all the time and not just when offering some water to her guests. Time would tell.

She folded her hand on the papers on her desk. "To what may I credit this visit?"

Edwin nodded at me. "Delaney met someone recently who has suffered the direst of fates. She heard that you might have known the same person."

Sara's eyebrows came together as her smile fell. "Direst?"

I nodded and jumped in as it seemed Edwin wanted me to do. "Murder."

"Oh?!"

I hurried to say, "Dr. Adam Pace."

Sara sat back in her chair. "Oh, yes, I heard about that. Such a pity." She paused. "I did meet with Dr. Pace a few times. In fact, I was hoping for a small business relationship with him, but he could never quite deliver."

Edwin and I shared a look before I continued, "What sort of business?"

Sara didn't seem sad but there was something distant about the way her mouth pursed and her eyes unfocused. Hidden so only I would notice, Edwin sent me a hand gesture that told me to be patient.

I got the message.

A long—very long—beat later, Sara's eyes reengaged and she sat forward. "Come with me."

She stood and made her way around the desk and out of the office. It took Edwin and me a moment or two to stand, put the papers back where we found them, and then follow Sara out into the hallway.

With her hands on her hips and an air of impatience, she turned and said, "Come on."

We followed her quick footsteps back to an elevator. None of us spoke as we rode back down to the main level. For whatever reason, and even though Sara hummed lightly as she seemed to be pondering something, the trip wasn't awkward.

Once out of the elevator, we followed her into a special exhibit room. About twelve by twelve, glass-doored shelving units like the ones in the main hallways took up the perimeter of this space. It was immediately clear, though, that there was something different about the items in these cases. I didn't think they were specimens.

Raised letters spread across the back wall: The Phyllis Bone Sculptures.

Sara stood in the middle of the room with the same stance from upstairs, though it didn't seem impatient now.

"Ah," Edwin said knowingly.

I had no clue what was going on, but I figured I just needed to remain patient.

"Aye. The sculptures in this room were created by Scotland's own Phyllis Bone." She lasered her attention to me, probably having figured out that Edwin knew about whatever it was she was going to get me up to speed about.

I stood straight and listened as she continued.

"Ms. Bone died back in the early 1970s. She was a talented artist, having learned her art under many sculpting masters here and in France. She loved animals, drawing and sculpting them from a young age. She was the first female academician of the Royal Scottish Academy."

I did not know what that meant, but I widened my eyes as if it was an impressive honor, which seemed to be the correct response.

"Aye." Sara nodded. "Ms. Bone was and still is beloved. We acquired this collection of her sculptures, which I think you will find magnificent. Take a look around."

The three of us made our way to the display cases, each of us to a different spot. Of the sculptures I looked at, the chimpanzee and the Indian elephant were my favorites.

"They are incredible," I said, breaking the reverie we'd all fallen into.

"They are. Ms. Bone is one of our beloved Scots, aye, Edwin?"

"Absolutely," he said, genuinely.

"This is some of what Dr. Pace and I spoke about." Sara made a big circle in the air with her hand. "Well, in a roundabout way. He originally approached me, asking if I would like to buy something he claimed to find regarding the Picts, but, as you can see here, we aren't so much about the Picts, though they were a fascinating group. Not our thing, though. When I told him that no matter the value of what he claimed to find, there was not a chance we would be interested in purchasing that sort of item. I sent him, instead, to a local artist of fame, Ryory Bennigan. You've heard of him."

I nodded.

"He told me he was already working with Ryory but wasn't sure anything would come of that either. He became . . . agitated when I wouldn't give him an offer for what he was trying to sell." She frowned. "I had to become quite stern with him, asking him to leave immediately. He did exit my office, but not as immediately as I'd wished. And then, only a few minutes after leaving—and I know he did originally leave as I heard him make his way down the hall—he burst back into my office. I was a wee bit frightened to be sure, but he came bearing a different twist, or so he said.

"He visited this room on his way out of the building and then came back up to tell me he could provide something similar with a 3D printer. Asked if I would be interested in some things like that. I told him that we simply were not interested in the Picts." She cleared her throat. "But he mentioned bones and fossils as well. If we wanted him to, and though he wasn't an artist, he could fabricate things that might be helpful in our students' studies.

"What more can I say other than I was intrigued. Could he? Could we, and I mean our students, benefit from having someone create things we didn't have or things we wanted to somehow upgrade?"

"You made a deal with him?" Edwin asked when she didn't continue right away.

Sara shook her head. "No, not at all. I told him to bring me something, a sample, and we could talk. Part of my excitement was feigned to get rid of him, but another part of me wished for something . . . I don't know, extraordinary."

"Sara. There are 3D printers everywhere, aye?"

She nodded. "Aye, we have quite a few here at the university."

"You could create the things you're talking about."

"Aye, but I'm always . . . open, I suppose, to looking at someone's work. I wondered if Dr. Pace had any sort of knack for creation or if he would just plug something into a computer and have a printer spit it out. Look around here. There's no question that we have benefitted from Ms. Bone's work, and there's no doubt in my mind that she was a cut above so many others. Do you not agree?"

"I agree," Edwin said.

"I do too," I added.

Sara sighed. "Though I have absolutely no professional interest in the Picts, I am always looking for ways to improve what we do here, add more items that will only advance the studies of . . . anyone who might be interested." She smiled.

"This would be a legitimate undertaking," I said.

"Of course," Sara said.

"I guess I mean that there was no reason to think he was doing something suspicious."

Understanding brightened her eyes. "Oh, no, lass, I didn't think so, at least not completely."

"I think that came out wrong. Sorry."

Sara laughed. "No need. I love a good mystery."

"So does Delaney," Edwin said.

"So, no, Dr. Pace did nothing that I or someone else would have found particularly bothersome here at the university. I did have to ask him to leave with a little force, but he listened. I was looking forward to seeing what he might bring me. He never showed me anything at all."

"How long were you waiting to hear from him?" Edwin asked.

She bit her bottom lip. "Maybe two weeks or so. I could check my calendar, but that feels about right."

"Ms. Shoemaker," I said. "Did Dr. Pace mention where he kept his 3D printer?"

"I didn't ask him, but, and as Edwin pointed out, there are many on the campus. Perhaps he was working with someone here who would let him use one."

"Sara, is there any way to send out a question, campuswide, asking if anyone worked with Dr. Pace on using a printer?" Edwin asked.

"That would be an easy undertaking, though sometimes folks are slow to respond." She tsked. "I will never understand laziness. Would you like me to send out a question?"

"Please."

"My pleasure."

There was nothing suspicious here, except the fact that

Dr. Pace might have had a legitimate business dealing if he'd made an effort to bring something for Sara to consider. I wondered why he hadn't, except that maybe there was more money in the Pict language translation stone.

I'd learned who Dr. Pace was by hearing about his dealings with others. They all seemed fairly consistent, but this one was different in that it was on the up-and-up, and Dr. Pace didn't follow through.

As I stood there and thought about all the things I'd learned, I knew there were only two people I'd spoken with in the last week who had enough money to make a bad lucrative deal more interesting than a legitimate one.

Edwin was one, and he hadn't even ever met Dr. Pace.

Ryory Bennigan was the other one. He was also the common denominator. Even Sara had brought up his name.

Sara Shoemaker was nothing if not succinct.

She said, "If there's nothing else, I must get back to work, though it was lovely to see you, Edwin, and meet you, Delaney. Could you show yourselves out?"

We nodded, and made our way outside, standing in front of the amazing doors only a few moments after watching Sara hurry toward the elevator in the other direction.

"Thoughts?" Edwin asked me.

"Two big ones at the moment. She was amazing, and all roads lead to Ryory," I said.

"Aye. I agree. Now what?"

"I think I'd like to talk to Ry, even if I'm not sure what questions to ask him," I said.

"Shall we try his place?"

"You have the time?"

"Absolutely."

Though I wanted to see Ry, there was also a part of me that was excited to be the one to show Edwin his studio and home.

I had no doubt that my boss was going to love it.

Edwin parked the car out on the street, and we made our way, but I came to a quick stop as we turned into the close. Ry was leaving his place.

The sun was setting behind thick clouds. Darkness was coming quickly, but Ryory Bennigan was easy to recognize. He was a big man, but now that I knew him the cover of black clothing, including a scarf and a hat, didn't disguise him at all.

I put my arm out in front of Edwin to stop him.

He seemed to understand the instruction and we both backed out, sticking near the building that currently housed a closed flower shop.

"I don't think there's a way out on the other end. He's coming this way," I said.

"A perfect opportunity to meet up with him. Ask him to join us for a pint maybe?"

I bit my bottom lip and then shook my head. "I think I'd like to follow him."

"I see. Should I get the car?"

I shook my head again. "I think he'll walk. I've heard that he does that sometimes. I'm curious what he gets up to. Are you game?"

Even with the encroaching darkness, I could see Edwin's eyebrows raise. "I think so, lass. I'll bow out if my legs can't keep up."

I had a hard time keeping up with Edwin when he was on a determined path, and he loved to walk. I was more worried about me than him.

I nodded for him to join me going up the three steps of the flower shop's entryway.

"If he comes this way, he might not notice us," I whispered.

"Aye," Edwin said, his tone sounding more game, or he was pretending to humor me.

Ry did not walk in front of us, but we could hear his movement as he exited the close and turned in the other direction. It was more than his footfalls, which did make some sound—he hummed as he walked.

"A lovely tune," Edwin said in a low voice.

We gave it a moment before I peered out of the entryway. Ry wasn't moving at a quick clip, but he had long legs too, so he'd almost reached the corner in record time.

He turned right, and I said, "Come on."

Edwin nodded and we set out in a quick clip. In fact, as I'd already considered, I had to work to keep up with my septuagenarian boss's strides.

The street we turned onto was busier than the one we'd come from, and it held many shops, restaurants, and pubs. Most of the shops were closed or closing, but the restaurants and pubs would be busy for a while.

Ry walked down the middle of the sidewalk with a confident stride. We were far enough behind him, and there were enough people out and about that, possibly, he wouldn't notice us if he turned around, but he was tall enough that we could hang back and keep an eye on him easily.

He didn't stand out, though. The cover of dark clothes as

well as his easygoing manner kept extra attention at bay this time. I didn't spot any picture takers. Maybe people paid less attention as the days turned into night.

"I wonder if he's going to his tattooist," I pondered aloud.

"That would be a fun discovery!"

It would be, but I suddenly felt sneaky. My knee-jerk reaction to following Ry was beginning to transform into something that felt like none of our business. I was about to suggest we stop when Ry turned and made his way into a restaurant, not a tattoo parlor.

"Oh," Edwin said. "I've been there before. It's a wonderful spot and I know why Ry would like it."

"Why?"

"Come along. We don't have to go in for me to show you."

We picked up the pace even more. I'd noticed a sign carved with a picture of fish and chips, and the name became clear as we got closer.

"Art's?" I said.

"Aye, that's the place."

"Do you know Art?"

"Art isn't the owner, it's the thing."

"The thing?"

"Aye. I'll show you."

We stopped a few doors down from Art's. As with all the other establishments on the street, it didn't take up a big space. Its boxy front was colorful with flowers painted over a bright blue background.

"It's an artists' hangout," Edwin said. "Artists are encouraged to work inside, their creations displayed and for sale. It's a lovely setup."

I looked at Edwin and enjoyed the smile on his face. "You have good memories of it?"

"Art's has been around a long time. About twenty years ago, I visited frequently. I was fond of an artist who displayed and sold her oil paintings."

"Fond?"

Edwin looked at me like he had a secret, but he spilled it quickly and it wasn't what I thought it might be. "It was Rosie."

"Rosie's an artist?"

"She used to be. I don't think she paints anymore, but for a while she did. Her landscapes were magical."

I thought about the painting in Edwin's foyer. "Do you display some of her work?"

"Of course. The one in my entryway is my favorite."

"It's spectacular."

"I agree."

I couldn't believe I didn't know about Rosie's talent. "Why doesn't she paint anymore?"

"Age gets the best of us if we're lucky enough to live that long, lass. Arthritis got into her fingers. It's not bad, but it hinders her abilities."

"I'm sorry to hear that."

"Rosie wasn't. She is one of the most content people I know when it comes to accepting the passing of time and its challenges."

Before I could say anything more, Ry came back out through the front door. We were far enough away that he wouldn't spot us right off, but if he went in the direction he'd come, he'd probably see us watching him. We sidestepped into a shoe repair shop entryway and stood there together looking terribly guilty as we watched him, indeed, turn back toward his home.

He held two items under one arm, and a bag of food in his other hand. It was easy to see that one item under the arm was a small painting, though we couldn't make out the details as he passed by us again. The other item was in a white box that was about four by four by four. Edwin and I looked at each other and then hurried back out onto the sidewalk to resume our curious chase. My curiosity won out again over my nosiness and I no longer felt sneaky; in fact, I was beginning to feel downright stealthy.

Ry stopped suddenly and began talking to a young couple— it didn't appear that they knew each other. Edwin and I stopped too and hung back. We watched as Ry and the couple nodded and seemed to be meeting for the first time. A moment later he handed them the picture. They were both surprised and behaved as if they were trying to give it back. But Ry wouldn't take it. The handoff complete, Ry nodded again and then went on his way as the couple admired their new painting.

"He buys and gives away art?" I asked.

"It appears that way. Should we continue to follow?"

"Can you tell what the other item was?"

"Well, I recognize the food bag, but the box is a mystery."

I put my hands on my hips. "I'd like to know. We could go back to Art's and see if we can figure it out, or we could follow Ry and ask him. I'd still like to show you his place."

"Ah." Edwin thought a moment. "I vote for leaving him to his meal."

I nodded a moment later. "Okay. Me too."

We turned again and made our way back to Art's, going inside this time. My imagination had conjured up an idea of the place that turned out to be not too far off from reality.

It wasn't a large space, but uncommon to most restaurants and pubs, the lighting was extraordinary, bright and clear. There were only ten tables, each with four chairs. Each table had one or two artists at work, most of them with a sketch pad and some drawing or painting materials. But one table held four diners with no art. The walls as well as a set of shelves were packed and stacked with all different sorts of creations. In another setting it might have felt claustrophobic, but in here it mellowed the bright light and gave the whole place a cozy feel.

Another time I would have wanted to look around, and probably buy something, but I had a mission in mind. I wondered how to figure out what Ry had taken with him.

"Is there any way to do this?" I asked Edwin quietly.

"I don't know, but look over there." He nodded to the corner, where a machine sat on a stand.

I looked in that direction. "Is that a 3D printer?"

"I believe it is," Edwin said. I looked at him with surprise. "I've been researching."

A server asked if we'd like to place an order or wait for a table. I said, "Could we just look at the printer?"

She shrugged. "Sure. There's a price list taped to the top."

Edwin and I wove our way to the corner. The server, maybe seeing our wide eyes, came up behind us. "People usually bring a laptop and hook it up. Do you have a design you want printed?"

I shook my head. "Not today, but is there another way to send it information? Via email or something?"

She nodded. "You can bring in a thumb drive and use the

owner's computer, but he vets people pretty well. He doesn't allow just anyone to load stuff on his laptop."

"I understand. Is that what just happened? I thought I saw someone over here before we came in?"

"Oh." She gave us a long look as if she wondered if we knew who the man had been. I thought Edwin and I managed to pull off clueless pretty well. "Well, sure, I suppose that is what happened. The man is . . . well, we all know him."

"I'm just learning about these printers," I said. "What did he print? I mean, if you can tell me. Or just give me an idea of what *can* be printed."

She nodded. "So many things can be printed. This is just a small machine, though." She laughed. "The gentleman who was just here comes in a lot, but he hasn't used the printer until recently. Today, he made a plastic hummingbird thing." She shrugged. "I didn't get a good look at it."

Edwin and I made almost identical sounds that didn't seem to be an exactly appropriate response. The woman's eyebrows furrowed. "So, any questions just let me know, but the price list is right there." She pointed and then turned to assist other customers.

"What do you suppose it means?" Edwin asked me.

"I could be very wrong, but I would bet that it's a gift for Ani."

"The police have released her?"

"I don't know, but I think I'm going to be bold enough to ask Inspector Winters."

Before I could type in a text, Edwin said, "How about a group dinner?"

"That sounds wonderful!"

"You ask Winters, I'll gather the gang."

CHAPTER TWENTY

In fact, Inspector Winters called me shortly after I sent the text. Edwin and I had moved outside so he might gather the troops as I spoke to the inspector on my phone.

"Aye, Ani has been released, lass, but that doesn't mean we're done with her. I can't give you details, but I feel like she and Mr. Bennigan might be up to something. Is it murder? I don't know, but be on your toes around them, lass."

"I will. Thank you." I realized the reason he'd called was to offer the warning and my gaze went down the street. Maybe we should have followed Ry to see if he really did go home. Too late now. "How's the evidence coming?"

"Not enough yet, but . . . be careful, lass," he repeated.

We ended the call just as Edwin sent me a thumbs-up. "Rosie and Hamlet will meet us there. Want to call Tom?"

"I'll do it on the way."

They didn't happen enough, these dinners, but when they did, it seemed we all lit up. We enjoyed each other's company so much that we collectively wondered why we didn't do it more often. Sometimes, my previous landlords Elias and Aggie would join us, but they were busy this evening. Artair and Tom were too busy too.

Edwin's lady love, Veronica, from Ireland herself, ran an Irish restaurant in Edinburgh. She had a room specifically made for large parties. Every once in a while we would gather for a dinner full of delicious food, laughter, and rousing conversation.

The only caveat was that none of the rest of us would allow Edwin to pay for these dinners. Neither did we want Veronica to give them to us free. The deal was simple—we would pay. Edwin and Veronica only tried to argue a little bit. They liked the idea that we wanted to spend time there. They knew we were serious about our terms and were more likely to be there if we didn't feel we were any sort of obligation to anyone else.

As we ate, Edwin and I told everyone about our short but intriguing chase, and I shared that Ani had been released.

I asked Hamlet, "Have you heard from her since?"

"Not a word. I have left messages and texts, and nothing back."

Hamlet shook his head. "Despite Inspector Winters's warning, I am more worried about her now that I think she might be up to something. She was in hospital, and she's been cagey, but she's not a bad person. I don't know. Now that I know she's been released, I think I'll stop by her flat tomorrow." He paused. "Do you want to come with me?"

"Right, well, be careful, and as much as I'd love to ask her about her time with the police, she might need just a friend."

Hamlet nodded and gave me a small smile. "I will let you know if I talk to her."

"Thank you."

Veronica had been busy, in and out, not able to sit down with us while we ate. She rejoined us and took the empty chair in between Edwin and me, sitting as though it felt good to take a moment.

"Dinner was delicious," I said. "Maybe the best pot pie I've ever had. Don't tell me what was in it, though. I'd hate to hear there was haggis or anything."

Veronica shared a smile with Edwin before she turned back to me. "I'm glad you enjoyed it. It's a new item on the menu."

"How often do you switch up the menu?" I asked. I'd never noticed one change.

"Very rarely, but with the seafood issue, we had no choice."

"Seafood issue?"

On the other side of Veronica, Edwin leaned forward, as he was curious to hear what she had to say next.

"It's been in the news," Veronica said as she glanced at the three of us who were most listening to her. "You didn't hear?"

Edwin, Hamlet, and I shook our heads.

"I don't think so."

"Well, it's an overreaction in my opinion because it's something so specific. Have you heard of torafugu?"

I shook my head. "No."

"I might have," Edwin said. "Is it the same thing as pufferfish?"

"It's tiger pufferfish," Hamlet added. "Aye?"

"That's right," Veronica said. "It's poisonous, deadly, but also delicious. Though it's served in Japanese restaurants, there are specially trained fugu handlers. Usually that means taking the skin off the fish and then washing away the blood before preparing and serving. Anyway, a couple weeks ago, someone was poisoned by tetrodotoxin from a torafugu. The restaurant who prepared it has been shut down and the rest of us were ordered to stop serving anything but cod. I don't even know why they chose cod, but maybe they know what they're doing. The authorities are investigating."

"Seafood is a Scottish staple," I spoke the obvious. With the North Sea right there, Edinburgh's seafood was the freshest I'd ever tasted.

Veronica shrugged. "We'll get back to normal soon. I do feel bad for the restaurant that got shut down. Someone made a mistake, though, and it does need to be investigated. I hope they get to reopen, but I worry about any customers returning."

"I can see how that would scare people away," Hamlet said.

"I can't believe I haven't heard a thing about this," Edwin said.

"Did the person who was poisoned die?" I asked.

"No, and I don't know the circumstances. I don't know if the poison was ingested or if they touched it. I heard they are fine, but I keep waiting for some sort of lawsuit," Veronica said.

"Sounds like a possibility."

"Oh, excuse me," Veronica said. "I think I need to help up front."

The upper half of the dining area walls were glass, so I could see out toward the front of the restaurant. She made her way in that direction as quickly as she could, but I couldn't quite see what had garnered her attention.

The place was busy, with customers and the waitstaff walking everywhere. Once Veronica was next to the podium, I could see her profile as she spoke with someone standing just inside the entryway—though I couldn't make out that person.

I did a double take when it seemed that Veronica started speaking adamantly, though I still couldn't spot who she was talking to. I watched a moment longer, hoping that whatever might be going on would be resolved soon enough—Veronica seemed more bothered than seemed reasonable.

Edwin noticed my frown and turned to look toward the front of the restaurant too. He sat up straighter, observed for only a moment, and then stood from the table. I stood too. Hamlet and Rosie were in another conversation as I followed Edwin out of the room and toward the entrance.

As we wove our way, it was still impossible to see exactly what was going on. In fact, we didn't even have a clear view of Veronica the whole time.

But as we got closer, we heard Veronica make a strangled noise, a yell but not defined by any specific word.

In an instant, Edwin and I sped up our approach. When we were next to her, we could immediately see that she seemed fine—no obvious injuries.

Edwin put his hand on her arm. "Are you all right?"

Visibly shaken, Veronica nodded. "I'm fine, but that was strange."

"What happened?" Edwin asked.

"A food delivery kid came in here but there was nothing for him to pick up." Veronica nodded toward a shelf behind the front counter. "He was angry and tried to leap over the counter and to take someone else's bag anyway. I pushed him back, but it wasn't easy. I . . . well, I just reacted. He fell back but picked himself up and ran away. It all happened so quickly."

"What did he look like?" I asked, thinking about the one food delivery person who kept appearing in my life lately.

Veronica shook her head. "He just seemed . . . average. Maybe in his twenties. He wore a knit cap and a big coat."

"Eye color? Height?" I asked.

Again, Veronica shook her head. "Average height. I don't know the eye color." She looked at a server next to her. "Did you see anything else?"

The young woman wasn't as shaken as Veronica, but she was clearly bothered. "I didn't. I didn't even catch the name of the delivery app. He seemed to mumble over the name of the app." She looked at Edwin. "It was a scam from the beginning, I'm pretty sure. Someone who just wanted food."

"If that were the case, if he just said he was hungry, I would have made sure he got something to eat," Veronica said.

The server nodded. "Yeah, Veronica does that all the time."

"Does that happen often, I mean do people try to steal deliveries or fake them?" Edwin asked.

"No," Veronica said.

The minimal description that Veronica and her server had offered up could have pointed to Layton, but also probably could have described lots of different guys in the city.

A thought occurred to me. "Did you, by chance, get the name of the person who was supposed to be on the order?"

Veronica and the server looked at each other.

"No," Veronica said.

"Like you said, it all happened so quickly," the server added.

Customers were both waiting to be seated as well as to pay their bills. Because everyone was fine, it seemed like it was time to move on and hope that none of the customers were bothered or upset by the scene.

"Excuse me a moment." Edwin stepped around the counter and made his way toward the door.

Again, I followed him.

We stepped out and into the cold night. I wrapped my arms around myself as Edwin looked up and down the street.

"I keep running into a food delivery guy," I said.

"Aye?" Edwin turned his attention to me.

I nodded. "They didn't give us enough of a description to know if it was him, but it could have been. His name is Layton."

"Layton?" Edwin's attention was now fully on me.

"Yes. Do you know him?"

"I don't know, lass. The name is familiar, but I can't place who it might be."

"Do you ever have food delivered to your house?" I asked.

"Never once have I done such a thing."

As was always the way, there was pedestrian traffic up and down the street, but we hadn't spotted anyone who seemed to be running away from causing a scene, though we both looked around again.

"Nothing," Edwin said.

"No."

"All right, let's go back in, but I do have something for us to do in the morning, lass. I just got a message back from a call I made earlier."

"Okay?"

"Want to see some ancient Roman items?"

"Always, but why?"

Edwin shrugged. "My friend Ian, the one I rang about the site up north, Knockfarrel, set up a meeting for us with a friend down here. I thought we could ask some questions about the site."

"I can't wait." I tried to hide a shiver.

"Aye. Let's get inside."

Once more, we looked up and down and all around, but there was no one suspicious in the area. Inside, the restaurant was back in its groove, no one any worse for wear.

I knew my boss, though. He would be bothered by this enough to search for whoever had interfered with Veronica's business and safety. I didn't know exactly what he would do, but it would be something.

I hoped he'd include me.

CHAPTER TWENTY-ONE

"I think I've seen a sculpture of a lion somewhere that noted it was from Cramond," I said as Edwin steered the Citroën toward the site of the same name.

"It's a lioness, but, aye, it's at Joshua's museum."

The National Museum of Scotland hadn't been "Joshua's" until he and I had become friends, but that's how we all thought of it now.

"That's right. In the Roman hall," I said.

"Aye. And it was found right here." Edwin pulled his car into an undefined spot and parked.

We were next to a building as we looked out over an open expanse of land. Edwin beckoned toward the space.

"That's the remains of the Roman fort." He nodded toward the building. "This is a visitors center, not really a museum."

I didn't spot anyone working outside, but it was cold. "Is this a working site?"

"No. Sometimes they uncover parts of the fort, but I think the last time was around 2000 or 2001, when they found some defensive ditches." Edwin smiled into the memory. "It was pretty exciting for a wee bit."

"Ian's friend works here?"

"He does." Edwin looked at me with a twinkle to his eyes.

"You look happy about that," I said, wondering about the twinkle.

"Oh, not unhappy. I was surprised by who our mutual friend turned out to be, though."

"Mutual? Intriguing."

"I agree."

As we made our way into the building, I got a better view of the open space. Grids were formed in the ground with the remnants of what had once been stone walls.

"That's the outline of the fort?" I asked.

"Aye. We're close to where there used to be water. Apparently, the Romans set up many forts along the river. It's very fascinating, though I doubt we want to get into all of that. There's something more important to our other investigation here."

Our investigation. I liked that but I didn't comment.

As I'd noted to myself just the night before, despite his age, Edwin's long legs moved quickly. Often I had to do a skip-hop to keep up with him. Today, it was even more necessary. He was anxious and excited. We could have followed Ry for a long time.

"The Romans were here for less than a hundred years, we think," Edwin added as he opened the door to the visitors center for me.

"Okay." I made my way inside as he followed.

The receptionist smiled from behind a desk. "Are you Mr. MacAlister?"

"I am. And this is Delaney Nichols."

"You are expected." She gestured toward a set of white double doors but didn't stand up from the chair that was behind a desk—not a desk that had seen the likes of kings and queens but one more contemporary and decidedly utilitarian.

There was no one else in the entryway that took up the entire middle of the building. Marble floors and a high ceiling made our voices echo a little and seemed to contradict the modern style of the desk.

"Ta," Edwin said.

The doors opened before we could make our way to them. "Hello, my friends!"

Birk, a friend of mine and Edwin's, came through, his arms open wide. He was fond of gold—the color as well as the precious mineral. Today, as on other days I'd seen him, he was covered in the color in shiny, glittery fashion.

"What a wonderful surprise," I said as we hugged each other.

"It is, isn't it? You should get to see me much more often than you do." Birk laughed.

"I agree."

He and Edwin shook hands. "Edwin."

"Birk, good to see you, lad. I didn't know you and Ian were mates."

"Aye, you too, my friend. It's a small world, indeed."

Birk led us back into the room behind the double doors. I expected to be taken into a lush space, rife with ornate decorations because that's what his house was like, that's what Birk was like.

But the room couldn't have been any simpler, with plain

cream-colored walls and a beige linoleum floor. Four chairs were tucked under a round table in the center, but they, like the desk out front, were made with simple, contemporary lines. There were papers on the table, but that was all that was in the room. We could see the open space outside with the fort's wall remnants—through tall, all-glass windows—which seemed to go on forever.

"So," Birk looked at me, "what did Edwin tell you about our meeting?"

"Nothing," I said.

"Ah, I thought he might handle it that way. Sit and I'll show you what I have. It's not much, but it's regarding the murder case you are looking into, of one Dr. Adam Pace."

Birk gathered the papers as we each took a chair.

"I'm intrigued," I said.

Birk smiled. "First of all, Ian told me that he looked into Dr. Pace's communications with his colleagues. There wasn't much to report. The communication took place a while back, maybe even a couple years, so memories might be sketchy, but all he could glean was that Dr. Pace seemed like a smart, affable gent."

"Did they remember what the communication was about?" I asked.

"Aye." Birk laughed. "Dr. Pace asked who he might speak with regarding the Picts. He was given a list of people who, according to Ian, were never contacted."

"That was a while ago, though," Edwin said. "Maybe that was the beginning of Dr. Pace's interest in the Picts."

"He was probably still in Kansas back then," I added.

Birk nodded. "He told Ian his questions were specifically

for a class at the university in Kansas where he worked, but if he had anything else, he must have found another way to find answers. Or, as Ian speculated, decided that so little was truly known that he could go with the scant information he was given. No one from that group ever talked to him again."

I nodded and pondered that idea. Considering what I had read about the Picts, I could see how there was only so much. There quickly came a point when everything else was just speculation.

"Thanks, Birk, and thank Ian too," I said.

"I will."

"You have a picture from Mr. Bennigan?" Birk said to me over the papers as he held them to his chest.

"Uh."

"I told Birk about the picture of Ry's sketch. I didn't think it was confidential."

"Oh!" I gathered my phone from my bag. It seemed like a long time ago that Ry had texted it to me. I found it and extended the phone to Birk.

It only took a moment of him studying before he nodded and gave me a knowing smile. "Aye, it's just as Edwin thought."

"I thought I'd seen it before and it's the main reason why we're here," Edwin added.

"What's that?" I asked.

Birk extended a different picture in my direction, one that had been copied onto a sheet of paper.

Both sketches contained the same words, but the one Birk handed me had a few more words.

The picture on my phone:

MATRIBALA
TERVIS ET

Birk's paper:

MATRIBALA
TERVIS ET
MATRIB CAM
PESTRICHCoH

"I don't understand," I said. "What is this?" I said.

"It's from an altar found here at this site. It's dedicated to a mother goddess or mother goddesses, I'm not sure. Certainly nothing about the Picts and their language."

"It's here?"

"Well, it's preserved, but you may see it if you have the proper credentials and get permission," Birk said. "I can get those for us, but I don't have them today."

"You think that's what Dr. Pace did? It wasn't that he created or found anything at the other site? He came here, took a picture, and just used it for his story?"

"I did confirm that he applied for and received access, but, of course, I can't know his motives."

"I think what you are thinking a distinct possibility, Delaney," Edwin said.

"Why?" I'd been infused with a spike of anger. It all felt so ridiculously made up. I could only imagine how Ry was going to feel when he heard the news. I wasn't sure I could be the one to tell him.

I was also impressed by Edwin's ability to suss such a thing out.

"It looks . . . interestingly authentic. It *is* authentic, I suppose, just not what Dr. Pace said it was," Edwin said.

"This tells me he was just after money. He didn't even have a faked item to give," I said. "He didn't 3D print out a stone."

"Oh, I don't know. He might have duplicated this item." Edwn nodded at the picture. "I don't think he dug anything up, though."

"Did anyone here talk to him?" I asked.

Birk shook his head. "Not that I know of, just gave him access. I'm on the board of this site. We are attempting to turn it into a real tourist destination, though we aren't there yet. Still, though, Jill is here a few days a week, just to give a presence, make sure nothing is bothered. People are in and out, though we have no guides or docents. She wasn't around the day he was. Delaney, Dr. Pace could have copied a picture of this from the internet. I believe even the Wikipedia site has a sketch of this."

"Wouldn't Ryory Bennigan know this?" I asked.

"Not necessarily. Those of us interested in such things would, but not everyone is as intrigued by all history as those of us in this room. He might not have even considered searching, or if he searched as it being something associated with the Picts, he wouldn't have found it."

"True."

"And, so you know, I did ring Inspector Winters this morning to tell him about this."

I nodded, wondering if it might be important or another diversion off the path of searching for a killer. "What did he say?"

"He was grateful for the information, but he didn't tell me anything else."

I sighed. "There is no interpretation of the Picts' language, is there?"

"There might be, somewhere, but I don't think Dr. Pace found it," Edwin said.

"No, I don't think so either."

"You are disappointed?" Birk said.

"Well, who wouldn't love to know what that language sounded like? But, more than that, I'm mystified. Who killed Dr. Pace, and why? Would it be as simple as he lied—which can be a motive for murder, I suppose. But unless someone gave him money, the lies seem harmless enough, able to be uncovered with a little digging deep by informed people. Maybe he convinced himself so much that he was delusional, but still . . ."

Birk's eyebrows lifted. "Well, based on what Edwin has told me about Dr. Pace, I sense he was desperate for money. Maybe a lot of money. I'm sure the police are digging deep to see if anyone gave him any."

I nodded but didn't share Theo's information about how Dr. Pace's account was being drained of money, not filled. Maybe he simply needed more. "I agree."

"But why did he need money? Your and the police's answer to everyone's question is there, I suppose," Birk said.

I nodded again.

"All right then." Birk sighed. "It's lovely to see the both of you, but that's all I've got. I'm happy to show you around the grounds if you're interested."

Birk's information had been good, but it certainly knocked out any hope that Dr. Pace might have had something amazing. Though I hadn't really believed it before, I'd had a few moments of imaginary dicovery—even with the soundtrack of crescendoing music in the background. Now I felt the weight of some disappointment. Nevertheless, I smiled.

"Love to, Birk. Thank you," I said.

Edwin agreed and we followed Birk outside.

CHAPTER TWENTY-TWO

After the interesting, but brief, tour that was rudely interrupted by a downpour, Edwin dropped me off at the bookshop.

Hamlet was excited to see me arrive and asked if I wanted to go with him—he was going to talk to Ani. Rosie didn't even give us the chance to ask if she was okay manning the store alone. She scooted us out of there, telling us to return with answers if there were any to find.

We left her and Hector in the quiet bookshop. I thought we were going to make our way to Ryory's or Ani's flat, but that wasn't the plan.

"We're going to a concert," Hamlet announced as we boarded a bus.

"Right now?" I asked.

"Aye."

The bus route took us directly to Dalkeith Road.

The Hidden Door Festival, of which today was the last day, was mainly being held in empty buildings. My plans for attending any additional events had been derailed by the initial invitation to Ry's studio and everything that happened after that.

At one time an expanse of business offices, the location for this event was made of modern hexagonal-shaped structures tucked together, with lots of windows.

"Ani is here to see a friend's band," Hamlet told me as we walked through the doorway of the first building. He gave me a sly smile. "Willa's."

"Oh, this could be interesting," I said. "How do you know Ani will be here?"

"She didn't answer a text last night but let me know this morning that I could meet her here. I didn't even argue and said I would see her soon. I didn't tell her you were coming along."

"Should I hang back? I don't want to do anything to interfere with one of your friendships."

Hamlet shook his head. "No, of course not. Come on."

I nodded. "Good, but just give me some sort of signal if I should walk away."

Hamlet frowned but didn't further respond.

The hexagon shapes were joined together, but we traveled through mazes of temporary walls set up between artistic displays. As we made our way through the first section, my eyes lingered on clay pots, watercolors, even some bottle cap sculptures. I wished for more time to look at everything, but Hamlet set the pace, and I kept up with him.

The second section held writers sitting behind tables upon which their work was displayed. Again, I wished for some time to look at everything more closely, but we didn't slow down at all.

The space between the second and third sections was closed off, but not enough to completely mute the sounds and beats of music coming from the other side.

Hamlet opened the door to the main entrance of the third section, and we were met with the full noise, a song that sounded pop to me, maybe eighties.

This section was the same size as the others, but only half of it was in use, tall dividers cutting off space on either side of the stage. I couldn't count, but it seemed that there were a couple thousand in the audience, all of them standing and dancing, singing along.

"Ani's here somewhere," Hamlet said to me, raising his voice.

"I don't see Willa." I nodded toward the stage.

Hamlet shrugged. "Maybe that's not her group. There's more than one playing today. Come on. Let's find Ani."

Again, I followed Hamlet, who checked his phone as he wove us through the crowd. "I think she's . . . there she is."

I followed his glance to a spot to the right side of the stage. Ani was moving and listening to the music. She seemed to be by herself.

When she noticed Hamlet, her eyes lit up and she pulled him into a loving hug. Her hair was pulled up into a ponytail and her bangs were swept back from her face. Her happiness upon seeing Hamlet made her seem like an entirely different person. She had more color than she had the last time I'd seen her too. She was healing well and seemed no worse for whatever time she'd spent either in the hospital or with the police.

She was clearly surprised to see me but still smiled my way. "Delaney."

"Hi, Ani," I raised my voice along with hers.

She nodded toward the stage. "Aren't they wonderful?"

"They are." I didn't recognize the music, but it sounded like lots of other tunes that I'd listened to. I wondered about Willa, but I didn't know what I was supposed to know, what was acceptable to ask about, and what I should keep a secret. I told myself to be patient as I sent lifted eyebrows to Hamlet.

"Ani." He put his hand lightly on her arm. "Are you all right? How did it go with the police?"

"Fine." She waved away the concern.

"How long were you questioned?" he asked.

"They kept me there for hours. It was scary, but it's all fine."

"Ani, I have a weird question for you," I said.

"Aye?"

"Did Dr. Pace give you a 3D printer?"

She stopped swaying with the music. "Why are you asking?"

"Long story."

Ani frowned but then answered. "Huh. He did. I thought that was why the police wanted to talk to me. He sent me one a while ago, as a bribe to talk to Ry." She frowned. "I never even opened it. At the time, I didn't give it much thought, but as time went on, I began to feel guilty about keeping it and about not telling Ry about it. I was going to, but the police came and got me right then. The timing was weird."

"Did he call you a bunch of times recently?"

Ani's eyebrows furrowed. "The police asked me the same question, but I told them that I hadn't spoken to Dr. Pace for a week or so. They looked at my phone. I handed it right over. Someone did call me a bunch, but I didn't have any sort of caller ID for them. I didn't know who it was, so I didn't answer."

"It wasn't a number that Dr. Pace used?"

"Not to my knowledge. If he'd called me, I might have answered, but I might not have. No, I didn't know who was attached to the number."

I nodded, registering to myself that if Dr. Pace did use the phone, it was to keep his identity a secret, which was the sole purpose of a burner phone.

I thought of another question. "Did you get an Oculudentavis tattoo?"

Ani's frown deepened. "How did you know that? How do you know—"

"I met Willa. She told me."

"Okay? Sure, I did, but I had it removed." She pulled up her sleeve to expose the back of her arm, where it appeared some laser removal had been done.

"Why did you have it removed?"

"I had it done based on something that Dr. Pace told me a while ago, back when he was first trying to get ahold of Ry. I thought it was cool."

Hamlet and I looked at her with questions in our eyes.

"When he first contacted Ry, he talked about not only having something from the Picts but also a partial skeletal specimen of the world's smallest discovered dinosaur. He sent me a picture of what it looked like. It was like a fierce hummingbird, with teeth. I loved the picture from the moment I saw it. I had Willa do the tat back then."

"And you had it removed when you realized that it wasn't true, or that it didn't look like a hummingbird but more a lizard?" I said.

"That's right. Delaney, really, how do you know so much?"

"I just . . ."

"You know, I didn't kill Dr. Pace, but he wasn't a good man either. I feel terrible, but that's because I'm the one who let Dr. Pace into Ry's life. I thought those bones would be so cool, that stone. Ry is obsessed with the Picts, of course, but since I'd started working for him he's been interested in many things. Anyway, Dr. Pace was a fake, a phony. I feel terrible for my part in that."

"So?" Hamlet interjected.

"Did Ry give Dr. Pace money for anything?"

She shook her head. "I don't think so, but I do think Ry was disappointed when the truth about Dr. Pace started to become clear. I was hired in part to watch for frauds, but I failed."

"You didn't fail. Things happen," Hamlet said.

"When did you start to realize that Dr. Pace was a fraud?" I asked.

"There is a little information about that on the internet, but not much. We didn't find it until a friend of Ry's told us what it truly was."

"Who's the friend?" I asked.

"She owns a bookshop. It's called Turn."

"Mary Katherine?" Hamlet and I said together.

"Aye."

"When did she tell you?" I said.

"About a month ago."

Mary Katherine had behaved as if it was news to her when I'd mentioned it two days ago. Maybe she forgot she knew? I didn't think that was correct, though. Her strange behavior came to mind. What was going on?

"When Tom and I first came to Ry's place, Dr. Pace was

leaving. I thought I overheard some raised voices, but it seemed like it had been a friendly visit."

"Well, Ry is polite to everyone. If it had been up to me, I would have told Dr. Pace to leave Ry alone, but . . . well, the possibility of that stone. It was too much, even if its existence did seem highly unlikely, at least to me. Dr. Pace was good at stringing people along. Ry thought that he was going to get to see the stone in person. He just kept hoping."

The act that had been on the stage finished to rousing applause, forcing our conversation to come to an end. When Willa and her group walked on, we didn't resume talking. Ani cheered and Willa smiled in her direction. She didn't seem to know Hamlet, but she sent me raised eyebrows as if to ask what I was doing there.

I just smiled and shrugged.

I'd thought Willa's voice might sound like Stevie Nicks, and I had been correct. Though the group didn't perform any Fleetwood Mac tunes, the music they did play was fun and folksy.

We listened and enjoyed the music for a short time, but I had so much on my mind that I couldn't appreciate the concert as much as I might have on another day. There were no other opportunities to ask Ani more questions, but I did think it was good to see her having a fun time.

We left a few songs into Willa and her group's set, saying we had to get back to work. I left Hamlet at the bookshop. I decided I needed a coffee with a friend, one of Tom's old girlfriends. I hoped Bridget was up for a visit.

CHAPTER TWENTY-THREE

"I'm starving," Bridget said to the server. "I'll have the biggest burger you have. Fries too."

We were at a restaurant known for its famous TV chef. The menu was distinctly American and the place to go if you wanted a good cheeseburger.

I wasn't quite as hungry, but I couldn't resist. "I'll have the same."

Once the server was gone, Bridget gave me a long look. "What do you need me to do?"

I smiled. "Believe it or not, I don't have a favor to ask. Well, nothing specific. I just wanted to talk about Ryory Bennigan and Ani."

"Oh." She took a drink of her water. "Well, I'm not going to gossip about a friend. I wouldn't do that to you. Ry's a friend, and I don't know Ani well enough to tell you much of anything."

"I know and I appreciate that, though I can't imagine anyone would find gossip about me interesting anyway. Okay, how about I tell you what I've been up to just to see what you think?"

"Sounds like a trick. You know I can't resist hearing what you've been up to."

"I don't think it's a trick, at least not consciously."

"All right. Go on."

"Well, most of what I've done has come from information I got from the university in Kansas where Dr. Pace worked as well as where I went to school, from Artair, and from a cellphone I found that might have been Dr. Pace's."

"I cannot deny that all of that is intriguing. I'm listening."

I started with the Zoom call with Theo, told her about finding the phone, adding how many times Ani's number had been called but that she had a different number for Dr. Pace. I shared how Ronny and Sara confirmed that Dr. Pace could have called them at the times listed, but that Mary Katherine couldn't be sure. I even told her about the stone that Ry had talked about and how Edwin and Birk debunked that one. Our food was delivered before I was finished.

"Wow, Delaney. That's a lot," Bridget said.

I nodded. "Right, and Ani was released. The phone could have belonged to the killer."

"Well, anybody, really. It was a burner, but I bet it was Dr. Pace's. Anyway, I talked to people attached to the other numbers on the log. Ronny didn't like Dr. Pace and Sara was disappointed in him. I'm only telling you that so you can see how lots of people might be angry at him. I don't think that either Ronny or Sara are suspects. I don't even know if the police have talked to them. There was one other number that Inspector Winters said hadn't been assigned for a couple years, but . . ."

"Give it to me. I have ways of searching."

"Oh. Okay." I'd memorized the number, so I sent her a quick text with it included.

Bridget confirmed she received it.

After Bridget took a bite and swooned for a moment, she said, "It's a big business, you know. Bones. Selling and stealing them."

"What about faking them?"

"I don't know, but your 3D printer idea is interesting. Let's think that through, though. Did Dr. Pace have one? Did he really give one to Ani? Where might he have used one?"

"There was no printer in the house. There are some around. I know about one at Art's restaurant. Do you know about that place?" I took a bite of the delicious burger. I didn't tell her about Edwin's and my spying.

Bridget grabbed a fry, chewed it, swallowed, and spoke. "I know about Art's, and I suppose there's more access to them than we might know. They're becoming almost commonplace."

"You don't think it would need to be . . . more sophisticated than the ones you can just buy for a home or a small shop?"

Bridget shrugged. "I have no idea. Pace was trying to sell a stone to Ry that would help people understand what the Pict language sounded like?"

"Yes."

"That's so farfetched but would probably need a big printer, maybe one at a university."

"I agree. What if it were real, though? It would be quite the discovery, and who in the world would want it more than Ryory Bennigan?"

Bridget nodded. "Ry is smart. He wouldn't have fallen for that."

"Okay, but what about Ani?"

"Is she smart? I have no idea. Wait, are you wondering if maybe Ani was in on something with Dr. Pace?"

I shrugged. "I'm wondering anything and everything."

Bridget's eyebrows lifted briefly. Had I been more focused on my food than her, I might have missed it, but there was something about the gesture that garnered my full attention. I set down the burger I'd picked up.

"What, Bridget? What is it?"

For an instant, Bridget appeared to regret her reactive eyebrows, but she nodded a moment later. "In fact, Ani didn't have food poisoning."

"What?"

Bridget shook her head. "I have a contact in the hospital. Ry called me after she was taken away in the ambulance, after you and Tom left. It took overnight, but my contact came through. And . . . oh boy, you can't tell anyone I told you this because people have a right to their privacy, but, Delaney, there was absolutely nothing wrong with Ani."

"I saw her. She was gray. She wasn't breathing right."

"I don't know what to tell you. They couldn't find anything wrong with her."

"According to your contact."

"Aye. I suppose I could be getting false information, but I don't think so."

"Does Ry know?"

"Of course. I told him right away."

"What's he going to do about it?"

"He didn't share that with me."

"Why would she do that?"

"Good question."

"Huh."

"Exactly."

Though I was now a lot more curious about Ani potentially faking an illness, I knew I had to ask Bridget the question I'd really wanted to ask while we were in the question/answer groove.

"Bridget?"

"Yeah?" she said around a mouthful of food.

"Are you related to Ry?"

Her eyebrows lifted again. This time I made sure to watch. She knew she'd been caught, whatever that might mean.

She swallowed. "Only distantly."

I nodded. "McBride Shipping, is that . . . both of you?"

Bridget sighed. "Aye, Delaney, but more Ry than me."

"Is it supposed to be a secret?"

"Not a secret really, but . . . well, my father is Ry's third cousin or some such thing. McBride Shipping was quite successful for a long time. When my father married my mother against his parents' wishes, he was disowned. My father sued McBride Shipping about ten years ago. In fact, Ry wanted my father to get his fair share. He's the one who actually suggested that my father sue. That's how we became friends."

"Did your father get his fair share?"

"He got some."

So, that was a no, but I didn't confirm. I could see the pain on Bridget's face. I didn't know what to say.

Bridget continued, "We all had to sign something promising not to talk about the results of the case. I can't tell you more, but though Ry had been distant family we didn't know, he's been a friend since then."

I nodded. I didn't really want more information about that anyway. I was sure after all I'd told Bridget that I'd learned and all that she'd probably uncovered on her own, my next question wasn't going to come as a big surprise.

"Bridget, do you think Ry has run into financial difficulties?"

Bridget smiled knowingly. "I've wondered the same thing, but I don't know, Delaney. The police probably know, but no one there is talking to me about that."

"Me either."

"I can't bring myself to ask Ry."

That was different. I'd never known Bridget to be shy about asking anyone anything.

"Hmm."

"Aye. Hmm."

If she didn't know about Ry's financial situation, I didn't know who else I could ask other than Ry, and I didn't see myself doing that.

Another fry later, Bridget said, "The police know the poison that killed Dr. Pace."

"They do?"

Bridget nodded. "They do, but no one's telling me. You?"

"No one's said a thing to me. Inspector Winters probably wouldn't give me quite that much information. I think he shares enough with me to keep him out of his hair."

Bridget laughed. "You're probably right."

We both finished every bite of the food on our plates. I was full to the brim, but Bridget considered ordering dessert. She didn't, deciding she should get back to work.

We gave each other hugs as we each went our separate ways. She hadn't proffered one dig at Tom the whole time.

As I made my way back toward the bookshop, my phone pinged with a text. It was from Tom.

Want to see a play?

I responded: I would love to see a play, but I can't imagine you do.

LOL. This one's different. Pick me up at six at the pub?

I'll be there.

"Hmm," I said to myself.

Tom didn't enjoy stage productions. Tom didn't like TV or movies. He liked books or newspapers, as long as he didn't have to read anything on a screen. I was intrigued by his offer and couldn't wait to see what he had up his sleeve.

CHAPTER TWENTY-FOUR

From the pub and in the fair-weathered darkness, we made our way up Victoria Street, climbed the secret stairway, and headed toward the castle. I glanced at Willa's door. I'd told Tom about Hamlet and Ani's and my visit to the festival and how great Willa's band was.

"We can knock on Willa's door on the way back if you want to. I don't want to be late to the . . . show," Tom said as we passed by.

I nodded. "I can't think of anything to ask her that won't just make everything more confusing. However, I'm very excited to see this play. This is very unlike you."

Tom smiled. "Well, it's not a traditional production, at least when it comes to stages."

"Oh?"

He laughed. "You'll see."

I spotted a crowd not far ahead. It wasn't an unusual sight—there were always things to see on the streets of Edinburgh, many of them street performers—but this gathering seemed a bit larger than some.

"Oh," I said knowingly. "A street show?"

"Aye."

"Well, I didn't even think you liked those, so I'm still intrigued."

"One of my customers spoke about it. It seemed like it was meant to be. You'll see."

"My level of intrigue only grows."

Tom lifted an eyebrow as he smiled. It was a good look on him.

Though the crowd was fairly thick, we found a path to make our way a little closer to the performance while not blocking anyone else's view.

A man sat on a chair, the skin of his torso fully exposed to the elements. It was nice enough outside that it didn't appear he was being tortured. In fact, he seemed comfortable.

The man cut quite a figure. Probably over six feet tall, his shoulders were wide and thickly muscled. He had a washboard stomach and legs with thighs that stretched the jeans over them. He was topped off with a head full of the curliest red hair I'd ever seen. If it was a perm, it was well done. I couldn't help but compare my naturally frizzy to his beautiful and tight (not frizzy at all) curls. He might have been in his early forties, but he was in such great shape it was hard to tell for sure.

Another man stood next to the seated one, though his back was to the audience. When he turned to face us, he held an item that I'd only recently become familiar with—a tattoo machine, or as most people called it, a tattoo gun.

I thought I'd seen him in the pub. I leaned closer to Tom. "Is that the customer?"

"Aye. The tatooist's name is Devan."

"Welcome, ladies and gentlemen," he said as he almost cradled the machine. "Thank you for coming tonight. Those of you who are new to my shows, a quick rundown. I will create a tattoo as I tell a story. Some call it performance art, some call it street art—for me, it's simply the job that I do."

A smattering of applause spread through the crowd.

I looked around, noting a few smiles of familiarity. This guy had a following. I was completely fascinated.

He continued, "As I work, a video of what I'm doing will display there." He pointed at a screen behind him—it was propped up a smidge higher than his head. His phone was attached to a mechanical extending arm, its camera aimed at the man's human arm.

"I'm Devan Loyola, and my associate tonight is Mr. Emmet Plant, from Glasgow."

Emmet smiled and waved. "I don't think I quite knew what I was getting into."

A chuckle ran through the crowd.

"I just wanted a tattoo and heard that Devan was the man to see."

"Aye," Devan agreed. "However, the public setting of tonight's artwork was approved by Mr. Plant."

Emmet nodded and shrugged at the same time. The crowd was intrigued.

"My specialty is the Picts," Devan said.

"Ah," I said as Tom smiled at me.

"I thought you might be intrigued. I just learned today that that's what Devan does. It was just by chance that I overheard him talking to Rodger. Apparently, Devan couldn't get a spot with the Hidden Door Festival this year. He wasn't happy about the rejection and was complaining. I overheard something about tattoos and Picts, and so I talked to Rodger later. Rodger says Devan's done quite well with his tattoo business. This is the way he drums up extra customers."

"It's quite a display. Do you think he's Ry's artist?"

"I don't know. Rodger didn't either. I thought we might ask afterwards."

I didn't know how Devan's setup could possibly be portable, but it appeared that a generator was being used for the gun, and though it was dark outside, a big spotlight had been aimed at Emmet's arm, where Devan began his work.

He started by talking about the Picts.

I wondered if all Scottish tattoo artists might be Pict experts. A familiarity washed through me as I watched a bird, done in bright blue ink, be created on Emmet's arm. Emmet wasn't shy, and it was clear to everyone that the tattoo came with pain, but he could take it.

Devan told a spotty history of the Pictish people who'd been a part of Scotland a long time ago. The brief tale was also familiar to me by now, but maybe not to the rest of the audience.

"Their impact is indelible," he said before he paused to be silent a moment, his gun turning an inked curve.

He then took a moment to make sure that Emmet was okay. Emmet nodded that he was.

Devan turned toward the audience. "I don't think we can quantify their impact on us. What we know of their colorful existence, as well as the stones they left behind, only makes what we don't know about them even more intriguing. We yearn to understand what we don't know, don't we?"

"Do you know Ryory Bennigan?" someone from the group of onlookers called out.

"I do." He turned his attention back to Emmet's arm.

"Have you done any of his tattoos?"

"Mr. Bennigan's tattooist is a secret. I'm only going to add to the secrecy by not answering."

Tom and I looked at each other. It was the Edinburgh tattooist conspiracy at work again. Our question had been answered, but the whole "show" was too interesting.

"If you're the expert, then you must be."

Tom and I shared another look before I turned to inspect the crowd for who might be causing the ripple of discomfort. I couldn't spot the culprit. The voice was female and rolled with a slight Scottish brogue.

Devan chuckled and turned to face the crowd again. "Well, I did say I was an expert, but I didn't say I was the best expert," he said, a playful tone to his answer.

"Uh," Emmet said, though it seemed he was somehow only playing along.

"Devan's the best," another voice called.

"Well, ta, friend," Devan said with a small bow.

"Why is Ryory Bennigan's artist such a secret?" I asked.

People in the crowd turned to look at me.

"See me after, lass."

I nodded but didn't say anything else.

I sent Tom an apologetic frown. Gently, he put his arm around me in a show of support. I appreciated it.

Devan was very good at what he did, and the bird was done in short order. I couldn't understand how anyone could create such precise lines and curves—no matter what tool they were using—freehand.

"What do you think?" he asked Emmet.

"It's ridiculously good, mate," Emmet said as he inspected the screen as well as a mirror that Devan held up for him.

"Glad you like it."

I didn't have any idea how to judge good and bad tattoos, but I knew preciseness and artistic ability. Devan had both in aces. Not only that, I felt like I was recognizing a style. Everyone had a style, a voice, even if they weren't aware of it themselves.

I leaned toward Tom. "That looks like the same style, doesn't it?"

"It does."

As the event finished up, a short line formed to a clipboard, where people could sign up to be put on a list Devan would call from to schedule other appointments, most of them in his parlor, he assured.

Once the rest of the crowd dispersed enough, Tom and I approached the artist.

"Ah, Tom, lad, good to see you." Devan extended a hand.

"That was wonderful," Tom said.

"Ta."

"This is my wife, Delaney."

"Lass, I've seen you in the pub," Devan said as we shook hands.

"It's good to meet you. You are very talented."

He bowed his head briefly. "Ta." He lifted his head and looked at me. "You want to know why Ry's artist is a secret?"

"I do, though I don't think I should have yelled out the question. Sorry. I couldn't help myself."

"It's fine. These events lend themselves to those sorts of

things." He hesitated. "Have you ever thought of getting a tattoo?"

Tom and I nodded, though I did so more eagerly.

"We're working up the courage," Tom said.

"Well, when you do, come find me," Devan said. "I'll give you a discount if only for the fact that Tom runs one of the best and friendliest pubs in town." He looked around. The crowd had dispersed, and I knew it was only because he liked Tom that he continued. "I know Ry Bennigan well, but here's why his artist is a secret."

He had us both on the line. I might have even been holding my breath.

"Aye?" Tom said when Devan didn't continue immediately.

"The answer is obvious. That's why people can't figure it out."

"What?" I asked.

Devan shrugged. "It's obvious. Think about it. I won't give you the answer, but you'll get it eventually."

"There's an NDA, isn't there?" I asked.

"Not that I'm aware of."

I thought about Ry's gifting the painting to a couple he met on the street. The obvious answer was something about generosity, I was sure, but I still didn't see it. The Pictish tattoos weren't all that difficult. If tattooing was your trade, you could most likely do something Pictish.

"Ry is a lovely man," Devan said.

Tom and I shared a smile.

"Thanks, Devan," Tom said.

"You're welcome. Come see me when you're ready for some ink."

We offered to help Devan load up his equipment, but he

sent us on our way, telling us that he'd done it so often that he couldn't imagine any other routine.

As we were making our way back down the Royal Mile, and I was digesting the news that only furthered Ry's seeming loveliness, I thought I saw something near the alcove in front of the secret stairway. As the turn that would take us to the stairway came more into sight, I spotted the edge of a wheelchair heading in that direction. Someone was accompanying the person in the chair, but it all happened so quickly that I couldn't be positive who I saw, though I had my suspicions.

"Tom, is there an elevator near the stairway?"

"No, I don't think so. Why?"

"Follow me."

I stepped up my speed and we were around and into the alcove only seconds later. There was no one in sight. My eyes went to Willa's door—there was no way to tell if anyone had gone inside it. There were three other unmarked doors.

I tried Willa's door, but it was locked. I knocked but no one answered. Without hesitation, I tried the other three doors, but they were also locked.

"What's going on, lass?" Tom asked.

"I'm pretty sure I saw Mary Katherine come around this corner."

"The bookshop owner?"

"Yes."

"Okay. So?"

"There was something about the person she was with."

"Familiar?"

I nodded again. "It's vague, but there was something . . . familiar, and something told me to hurry and catch up to them."

"Why did you ask about an elevator?"

"Mary Katherine is in a wheelchair."

"I saw a lass at Devan's presentation in a chair. Dark curly hair."

"That could have been her."

Tom's eyebrows came together as he looked around. "If they came this way, they must have gone through one of the doors."

"I agree."

Tom tried Willa's door too and then knocked on the others. None of them opened.

"What do you want to do?" he asked. "Want to hang around here and see if they come out? We can find a perch somewhere?"

I thought for a long moment. "Let's go home, Tom. I can't help but wonder if I'm overthinking everything. I might just need a break. Am I seeing things?"

"No, lass, but a break doesn't sound like a bad idea. Home it is."

CHAPTER TWENTY-FIVE

I slept so fitfully that I wasn't sure there was enough coffee to get me through the day.

"More?" Tom held up the carafe.

I nodded, but before he could pour, my phone buzzed on the kitchen table. A call was coming in, which though infrequent, was Edwin's preferred way to communicate. Hurriedly, I set my mug on the table and grabbed the phone, expecting it to be my boss.

But it wasn't. "It's Inspector Winters." I couldn't hit answer fast enough.

"Hello," I said.

"Good morning, Delaney."

I paused. "Uh, good morning to you too."

"We've found something I thought you might like to see."

Without even knowing what it was, I said, "Absolutely. Where should I go?"

"I'll ping you the address. Can you leave now?"

"Yes." I nodded and looked at Tom, who nodded as well even though he had no idea what was being said on the phone.

"See you in about fifteen." Inspector Winters disconnected the call.

His text came through a moment later. I showed it to Tom.

"That's not far. Are we going there?"

"Do you have time?"

"Aye. I'll ring Rodger on the way, let him know I'll be late. What are we getting ourselves into?"

"I have absolutely no idea."

"All right then. Let's go."

About fifteen minutes later, we were pulling into the parking lot of the tallest building I'd seen in Edinburgh.

"Jenners Depository?" I said. "What is that?"

Tom nodded and smiled knowingly. "Well, it used to be a place for horses, but it was transformed a while ago into a self-storage facility."

"Even the self-storage in Edinburgh is in a cool building."

It was simple architecture, made with red brick and white-paned windows, but there was nothing boring about it, nothing institutional, like how I might describe the facilities in the States.

"I don't disagree."

The lot held one white-paneled truck and three police cars as well as a forensic van.

"I wonder what they found," I said.

"I doubt it's anything gruesome," Tom said. "We wouldn't be invited."

"True."

Tom parked away from the official vehicles, and we made our way inside. We were greeted by a young, visibly upset woman.

"We're closed," she said, her words clipped. "Police business."

"Thanks," I said. "I think we're expected, though. Delaney Nichols."

"Let me check."

She made a move to get around the desk she'd been standing behind, but an elevator at the end of the hallway dinged and Inspector Winters emerged.

"Delaney, Tom, this way," he signaled.

The receptionist returned to her spot as Tom and I hurried to join the inspector.

Once the elevator was on its way up, he said, "It was the mystery phone number. Since it didn't lead anywhere, we figured it was a misdial. We had someone going through the number, moving things around, looking things up—by hand even. It was tedious, but our man Blake came up with this number. He rang it and found that Dr. Pace had rented a space. Once we had what we think is the right number, it seemed easy."

"What seemed easy? Did you solve his murder?" I asked.

"No, not that, but something in this space might lead us in the right direction. There's a lot of stuff."

"I can't wait to see," I said.

"Well, I can't let you inside the spot, but I wanted you to have a chance to see it at least from the hallway. If you hadn't gathered the phone, which to be honest with you, we should have found, we might not have ever discovered this place."

Tom sent me a smile. He'd spent a considerable amount of time worrying about me, but I'd promised him I would be safer than I'd been before. Now, his cobalt-blue eyes shined with something I thought might be pride. Whatever it was, it certainly gave me plenty of warm fuzzy feelings.

"I'm glad it helped," I said.

The elevator went all the way up to the top floor. When the door opened, we made our way to the right.

Large spotlights had been set up, aimed down the hall and at two people in white crime-scene coveralls who were looking at the items placed on a canvas on the floor.

Inspector Winters walked in front of us. He held his hand in our direction. "A moment."

We waited away from the action as he approached one of the forensic investigators. Shortly after, he signaled for us to join him again.

He pointed down toward the outer edge of the spotlight's reach. "Stand here. The lights are bright. You'll be able to see a lot. Though I invited you here because I thought you'd want to see what was in here, I also want you to let me know if anything you see pings with regards to something else you might have learned."

I nodded. Tom stood a little behind me as we both peered inside.

The space was probably ten feet by fifteen, deeper than it was wide. My eyes had looked over the items on the canvas. I wasn't surprised to see bones, or at least things that looked like bones. Considering everything, of course, they might not be real.

"That's a big printer," Tom said.

The 3D printer took up almost the entire back wall, except for a slot next to it that held a generator.

"Is it legal to have a generator in here?" I asked.

"I think it's against the rules of the facility," Inspector Winters said. "But I doubt much is checked. We're looking into it."

Tall shelves lined the side wall and were packed with bones and books. The bones might have been an odd sight to many, but they weren't strange to me. Even the Wichita museum where I used to work had a basement room full of bones.

"Are they real?" I asked Inspector Winters.

"Don't know yet. We will figure it out."

I might be able to tell by touching them, but I wasn't going to offer. The police had experts enough. I zoned in on some of the books, most of them seemingly dinosaur books. I couldn't see any about the Picts, but that didn't mean there weren't any.

Bones and books. And a 3D printer with a generator.

"This is where he worked, I guess," I said.

"Aye. We hope we find something that tells us more, but this must be it."

I looked over all the bones again. Some were big, some small, but I didn't have any idea to what creature any of them belonged.

"Take your time. Please look the best you can." Inspector Winters walked away as I began another once-over, slower this time.

Bones and books, bones and books, and . . . what was that?

I called him back over. "What is that on the bottom shelf over there, under the giant bone?"

Stepping carefully and then checking with an investigator inside, Inspector Winters asked if he could reach for the black item with the red stripe that had been tucked under the bones. The other investigator took a couple pictures of the area and then handed Winters some gloves. He put them on and then reached for the item.

He brought it toward Tom and me as he unfolded the

vinyl. "It's a delivery bag, or carrier. I'm not sure what you call them."

He held it up so we might look at it. It was a bag, maybe fifteen inches high, eight wide, and six deep. The name of the food-delivery company was emblazoned on its front.

"I've seen that before," I said. "I've seen it a few times, in fact."

"Okay," Inspector Winters said.

"Do you know what poison killed Dr. Pace yet?"

"We do." Inspector Winters hesitated. "We aren't making it public and it's strange . . ."

I thought back to the dinner at Veronica's. "Was it by chance tetrodotoxin?"

Inspector Winters furrowed his eyebrows at me. "How did you know?"

"We heard about the seafood issue, the restaurant that was shut down because of the poison . . . anyway, I was guessing maybe because of food delivery." I nodded at the delivery bag. "Maybe the poison was in a food delivery that Dr. Pace ordered." I paused. "He had another phone, right?"

"He did."

"Did he order food from that phone?"

Inspector Winters's eyes lit with what I thought might be a little awe. "We are trying to figure that out, but we don't have forensic access to his American bank accounts yet. We're working on it."

"But . . ." I looked around. "The phone led you here."

"The number on the burner phone did." Inspector Winters smiled.

"Maybe someone was working with Dr. Pace. They used the phone."

"Or something like that. We really don't know yet, but I do believe you're caught up to where we are." He looked at the delivery bag. "Although, we hadn't gotten this far yet."

"Someone must have delivered food to his back door. That someone might have worked with him. They used a burner phone and called numbers that Dr. Pace might have called."

"It's possible."

I looked at Tom, who'd been watching and listening patiently. "G'on, love."

"I keep running into a food delivery guy. His name is Layton."

"You think he's involved?"

"I have no idea." Another thing came to me. "Layton delivered food to Ry's studio. That's the first place I saw him."

"Lass, how did you . . . never mind." Inspector Winters sighed. "According to Ani, she wasn't faking anything. She didn't feel well."

"But they couldn't find anything wrong with her, right?"

"I'm not at liberty to confirm that."

I nodded, not wanting to tell him what Bridget had already shared with me. "Okay, so maybe Layton is somehow involved. Maybe not, but it looks like there's something with food delivery going on."

Inspector Winters nodded. "I don't think you're wrong, lass. Good work. Thank you."

"You're welcome." I was on an adrenaline high; the sense of discovery or understanding was buzzing through me.

"Take your time. Keep looking."

I nodded.

Inspector Winters turned and communicated with other investigators. I watched as one tech picked up a bone. "This isn't real," he said.

Tom and I were there for only a few more minutes but we didn't have anything else to add. I tried to calm my swirling mind—discoveries mixed with more questions.

A killer hadn't been caught yet. There was so much more to do.

CHAPTER TWENTY-SIX

"The only real valuable thing is intuition," a voice spoke in my mind.

"Hello again, Mr. Einstein," I said quietly as Tom steered the car toward his Grassmarket parking spot.

"What's that?" Tom said.

"Nothing." I laughed. "Just working through things in my head."

I loved my bookish voices, but the redundancy of listening to my intuition telling me to listen to my intuition was suddenly irritating and confusing.

Tom parked the car, and we parted ways with a quick kiss. He watched me walk into the bookshop, and I waved before he turned and made his way up to the pub.

As I went through the door and Hector trotted to meet me, I spotted Rosie on the shop's phone. She frowned as she listened intently.

"What's going on?" I whispered to Hector as I lifted him to my cheek.

He cuddled close as I made my way closer to Rosie.

"Aye, but Edwin isnae in this morning. I'm happy to give him a message if . . . oh, aye, one moment, let me see if she's in."

Rosie pulled the handset away and covered it so the caller wouldn't hear.

"It's Mary Katherine from the bookshop. She's upset about something, but I'm having a hard time understanding why. She wanted to talk to Edwin. Now she's asking for you. Are you in?"

I nodded eagerly, hoping I could ask her about the night before and maybe seeing her, and reached for the handset. "Mary Katherine?"

"Delaney, do you know where Edwin is? Can you reach him?" Her voice was tight with anxiety.

"I'm happy to try to find him, but can Rosie and I help you? What's going on?"

Mary Katherine didn't speak for a long moment. Finally, she sighed heavily. "No, I don't think so. I would like to talk to Edwin. It's about an employee issue."

"Oh, I see."

I had no idea what the employment laws were in Scotland. I knew laws in the States were different depending on which state was being discussed. Rosie might know, but Edwin would most definitely be able to guide her.

I continued, "I'll track him down right away. Will that help?"

"Aye, but I do need his help immediately. He's . . . in the back."

"Who? Are you okay?"

"I am. But, Delaney, I have an issue and I need to deal with it. As soon as possible."

"Okay, should we call the police?"

Mary Katherine was silent long enough that I knew she was

pondering the necessity, which was enough for me to think she probably did need the authorities.

"Maybe," she finally said, unconfidently.

"Are you at the bookshop?" I asked. "I'll just ask Edwin to go there."

"I am. I don't know, though . . . just have him ring me if you wouldn't mind."

"Not a bit." I hesitated. "Should we stay on the line? Rosie and I can use our cellphones to try to reach Edwin."

Rosie mouthed that she had already tried.

"No, that's okay. Really, a phone call might be enough, but I wouldn't mind if Edwin could stop by. Maybe. I'm worried I'm overreacting."

"Count on it," I said.

I let her disconnect the call, which she did without saying goodbye.

"I'll have to leave him another message," Rosie said to me. "He's not answering, and I don't know what he's up to this morning."

I nodded and tried to think of another way to reach Edwin, but there wasn't one.

Rosie left a message for him, putting enough urgency into her tone that I knew he'd pay attention. Once she finished the message, she also texted him with a 999. If he was anywhere near his phone, he would respond quickly.

Once that was done, I asked her, "What did Mary Katherine say to you?"

"Probably the same thing she said to you, that she had an employee issue and wanted to talk to Edwin."

"Did she sound scared to you?"

Rosie nodded. "Aye, a wee bit."

"I'm going to her shop. Edwin will get the message and be there soon, but I'm worried about her."

"Should I call Inspector Winters too, or are we over-reacting?"

"Maybe we are, but call him. He's working on something, but this seems urgent. Just give him the details and he can determine what the police might need to do." I paused. "She would have called the police if she thought she was in trouble, wouldn't she?"

Rosie nodded. "Probably. Maybe we really are overreacting."

I'd been holding Hector the whole time. I set him on the ground at Rosie's feet. "I don't care if we are. I'd rather over-react than under. I'll head over there."

"By yourself?"

I thought about Tom, whose morning I had already inter-rupted. He would go with me, but I knew he had things to do. He needed to help Rodger, who'd come in early to help.

"I won't even go inside the bookshop if I think there's a problem. But I can't just wait here."

"All right. I'll call the inspector." Rosie had already started to dial.

Turn wasn't far from The Cracked Spine, but being in a hurry automatically slowed everything down. I felt like I was slogging through wet concrete as I made my way.

Once in front of the windows, I first looked around for Edwin's car, but it wasn't there. I hoped he got the message quickly. I hoped the police also took this seriously and showed up, even if it might end up being a waste of a call.

I pulled on the door, but it was locked. I knocked and put

my face to the window. I couldn't see anything on the level up the ramp, but I could tell the lights were on.

"Mary Katherine," I called and knocked.

There was no answer, and I didn't know what to do. Finally, I grabbed my cellphone and dialed her number. It rang four times before it picked up.

"Mary Katherine? It's Delaney. I'm right outside the front door of your bookshop. May I come in?"

But she didn't answer. Instead, I heard her voice as if she held the phone a distance away.

"I'm sorry," she said. "I didn't tell anyone. I wouldn't do that to you!"

"You told Willa!" a male voice yelled.

"I didn't, though. Think about it, I didn't tell her anything. She was just guessing. She doesn't know."

"You didn't deny it!"

I didn't need to hear more. I didn't end the call, though I held the phone away from my ear as I tried to figure out what to do. Mary Katherine needed help, and I was the closest help available. I hoped Edwin and Inspector Winters were on their way as I tried to figure out how to get inside.

I couldn't bust through the door. I *might* be able to break the glass, but it was thick, and I certainly couldn't do it with my bare hands.

I looked around for something I could throw, but there was nothing nearby.

My mind whirled as I glanced over the nearby pedestrians. I was looking for a big burly someone who could break the door down without much effort. There was no such person.

I needed another door.

I ran to the side of the bookshop and found a close, an alleyway. It was so narrow that I hadn't noticed it before. I could fit, but just barely.

My shoulders grazing the walls on each side of me, I hurried through and found my way to the back of the entire row of buildings. I was suddenly in the space in between, where back doors and garbage bins were located. The space was barely big enough for a garbage truck to make its way through.

I found the back door, but it was locked too. Now what?

I put the phone to my ear, but it seemed the call had been disconnected.

"Shoot!"

As I went to try to call her again, my phone buzzed exuberantly with texts. I had three.

One from Rosie said: Edwin is on the way.

One from Inspector Winter said: I've sent some officers. Do not go into that bookshop!!!

And then another one from Edwin: I'm on my way.

No matter what anyone said, I was certain that Dr. Pace's killer was inside with Mary Katherine. Nothing was going to stop me from trying to stop another murder.

I grabbed a nearby discarded and dirty pail and lifted it high. I brought it down hard onto the doorknob, which only bent it, making it worse than if it had just been locked.

I lifted it again and put everything I had into it. The metal knob flew off and clinked as it rolled over the alleyway.

I had to maneuver my finger into the mechanism, but I finally got the door open. I propelled myself inside, entering what appeared to be a small storage room, though I didn't see any books, just boxes. If there were books inside them, I didn't take the time to look.

I hurried to the door that led into the shop, sending up a silent prayer as I went. Not another locked one, please.

My prayer was answered, and I was able to pull it open easily. I entered the back of the shop. I could hear voices, but they were muffled by what I thought were about five bookshelves in between me and them.

I squelched the desire to yell out, tell Mary Katherine that help was on the way, but I probably wasn't as stealthy as I wanted as I hurried to where I hoped to find her—unharmed.

"Look, Layton," Mary Katherine said as I came upon the last set of shelves between us. "No one knows what you did."

"You do!"

"Only because you admitted it. I would never have put the pieces together with certainty. You are a valuable employee. You are a friend. I'm on your side. Always."

"You didn't even like the man."

"I didn't! I won't tell a soul, Layton."

"No, you won't!" Layton made a growling sound.

I peered around the shelves, my eyes first seeking out Mary Katherine. She was fine. She was in her chair, and the counter was in between her and Layton. He didn't have a weapon, but he was obviously angry and had an advantage simply because Mary Katherine was in a wheelchair. He was wound tight, his hands in fists, his face tight and ruddy.

Hadn't Mary Katherine told me that she was going to ask her employees about Dr. Pace calling? I hadn't given a second thought to who those employees might be.

It appeared that Layton—the delivery guy I kept seeing, the same one I'd just spoken with Inspector Winters about—worked here too. And, from what I was hearing, he'd killed Dr. Pace. The *who* was answered, but the *why*?

He started pacing a short line back and forth on the floor in front of the counter. He kept swiping his hand back through his hair. He was far enough away from Mary Katherine that I thought I could tackle him if he made a move in her direction. Until then, I decided it was wise to stay back, listen, and hope that Edwin and the police arrived soon.

As covertly as possible, I texted both Inspector Winters and Edwin again: back door.

"That man. If only I hadn't ever met him," Layton exclaimed.

"I know, and I understand."

"What do you understand?"

"You thought the two of you had a business transaction. He stopped . . . paying. You had a right to be angry."

Layton laughed. "I can't deny that's how I saw it, but bottom line, I was blackmailing him. You know that. It wasn't a business transaction, no matter how—"

"Okay. Okay. You work so hard, Layton. All the jobs you do. You deserved a break."

"I did! I do! I work all the time, but still can't afford anything. If he'd just kept paying me, I might have gotten . . . something. Do you know what he did, though? Do you have any idea?"

"I don't, honey."

"He went behind my back and tried to sell fake artifacts."

"Maybe he had bills too, and maybe he wanted to keep paying you."

"He didn't tell me about any of it. He and I could have made so much money, Mary Katherine. I suspected he was up to something on his own, and when I followed him to that artist's place and saw him in there, I knew it!"

"Aye, lad, he wasn't a good man."

"He made me so angry, and I knew the poison would make him sick. I didn't think it would kill him. He was going to have to bring me into his scam or pay me more! I can't believe he died!"

My gut—just my intuition, not a bookish voice—told me that Layton didn't want to hurt Mary Katherine. But given the tension in the air and Layton's building anger, I couldn't say for sure that something wouldn't happen anyway. Something everyone would regret. Myself included if I didn't at least try to stop it.

I stepped out from behind the bookshelves. "Layton?"

Layton and Mary Katherine looked at me with equal surprise.

"What are *you* doing here?" he bellowed.

"I was shopping in the back."

"No, you weren't," he said without missing a beat.

I realized he had been the one with Mary Katherine the night before, and from what I'd heard them say, they had visited Willa. Every time I'd seen him, he'd been wearing that jacket—black with a red stripe around the arm. While the matching bag that he carried food in typically stood out more than what he wore, the jacket was recognizable as well, now that I really looked.

"How did you get in here?" Layton demanded.

I held up my hands. "The back door. Look, I overheard what Mary Katherine was saying. It sounds like you didn't mean to kill Dr. Pace. That's good news. It really was an accident. Accidents are much less serious than murder."

He huffed a laugh. "I'm sure the police will believe that."

"Mary Katherine will talk to them. Layton, there's a way out of this. I don't really know what happened, but I do know some things about Dr. Pace. He wasn't a good guy." I swallowed because he probably was a decent enough man who just got caught up in something horrible and shortsighted.

Layton squinted at me. "You knew him?"

"He worked where I went to school."

"In Kansas?"

I smiled and nodded. "Small world, huh?"

"Yeah." His eyes went to the ground as he raked his hand through his hair again. "I just wanted to make him sick. That's all I wanted to do."

"I get it." Just to keep him talking, I continued, "Did you meet Dr. Pace here at the bookshop?"

Layton nodded. "Then I researched him. I found what he'd done in the States, the trouble he was in."

I'd searched Dr. Pace on the internet too but hadn't found any of what he'd done with the T-Rex bones. Theo had said it had been mostly swept under the rug, but Layton must have known how to dig deeper.

"We hit it off. We both liked dinosaurs, and I knew about the Picts. I told him all about Ryory Bennigan, but then he didn't let me in on that scam. I'm the one who told him all about Ryory!"

I'd heard a couple people mention that they'd told Dr. Pace about Ry. I wondered who'd been the first one. "I'm sorry." I looked at Mary Katherine, who still appeared to be scared, but not as much. I turned back to Layton. "What happened, Layton? It was just a bad mistake, right?"

For a long moment, I didn't think Layton would say anything, but then he did.

"I thought something was up. I called the numbers I saw on

his phone but couldn't figure out what was going on, so I had to follow him."

When he fell into angry thought, I said, "Right. So, see. Not on purpose."

He looked up. "Sure. Whatever."

"Really," I said, prompting him to continue.

"There's a camera on the front of the house, so I always went in through the back, but when he saw me at Bennigan's, I think he realized that I'd be there that night. He locked the back gate! I had to jump over it—even lost one of my phones."

I didn't mention that I'd been the one to find it, but I liked knowing whose it was. "Okay."

"When I pounded on the back door, he had no choice but to let me in. I'm not stupid. I knew he was up to something with Bennigan. He told me all about it, all proud-like. I told him we would do it together. All of it. I would help him sell fake bones, fake stones, whatever. We were partners!"

"That makes sense," I said. It didn't, of course, but appeasing him seemed the right way to go. "You must have needed the money."

"Of course I needed the money! Doesn't everyone? It's just so hard to do . . . anything."

I nodded.

Layton looked at me with a fiery hatred in his eyes. "Pace laughed at me, told me I was crazy to think we were partners, that he'd had enough of me, my blackmail. He didn't care anymore if I exposed him. He said he was just tired of all of it . . ."

"Layton?" I said, again to keep him talking.

"I gave him the sandwich, but I wasn't even sure he'd eat it, and then I didn't think it was enough to kill him. I just thought he'd get sick and be scared into letting me work with him. He took it and put it in the fridge. I didn't even think he'd eat it, but he must have at some point overnight."

"See, you didn't do it on purpose."

I hadn't heard anyone enter, but suddenly Edwin and an officer came through the back, the same route I had taken.

"Lad—" Edwin began.

"No!" Layton yelled before he took off for the ramp to go out the front of the store. The officer gave chase and Edwin and I hurried to Mary Katherine.

"Are you okay?" we both asked her.

"Aye, but he was so upset. I didn't know what might happen. I just . . . called The Cracked Spine. It was the first number that came to mind. I'm sorry, but . . . Layton was . . . oh, I'm so sorry."

"I'm glad you rang," Edwin said. "And I'm very glad you're okay."

A ruckus came from the front door, and I was pretty sure Layton was apprehended by other police coming in that way. Inspector Winters appeared from the ramp a moment later.

"We got him," he said.

Those were three very welcome words.

CHAPTER TWENTY-SEVEN

"In fact, Layton didn't know about Dr. Pace's storage facility," Inspector Winters said. "He'd tried to call the number based on seeing it on Dr. Pace's phone, but he hadn't written it down quite right with his quick look at it. During his confession, he said that the delivery bag had probably been his. He'd delivered a lot of meals to Dr. Pace, and it must have been left behind at some time. Dr. Pace might have taken a meal with him to his storage facility, using the bag to keep it fresh. Layton really did think they'd turned into . . . maybe not 'friends,' but work partners, even if the bribery couldn't be disguised as anything but."

It was the next day, early in the morning, but Edwin, Rosie, Hamlet, Hector, and I were at the bookshop when Inspector Winters showed up. Ry came in only a few seconds later, bringing a box of pastries. He'd come to apologize but we were all, including Ry, more interested in what Inspector Winters had to say than Ry's concern over disrupting our lives.

"Where did Layton get the poison?" I asked Inspector Winters.

"A sushi restaurant. Lots of the restaurant folks know him. No one seemed to notice the theft, which is scary, but food safety is another issue for another day."

"It was all about money?" I asked.

Inspector Winters frowned for a moment. "Yes and no. Layton wanted the money, but as strange as this sounds, I think it hurt his feelings more than anything when Dr. Pace said he wouldn't pay him any longer, and, of course, when he wasn't invited in on the fake bones scam, he felt very disrespected. It's sad, really. Layton doesn't have any family. Mary Katherine is as close as anyone, and she helped him through some earlier darker moments in his life."

"I'm sorry to hear that," I said.

Inspector Winters continued. "And, despite his behavior, I really don't think Dr. Pace was a terrible person either, just . . . searching for some sort of fame, perhaps. People who worked with him were fond of the man."

I nodded but didn't add that I'd heard the same.

"Sad all around," Rosie said.

"Aye."

Ry had been silent as the inspector had spoken, but he piped up as we all seemed to turn our attention his way. "Oh. It's a tragedy to be sure. I admit that I was close to giving Dr. Pace some money for his 'discovery,' but I doubt it would have ever gotten that far. I would have needed proof, and . . . well, he was likable."

"Ry," I said. "Did you give Ani a 3D-printed Oculudentavis?"

"Delaney. How in the world do you know about that?" Ry asked.

I shared a look with Edwin who would give up our secret spying mission. I looked back at Ry. "Long story. Did you, though?"

"I haven't yet, but I plan to. She was so disappointed when the creature turned out to be different than what she thought. She even had a tattoo of it removed, though most of the body was made-up, hummingbird-like. She felt so bad for allowing Dr. Pace into my life that I wanted to let her know that I have no ill feelings toward her or her job performance. I thought a model, done like the tattoo, to let her know I liked the idea of the creature too, might be helpful."

"That's thoughtful of you."

Ry shrugged. "Is it? I don't know. I'm happy to have her around, but I'm navigating this world of not being alone all the time. I'm figuring it out as I go."

"It's better not being alone, isnae it?" Rosie said.

Ry smiled at her. "Aye. It is."

I'd emailed Theo. We were Zooming again in an hour. The turn of events would sadden him and everyone at the university. No one there would be thrilled about some possible notoriety. I was sure Bridget would write a big article.

"How's Mary Katherine?" Edwin asked Inspector Winters.

"She's fine. Sad but fine. She wishes she had figured out what happened before the night she and Layton visited Willa. Apparently, a discussion about Ani's tattoo and its removal seemed to make things come clear to Mary Katherine. Well, she'd had suspicions since she first spoke with Delaney, she told us, but she didn't want them confirmed. Of course, they were."

"What will happen to the lad?" Rosie asked.

"It seems there wasn't intent to kill, but murder happened. I don't know yet, but he'll be in big trouble." He glanced at his phone. "Ah. I have work to do, but I suspect we'll want to talk to you again, Ry. Maybe you too, Delaney."

"I'm at your disposal," Ry said.

"Same," I said.

Inspector Winters sent me a smile of gratitude before he left the bookshop. He had become such a good friend, and we were all grateful for his early-morning visit.

When he was gone, the rest of us looked at each other a long moment.

"So, no Pict language translation," Hamlet said.

"No, I would expect that language is lost to history, as many things are. It was too good to be true," Edwin said.

"Aye," Ry said. "I thought the same, but still . . ."

"It's hard to find much that's as interesting historically as the Picts. All the mystery around them is compelling," Hamlet said.

"I have a message from Ani," Ry said with a small cringe. "She's sorry she faked being ill."

"Why did she do it?" I asked.

"She was concerned about you and your husband's involvement with Dr. Pace. She was overwhelmed by him being there right before you, and then when you and he were from the same place in the States . . . She told me she made up monsters in her mind. Faking an illness was the only thing she could think of to get you out of there. She knows now she was wrong, and she will come in to apologize herself, but for now . . ."

"Apology accepted," Rosie said. The rest of us nodded.

"Ry, who is your tattooist?" I asked.

"I still can't share that."

"You could, but you don't want to. I've heard the answer is very obvious."

Ry thought a moment. "That's an accurate statement."

I looked at the others. "What would the most obvious answer be?"

They all fell into thought, but it was Rosie who spoke up first. "I ken."

"You do?" I said.

"Aye."

"Spill the beans, Rosie," I said.

She smiled at Ry. "There's not one. You go to a different artist for every new tattoo."

Ry's eyebrows rose. "That's impressive, Rosie." He pulled up a shirt sleeve. "They are easy tattoos, and when I started to gain extra attention, I couldn't imagine forcing the spotlight on anyone else."

"They might like the attention," Edwin said.

"Or they might not." Ry pulled his sleeve down again. "It can be a lot. So, I don't give out names, and I make sure I'm never seen with any artist more than once."

"That makes sense." Hamlet smiled. "I like that answer."

"Lass, are you and Tom still considering some body art?" Ry asked.

I shrugged. "Our anniversary is coming up, and Tom has been asking for ideas. Maybe."

"I'm sure that will go over well," Rosie said.

The bookshop's phone rang its landline jangle. We all watched as Rosie answered.

"The Cracked Spine. Aye. Aye? Weel, lass, ta for calling, but I believe you've come across an old advertisement. That position was filled a long time ago. Aye. Same to you." She hung up the phone.

The rest of us looked at her curiously.

"Oh, a young woman came across the ad that Delaney answered long ago, the one that mentioned the desk and kings and queens. You remember it?" She looked at me.

"Of course," I said. "Nothing ever goes away on the internet, I guess."

"No, that's why I stay far away from it. Anyway, I told her the job was filled. You heard."

"I did."

"We all did," Edwin said.

I looked at everyone else then, one at a time. There was something about that call that at least momentarily made me forget about murder.

I was suddenly rattled, though. What if I hadn't answered the ad? What if I hadn't seen it? Surely the position would have been long filled by someone else by now, right? Would the woman on the other end of the phone have been granted an interview? Was there someone else out there who was *almost* destined to live what I had lived, or had it been meant only for me the whole time?

I looked at everyone again. I took a moment to smile at each person, and they smiled back. I wished Tom, Elias, and Aggie were there. Artair too. Oh, and maybe Bridget. But I'd remind the rest of them later how much they meant to me.

A tragedy had occurred, but one with Mary Katherine had been diverted. There was work to be done, and we all needed to get to it, but I'd just been gifted a few moments of real gratitude, and, boy, did it feel good.

It was a long journey from Kansas to here, not just because of the miles but because of the person I had become. I liked me beforehand, but now, well, now I was coming into my own in so many ways. How fortunate could someone get? I blinked back a few tears as Hector let me know he wanted me to pick him up. The bell above the door jingled. We had customers. It was time to get to work.

Oh my goodness, it had been a good run.

ACKNOWLEDGMENTS

I feel so lucky to work with Minotaur. Everyone is amazing. My editor, Hannah O'Grady, and her assistant, Madeline Alsup, are extraordinary. Kayla Janas, Sara Eslami, and Allison Ziegler have always been on top of everything needed to spread the word about my books. Many thanks to Juchole Gaines and Sarah Melnyk. I have worked also with many great copy editors over the years, and I can't believe how good copy editor Alda Trabucchi, proofreaders Tania Bissell and Shawna Hampton, and senior production editor Kiffin Steurer are at finding all the tiny details. What a fantastic group. Thank you to everyone there.

Thanks to all the booksellers. I love the passion you have for books, writers, and readers. A special thanks to everyone at The King's English in Salt Lake City. I lived there when I was first published, and I so appreciate their support of my books.

Another special thanks to the Poisoned Pen in Scottsdale, Arizona. Barbara Peters, Rob, Bill, Patrick, PK, Susan, Sharon, Chantal, Ian, Jen, Deb, Karen, and the amazing and wonderful John Charles. Thank you all for everything.

Thanks to my readers. It's obvious, of course, but I couldn't do this without you. I so appreciate your kindness and friendship.

Thanks to my Booktalk buddies, Kate Carlisle, Jenn McKinlay, Hannah Dennison, and Jenel Looney. How fun has that been!

And, thanks to my family. My husband is a numbers guy, but if I need a word person, he gives it his best. He also has an uncanny knack for synonyms, and that's a handy skill. My son and daughter-in-law, and their growing family, fill my heart every day. I didn't expect so many blessings. Thank you, and I love you all.

ABOUT THE AUTHOR

Jacqueline Hanna Photography

Paige Shelton is the author of the Scottish Bookshop Mystery series and the Alaska Wild series. Her other series include the Farmers' Market, Country Cooking School, and A Dangerous Type mysteries. She lives in Arizona with her family. Find out more at paigeshelton.com.